Published by GladEye Press
Interior Design: J.V. Bolkan
Cover Design: Sharleen Nelson
ISBN-13: 978-1-951289-26-3
Library of Congress Control Number: 2026930743

10 9 8 7 6 5 4 3 2 1

The body text is presented in Garamond, 11 point for easy readability.

DYING *for* LOVE

PATRICIA BROWN

GladEye
Press

Springfield, OR

For my amazing daughters, Nikki and Jennifer, who have their own stories to tell.

"The essence of romance is uncertainty."
~ Oscar Wilde

"The condition of women affords, in all countries, the best criterion by which to judge the character of men."
~ Frances Wright

Klara Kay Kent sat at a table at the Boat House checking her phone for a message from her husband, Tip. Nothing, there was nothing from him and he hadn't come back to the rental last night. Maybe she should be worried, but she was used to his free-spirited ways by now. Perhaps Tip and her son, Jesse, were together bonding over a late-night gabfest or poker game with Jesse's friends. She refused to text Jesse to find out because she truly didn't want to know. In all honesty, Tip and Jesse didn't know each other well and had little in common so if they were spending time together, she was all for it. Jesse was grown when she remarried and moved from Waterton back to her home town of Atlanta after retiring from her job as a behavior specialist for the Waterton School district. She had felt lucky to find someone to spend her golden years with then, but not so much now. Critics were right when they claimed marriage was like sitting in a bathtub. Once you got used to it, it wasn't so hot.

She was so engrossed in her own thoughts, she was surprised to find Pearl standing by her table smiling from ear to ear. "Well butter my butt and call me a biscuit!" she said loudly.

"I thought that was you, Klara," Pearl said. "There's a group of retired ladies over by the fireplace that would love to catch up with you. Please come join us."

Klara looked over to four older women, displaying warm smiles and waving at her. She was familiar with Cleo and Dede through her work in the schools, but didn't recognize the other women. How could she refuse? She approached the table and greeted them.

"You remember Cleo and Dede who taught in elementary schools," Pearl said. "Dede's the mayor of Waterton now."

"Of course, you two haven't changed much since I saw you last," Klara said, taking in Dede's short white hair and Cleo's tousled chestnut curls and concluding it must be dye that kept Cleo looking so young.

"Josephine Flutter is a therapist and Eleanor Penrose is a poet." Pearl said.

"I remember you, Josephine," Klara said. "I'm certain we worked together on a student referral at one time." Klara simply nodded at Eleanor whose classic poise and beauty seemed impenetrable.

"This is Klara Bomotti," Pearl said as she gracefully tucked her long legs under the table.

"Klara Bomotti, I haven't seen you in the longest time," Cleo said, thinking Klara hadn't changed much from the small, sassy, white-haired woman she remembered. "How's life been treating you?"

"Well, I guess you could say the sun don't shine on the same dog all the time," Klara said. "It's not Klara Bomotti anymore. Got married. It's Klara Kent now."

No one noticed Josephine's eyes widen in surprise as she spied the ring on Klara's left hand. "How long have you been married?" Josephine asked as she tidied the braid on top of her head.

"Long enough," Klara said. She could hear her mother's voice advising her: Don't complain, don't explain. "I met Tip through friends here in Oregon and we decided to move to Georgia after the wedding. Jesse stayed here and works as a financial advisor. You've probably heard of the Gerald Park Challenge."

"That's the treasure hunt offered by Gerald Park, Oregon's famous billionaire. It's supposed to get people off their couches and into the great outdoors," Dede explained. Because she was the mayor of Waterton, she made it her business to know everything that was going on everywhere.

"Yes, Jesse is into it big time and since the only thing the two have in common is the love of money, Tip decided he wanted to be a part of it, so I'm a part of it too." Klara lowered her voice, "All the clues have led us to this area. I really can't say more than that."

"How interesting," said Eleanor. "Do you know what the treasure is?"

"One million dollars goes to the first person to use the clues to find the location of the treasure, which is supposedly hidden somewhere in Oregon's great outdoors," Dede added.

"Are you saying that there is one million dollars hidden somewhere nearby?" asked Pearl in amazement.

"Is a frog's butt watertight?" Klara answered."

"You mean it's here in Waterton?" asked Cleo.

"I don't chew my tobacco twice," said Klara as she checked her pinging phone for its latest text. "It's been a real treat, ladies, but it's time to pee on the fire and call in the dogs." With that said, Klara stood up and left the Boat House.

Once she was gone, Eleanor said, "Klara must have spent a great deal of time in the country. I don't think I've ever heard anyone use so many colloquialisms in one conversation."

"Yes, but did you see her ring?" asked Josephine who had been relatively quiet.

"It was a lovely piece," said Cleo. "I'd guess it was at least a three-carat diamond."

"Five, it was five carats. I know because it once belonged to me," said Josephine. The coffee ladies leaned in for the scoop.

"I was very young when I met Tip Kent. We dated a few times over the course of the summer I turned nineteen. He was older, more experienced, and a very charming Southern gentleman. I was bored and angry with my parents who didn't want to pay for a trip to Europe before I started my sophomore year in college. Anyway, he was a diversion for me, but, evidently, I was much more than that for him. You can only imagine my surprise when he pulled out that ring and asked me to marry him. What can I say? I wanted that ring. It was huge, unique, not to mention beautiful, so I said yes." Josephine paused here and shook her head. "Don't judge me, now. I know it was shallow and cruel. I didn't love him, didn't even like him much, but I loved that ring."

"Was he your first husband?" asked Pearl knowing that Josephine was on her third but had kept her most personal history private.

"No, I couldn't go through with it," Josephine continued, "I knew the ring was valuable and when I found out it was a family heirloom, I broke off the engagement and gave it back to Tip."

"It's a beautiful piece of jewelry. I can understand why you would want it," said Cleo trying not to sound judgmental.

"Have you seen Tip since?" asked Eleanor.

"No, I totally lost touch with him and to be truthful haven't thought about him at all over the years, but I still have dreams about that ring." Josephine gazed thoughtfully off into the distance absently turning her wedding ring round and round.

It was dark when Eleanor woke from an uneasy sleep. She hadn't been thinking about Klara, Josephine's ring, or the mysterious challenge presented at the coffee group although any or all of those things might have entered into her dreams. Her friend, Angus, invited her to go woodcutting at the crack of dawn, but Eleanor didn't know exactly when the dawn cracked. She gave up on sleep, stretched her seventy-plus year-old body and shuffled into the kitchen to make coffee, then ventured out into the cool spring morning to fetch the newspaper. It was her habit to work the crossword and other puzzles while she drank her first cup, but brain exercises would have to wait because Eleanor could see a light in the sky toward the east and didn't want to be caught in her nightgown when Angus was ready to go. She hustled into her house, perched on the hill overlooking the Pacific Ocean, and quickly dressed in what she considered appropriate woodcutting attire. She was ready for the crack of dawn.

An hour passed but still no sign of Angus. Eleanor had finished the crossword, jumble, and Sudoku. Feathers, her African Gray parrot, muttered obscenities as he looked out over the calm ocean and clear blue sky. "Where's Angus?" he mimicked. Eleanor stroked his sleek feathers and began to worry. Angus was always on time. It was one of the many qualities she loved about him. Maybe he had overslept ... or worse. He was older than Eleanor yet she never thought of him as old because he exuded such health and vitality in all his actions. Eleanor picked up the phone, then put it down as she caught sight of Angus finally pulling into her driveway and making his way to her door.

"Good morning, Ellie." Angus greeted her with a smile and a peck on the cheek. "Are you ready to hit the road?"

"I've been ready since the crack of dawn," she said.

"Let's go, then. We're burning daylight," Angus said as he looked her up and down to see that she was wearing the right clothing. At least that was what he would have told Eleanor, but he just liked looking at her. She thought he was very handsome in his buffalo plaid shirt and blue jeans. Eleanor almost forgot she was irked with his tardiness when he flashed his dimpled smile and winked one of his green eyes.

"Where's Bones?" Eleanor asked as she crawled into the pickup cab and noticed Angus' dog was not there.

"I don't want him getting in the way," Angus answered as he shifted the truck into gear and drove down the hill and out of Sand Beach.

"Why would he be in the way?" Eleanor asked. She had never been woodcutting before and didn't know what it involved exactly. She and Walter, her late husband, always paid someone to drop off a cord of wood or two.

"You'll see soon enough," Angus smiled as if he knew a secret he wasn't telling. It made Eleanor uneasy. She sat quietly watching the scenery, enjoying the beauty of various trees and early blooming flowers along the road. Oregon sported endless shades of green, all fresh and vibrant.

"I'm curious to know what you mean when you say 'the crack of dawn'," Eleanor said finally.

Angus glanced over at her with concern. "Is that what I told you? I'm sorry if you took me literally, Ellie. That's just a term I use that has no definite time and means whenever I get around to it. Have you been waiting for me since daybreak?"

"Yes," she admitted.

"Are you mad?" Angus seemed seriously contrite.

"No, I'm not mad. It just wasn't like you to be late and I worried that something might have happened to you." She explained.

Angus let out a sigh of relief. He never wanted Eleanor to be angry with him or cause her any grief. He loved her in a way he never loved any women before her, and there were many including his ex-wife, Margo. Margo would have been angry and she would have made him pay in a hundred hurtful ways.

"This is where we turn off," Angus said and Eleanor noted the sign that read **Jordan Creek**.

The gravel road followed a clear stream that flowed over mossy stones and fallen trees. Alder trees and evergreens flanked the narrow lane and provided a leafy canopy where the sunlight filtered through casting light and shadow along the way. It was a bumpy ride but Eleanor loved the beauty and the sounds of the forest.

"Ellie, look ahead," Angus said, pointing to two spotted fawns trailing closely behind a mother deer along the edge of the narrow road.

"Oh my, they're so small!" Eleanor said as she watched them stumble along on their wobbly legs. Angus slowed to a near stop and followed from a distance until they ambled off the road and disappeared into the thick underbrush.

After they turned left and crossed the creek by way of a wooden bridge, the road began a steep rise and Angus shifted into 4-wheel drive. Eleanor looked down and watched the creek get smaller and smaller as they climbed higher. There were no guardrails to keep them on the road—nothing but trees would break their fall if they drove too close to an edge that dropped abruptly hundreds of feet down onto the valley floor. Eleanor gripped the door handle so tightly her knuckles turned white.

"Don't look down," Angus said as he glanced her way.

"I'm glad you're driving, Angus," Eleanor said, trying to sound braver than she felt. "Just keep your eyes on the road, if you can call this a road." Angus smiled and seemed to be enjoying her discomfort. He was evidently confident in his ability to get them safely to wherever he planned to go. As the way leveled off, Eleanor began to relax but when they rounded a sharp curve, they suddenly met another vehicle coming toward them. Angus stopped and backed carefully over to a wider spot until the other truck could safely pass. Eleanor let out an audible sigh. "Please don't have a heart attack up here, Angus. I'm not sure I could back up on this narrow road without falling off the side."

"Don't worry, Eleanor, no one is dying today." Angus' words were meant to reassure her, but Eleanor wasn't convinced. They were both in their seventies. All kinds of tragic things could happen and hundreds of them flashed through her mind in the minutes that followed. Suddenly they reached a clear-cut where loggers had left piles of logs deemed unworthy to take to the mill. Stumps, branches, and other logging debris scattered the area like a sore on the landscape. Angus slowed and checked out each pile. When he saw what seemed to be a mass of wood, he stopped the truck and jumped out for a closer look. Eleanor climbed out too, avoiding the muddy areas as best she could. While Angus investigated, Eleanor breathed in the fresh woodsy scented air and gazed out over the tree-covered horizon. Everything beyond was lush, green, and pristine. In the far distance she thought she could see the ocean and below were layers of fir trees growing out of what looked like the folds of a blanket. Low-lying clouds floated below like wisps of smoke. Beautiful.

"This is a nice bunch of fir. We can yard out these five logs and they would probably give us a full load." Angus didn't wait for Eleanor to reply or ask what he meant by "yard out". He simply put down the tailgate and unloaded the gear by the side of the road while she stood by and watched. Then he tied a thick rope to one of the logs, hooked the other end to the trailer hitch and got back in the truck. "Better stand out of the way," he ordered. Eleanor wasted no time moving away from the area as Angus pulled the rope taut and the log began to slide from the pile and onto the edge of the gravel road. He did this again until all five of the fir logs lay along the road ready to be cut into lengths that would fit into Eleanor's fireplace. Then he handed Eleanor a pair of gloves and a stick with a nail at the end and showed her how to mark the logs using the nail so he could cut them into the proper lengths. By the time Eleanor had finished marking the logs, she had worked up a sweat and Angus had cut several pieces with a chain saw. She stretched her back and admired Angus as he worked. He was a fine specimen of a man. She couldn't see his face under the helmet and face guard but his strength was apparent as he wielded the saw with the ease of a man who knew how to use a power tool. Wanting to be useful, she began to carry the pieces to the truck bed. It wasn't long before Angus had all the logs cut and began to help load them.

"It got warm," Angus said as he opened a bottle of water and handed it to Eleanor.

"I'm tired," she admitted. Angus looked approvingly at the load of wood.

"We've made good time. Let's load up the gear and find a place to eat lunch."

They settled on a shady patch of grass a little way down the road away from the clear cut. Angus grabbed a blanket and a picnic basket from the back of the cab while Eleanor wandered into the bushes to relieve herself. It wasn't her first time in the woods. On her way back to Angus, something colorful caught her eye. Stuck among the branches of a low-lying shrub was something similar to a playing card that looked familiar. She picked it up, noted the words *The Lovers* at the top and put it in her pocket when she heard Angus call out to her. "Are you alright?" he asked. "I was worried you might have gotten lost." He had unpacked lunch on the blanket and gone searching for her.

"I like a little privacy," she said looking at the delightful array of treats Angus had prepared for their lunch. "Wow, you really went all out. I'm suddenly famished." Angus beamed. Eleanor usually cooked delicious dinners for him so it was gratifying to please her with a meal. He didn't tell her he had picked most of it up from the grocery story deli. Ham and cheese croissant sandwiches, fresh strawberries, a bag of Cheetos, brownies, and a small bottle of red wine completed the feast. Angus opened the wine and poured it into a glass for Eleanor. He knew she didn't approve of plastic. Then he opened a bottle of beer for himself and watched as Eleanor ate.

"I'm feeling a little nappish," Angus said after eating his fill. He stretched out and drew Eleanor into his warm embrace. It was a perfectly peaceful afternoon for a snooze under the dappled shade of alder trees and lullaby of bird song … until the sound of civilization woke them. Angus sat up and looked off into the distance. Far on another logging road, he could see what looked like a group of four wheelers. The sky had clouded up and the wind had changed direction. "I guess the party's over. We better head home."

"I don't think I can move," Eleanor said. "Every muscle in my body hurts." Angus stood and gave her a hand up. "What's that smell?" she asked, wrinkling her nose in disgust.

"It's not me," Angus said, sniffing his armpits. "Probably a dead animal, we *are* in the woods." Eleanor began to pack up and put things in the truck while Angus wandered away following the scent of decay. She watched him look over the edge of the road and then disappear down the slope. A feeling of foreboding swept over her as she hurried to catch up to him. "Stay there," Angus called when he saw her peering over the edge. All Eleanor could see were rocks, dirt, and pieces of wood, but the stench of death was unmistakable. She waited as Angus climbed back up the slope sliding on rocks and debris. "What is it?" She asked.

"A body," he answered calmly. "It looks like a girl or woman by the clothing, but she's been here a while."

"Oh no," Eleanor gasped. "What should we do? There's no cell service up here." Angus took her arms and looked into her panic-stricken eyes.

"We can't leave the body, Ellie. I'm going to stay here and you are going to drive down to the highway and call the police as soon as you can get a signal on your phone. Make sure to tell them there is a possible homicide at Archer's Camp. Then drive my truck home. I'll get a ride back with the police. It will probably be a while. Don't worry about me. I know you can do this. Just go slow." Angus spoke in a slow, reassuring manner.

Eleanor couldn't speak. She was terrified of driving down that narrow road with a drop-off on one side and rocks on the other, but she knew Angus needed her to do this. He was a retired homicide detective and he believed this woman had been murdered. That was enough for her. She climbed into the driver's seat and gripped the steering wheel. Angus took his jacket, a bottle of water and his gun from the truck. "You won't need 4-wheel drive going down, just keep it in low gear and take a right at every crossing." Angus closed the door and kissed her through the window. It didn't feel like a goodbye kiss or even one for good luck. Eleanor didn't feel anything but dread.

"I can do this, I'm a strong capable woman," she told herself, gripping the wheel tightly as she drove slowly away. She glimpsed Angus in the rearview mirror giving her the thumbs up. She had to do this. Failing was not an option. She pushed all negative thoughts from her mind and visualized reaching the highway, calling the police, then pulling into her driveway at Sand Beach, unloading the wood and driving Angus' truck to his house. She would walk back with his dog, Bones.

As she successfully maneuvered each zig that zagged down the steep grade, her confidence grew. The drop on her left didn't exist as long as she focused on the gravel road ahead. When she came to a fork in the road, she remembered Angus' words to go right. How did he know she wasn't paying attention and needed that information? She silently thanked him for his amazing forethought. The woods were a maze of logging roads that led to places Eleanor didn't want to visit and most likely ended in mires too difficult to escape or her worst fear—dangerously narrow and impossible to turn around in without backing up to the very edge of an abyss. Gradually she relaxed her hold on the steering wheel and flexed her stiff fingers. She crossed the wooden bridge and took another right turn following the creek that led to the highway. It was slow going but she was almost there.

Her mind returned to Angus. What had he seen that caused him to suspect murder? Perhaps a retired homicide detective always thought the worst. He said the clothes suggested it was a woman. Eleanor wondered what she was wearing and what business she had up there all alone. Angus had taken his gun. Was that to protect him or the body? Did he think the killer would come back, or was he preparing to keep animals at bay? Her mind created a variety of reasons for a body to be in the woods and before she knew it, she had reached the highway.

It seemed like the drive into Waterton would never end, but Eleanor was gratified to know someone was on the way to Angus when a police rig and rescue vehicle passed her with their lights flashing. Officer McGraw had listened to her directions carefully and reassured her that they would hurry. Now all that was left for her to do was drive home and unload all that wood.

"Her name was Monica Fischer," Eleanor told the coffee ladies as they ate their breakfast and sipped their coffee.

"She worked for the city," Dede added. "Hadn't been here long but she really made an impression as an efficient, no-nonsense, hard worker."

"Was she tall, blonde, and beautiful?" asked Cleo. "I'm sure she was taking an art class with me at the community college during the winter term. She dressed like a fashion model right down to her Louboutin pumps."

"That must be her," Eleanor said. "According to Angus, they found one red velvet high-heeled shoe near her body."

"How awful," said Pearl. "She certainly wasn't out for a hike in the woods wearing only one shoe."

"What a shame," Josephine said. "The poor girl was obviously murdered and dumped in the woods."

"Do we know how she was killed?" asked Pearl.

"They must be doing an autopsy to determine the cause of death. Angus didn't say. I just assumed it wasn't obvious because animals had gotten to her," Eleanor said.

"Who would do such a thing?" asked Dede, "and why?"

"Why does anyone kill?" asked Josephine. "Passion, money, revenge, hatred, I could go on."

"I wonder where the other shoe is," Cleo pondered.

"I don't like the way this conversation is going," said Pearl. "It's sounding more and more like a murder mystery and you know how I feel about those. Pretty soon there'll be stakeouts, disguises, break-ins, and heart palpitations."

"If we find the other shoe, I bet we find the murderer," said Cleo. And so … they began to make a list.

"We need to know who she worked with and if she was seeing anyone romantically," said Josephine.

"I know who she worked with," said Dede, who had access to that information as the mayor.

"Her close friends may have information. Do we know anything about her personal life? Was she married or divorced? Did she have a roommate? I must say I know nothing about this woman," admitted Pearl.

"How old do you think she was?" asked Josephine.

"I'd guess she was late forties or early fifties," said Cleo.

"That's about right," said Dede. "Old enough to have a past. I only know she wasn't from here and hadn't been here long."

"This could be very challenging. I have no idea where to start. Maybe we should Google her," suggested Josephine.

"I'll see if Angus has any information he can share," said Eleanor.

"Let's each do a little research and meet again later this week," said Josephine.

Eleanor walked quickly along the shoreline. She could see rain clouds looming on the horizon and didn't relish the thought of walking home in a downpour. Just ahead was another beachcomber hurrying past the frothy waves to reach shelter before the rain fell. Eleanor picked up her pace as the wind from the west began to usher in the squall. She ducked into Suzanna's just as the first large drops plopped down leaving dark spots on the sidewalk.

"Well, hello there," said Klara. "I see we are both victims of the weather." Eleanor glanced around the restaurant looking for her Do Nothing friends, Mattie, Sylvia and Mavis, who usually sat at a table near the window. Seeing no one there, she decided to invite Klara to join her for a cup of coffee.

"Let's take advantage of this time to share something warm and get to know each other," she said. "This squall will blow over before you know it."

"Just throw me in a chair and call me a sack of taters," Klara sighed. "I'm afraid I've overdone this walking on the beach business."

"That last scurry to get inside did me in as well," admitted Eleanor as she led them to a table near the window with a view. "Are you staying in Sand Beach?"

"Yes, we could have stayed with my son, Jesse, but decided it might cramp his style. He does have a life and a lady friend, or maybe I should say had a lady friend." Klara let out a long sigh. "Honestly he's never without a lady friend for long."

Eleanor didn't want to pry, waiting in silence to see if Klara wanted to talk about it. They sipped their coffee and looked out the window at the gray sky and crashing waves. Finally, Eleanor said, "It's difficult to see your children suffer."

A tear rolled down Klara's cheek. "Every man needs to skin his own skunk, but I worry about Jesse. He's my only child. He's bigger than life and twice as handsome, funny, smart and so precious. Here's a picture of him," she passed her phone to Eleanor who saw an attractive, tall, dark-haired man with striking blue eyes and a sexy smile. "His lady friend was found dead up in the woods and I'm afraid he may be a suspect."

"I heard about that," Eleanor said, "but I didn't know your son was involved with her."

"He hadn't known her long. We met her when we first arrived. She was as smart as a tree full of owls and easy on the eyes. I'm sure Jesse is sad to lose her but the police always assume it's the spouse or the lover when murder is involved, and I know Jesse and if he tells you a rooster dips snuff, you can look under its wing and find the can."

Eleanor took a minute to translate that in her head. "I'm sure the police have other suspects. There must be an explanation for what happened. Perhaps someone from her past had a score to settle. We just don't know, but it's early on and the professionals will certainly find out more as they investigate," she said hoping to comfort Klara. "Have they talked to him, your son?"

"Not yet, like I said, he hadn't known her long and he was actually still seeing Molly Fiori. Maybe you know her. She has a pottery shop on Main Street. Such a beautiful young lady and livelier than a puppy with two tails. I really liked that girl and hoped he'd found the one, but Jesse's a hard dog to keep on the porch. Usually, he's only serious with one at a time and treats them so respectfully. I think he was getting to know Monica and probably they were just friends. I really don't pry into his romantic affairs. Now someone has killed that poor girl and dumped her body in the woods."

"What did you actually know about her?" Eleanor asked.

"Not much really," Klara said. "We only met her that one time. She worked for the city. I got the impression they hired her to do some financial work for them. Grew up in California, some small city I can't remember right now, but it'll come to me. Jesse never said if she'd been married, divorced, or widowed. Didn't matter anyway. We mostly talked about the weather here and joked about Jesse's idiosyncrasies." Klara paused as if remembering something from the past. "He always had to stop at every historical marker when we drove any place. He called them hysterical markers. Then there was his pet chicken, Herkimer, who went everywhere with him, even sat on the handlebars of his bike as he rode around our neighborhood. That was until he hit a pothole and Herkimer fell off and Jesse ran over and killed him. He was so sad. Jesse made a cross to mark his grave but changed his name to Ivan because he couldn't spell Herkimer. So many funny memories from the time it was just the two of us. You know I just love that boy." Klara wriggled like a happy puppy.

Eleanor and Klara sat at the table, ordered lunch and continued to share information with each other. Each story leading to another until Eleanor looked at the time and realized there was some place she was supposed to be and hurried home. On her trek back, she thought how much she had enjoyed Klara's company and how much she learned about Jesse Bomotti and how little she had actually learned about Monica Fischer.

Eleanor could not sleep. It was the middle of the night and the moon appeared brightly between clouds illuminating the waves on the ocean below. She pulled on her robe and stepped out onto the deck where the rhythm of the waves grew louder. As she gazed at the full moon, she recited a poem as if it were a prayer.

> Mother Moon
> You shine with a reflected light
> Cool white
> Against the indigo night
> Humble Beacon
> You take no glory for your glow
> Illuminating the darkness here below
> You change your face with every day
> Waning and waxing
> And yet you stay the same
> Complete
> You are full and whole through every phase
> Nighttime Goddess
> Bless us with your silvery gaze
> So we may see in darkness—light
> And never fear the demons of the night.

Stepping back inside, she wandered into the kitchen for a glass of water. In the darkened window, she saw her face reflected and was reminded of her age and station in life. She was a mother and a grandmother. Her mind returned to the conversation with Klara about a mother's love for her child. Eleanor loved her children and admitted she would do anything to protect them. Was it possible Klara was involved in Monica Fischer's murder? Was she protecting Jesse from an unscrupulous woman? At this point anything was possible but Eleanor hoped it wasn't true. A noise interrupted her nighttime musings. Someone was at her door. Who could be calling at this time of night? She saw Angus through the stained glass of the door and opened it.

"Good grief, Ellie! What are you doing up at this hour?"

"Couldn't sleep," she replied. "What are you doing up at this hour?"

"Just getting home from a poker party with a few friends. Saw your light on and thought I'd check to see if you were all right."

"I'm not exactly on your way home," Eleanor said.

"Sometimes I like to check on you, but you're usually asleep," Angus admitted reluctantly. He knew Eleanor would not approve.

Secretly Eleanor thought it was sweet, but didn't want Angus to think it was okay to spy on her. "Well, I'm just fine, thank you. I'd invite you in for pie but I don't have any."

Angus got the message, gave Eleanor a quick kiss and said goodnight.

Eleanor ambled into her office, pulled out paper, and began making a list of guests to invite to a dinner party. Entertaining always gave her purpose and she decided she really wanted to know more about Klara and her husband Tip Kent.

The scene was set for a delightful evening. Eleanor lit the candles as a finishing touch to her dining table set with white and green China and decorated with magenta pink orchids, white magnolia blossoms, and dried yarrow. She stepped back to take in the full effect of the green napkins and delicate wine glasses. Everything met with her approval.

Angus was the first to arrive with a bottle of Chardonnay which he had researched as the perfect pairing for chicken and dumplings.

"Something smells delicious," he said as he buried his nose in Eleanor's neck. Eleanor smiled knowing he was referring to her cooking and not her specifically. Feathers, her African Gray Parrot, flew into the room complaining, "Not you again!" and landed on Angus' shoulder giving him the stink eye as a friendly greeting.

"I think he likes me," Angus said.

"I'll pour you a drink," Eleanor said, shaking her head at the silliness that defined the relationship between man and bird.

Angus sipped his Crown Royal and took in the heavenly aroma of chicken and dumplings and mashed potatoes, while admiring the beauty of the flowers and the candlelight that reflected off the crystal glasses as Eleanor welcomed the other guests: Klara and Tip, and the members of her coffee group and their husbands. Eleanor thought it best not to include Josephine and Richard considering Tip's earlier proposal and the awkwardness that might ensue.

"What a lovely home you have, Eleanor!" Klara said.

"And a charming and gracious hostess to live in it," drawled Tip as he took Eleanor's hand and raised it to his lips. Eleanor was amused but immune to the flattery of Southern gentlemen. She smiled and offered Crown Royal since she had no Southern Comfort.

The dinner party continued with drinks, small talk, a little entertainment by Tip at the piano and, of course, the delectable food.

"I declare, this lemon pound cake is as exquisite as my grandmother's," Tip gushed as he put the final piece in his mouth.

"It truly was a divine meal, Eleanor," added Klara. "Would you tell me how you prepared the chicken?"

"I just told her, 'You're going to die'," Eleanor said. Everyone laughed and Eleanor avoided giving her the recipe.

"You live in Georgia. I hear there are spiders and snakes there," said Cleo, who knew Eleanor would appreciate a change of topic.

"Oh yes." Tip spoke slowly as he leaned back in his chair. "We have spiders and snakes that will kill you. Let me show you something." He reached into his pocket and pulled out his phone. "See here, this is my friend's hand. He was working in the yard and was bitten by a little copperhead snake." A large swollen hand with a blackened fingertip appeared on the screen.

"Oh my," said Pearl. "Did he lose his hand?"

"No, but the antidote cost him $65,000 dollars," Tip said.

"I have no desire to go to Georgia," said Dede. "I hate snakes and spiders."

"I understand you are here to find the treasure offered by Gerald Park," Cleo said. "Are you having any luck?"

"You done chewed the bark off the tree, lady," Tip said pausing to put a wad of snuff in his cheek, "Can't say much about it now since the whole area has been closed due to the recent events up there."

"Well, that says a great deal," Dede said. "Now we know where you've been looking."

"Oops, guess I let the cat out of the bag," Tip said laughing. "Now I heard Angus is a detective. Maybe he can shed some light on when we might be cleared to go back in there to search."

"Sorry," Angus said, "Can't comment on it. For all I know, you might be involved."

"Don't get your tail up and stinger out!" Tip said. "I'm not one to go 'round spreadin' rumors, so you better listen close the first time. I understand that Monica Fischer was runnin' away from an abusive relationship. If you think I'm involved, you might as well be fishin' in the clouds."

That raised some eyebrows at the table. Angus merely cocked his head. Eleanor knew this meant he knew something he wasn't going to share and was suddenly eager for the guests to go home so she could get the scoop.

"Would anyone like a nightcap?" she asked.

"Oh, no thank you, Eleanor, we should be going. I see how late it is," said Klara who had been relatively silent most of the evening. Eleanor wondered if she felt intimidated by Angus' presence in light of her desire to protect her son. Maybe she was afraid she might say something that would incriminate him, or perhaps she just deferred to her husband, although Klara didn't appear to be the type of woman to let a man speak for her. Nevertheless, Eleanor's question precipitated a mass exit.

Later, while Angus and Eleanor tidied up the kitchen, she innocently asked, "So what do you think of the Kents?"

"Charming couple," he said. "Very Southern."

"Huh," Eleanor muttered. "Do you think they murdered that woman and dumped her in the woods?"

Angus turned to her with wide-eyed wonder. "Is that why you invited them here tonight?"

"Of course not," Eleanor admitted, "I wanted to get to know Klara better and meet her husband."

"I see," Angus said. "The fact that her son, Jesse, is a person of interest didn't play any part in that decision?"

"Maybe it did," Eleanor admitted. "Klara is worried. Do you have any new evidence to report?"

Angus wiped his hands on a kitchen towel and used it to draw Eleanor close. "What are you willing to exchange for that information?" He lowered his head and kissed her.

"Angus McBride, I think you're trying to seduce me!" Eleanor said in mock indignation.

"Is it working?" he asked looking into her eyes.

"Tell me about the investigation first," she conceded.

Angus released her and sighed. "Some interesting impediments have cropped up."

"Do tell," Eleanor prodded.

"Promise you won't laugh," he cautioned.

"Of course!" Eleanor could hardly contain her curiosity.

"Some unusual footprints were discovered near the crime scene."

"Yes …"

"They are exceptionally large ones."

"What are you saying? Do you suspect Bigfoot?" Eleanor began to chuckle.

"You promised you wouldn't laugh." Angus gave her a hard look.

"You're serious?"

"Absolutely. A cryptozoologist is coming tomorrow to verify their authenticity, but that's not all. We also found evidence of pagan rituals near the site."

"What? Witches might be involved, too?" Eleanor was stunned.

Angus merely rolled his eyes.

The coffee ladies sat at their usual table at the Boat House eating their usual breakfasts. Josephine was eager to hear the details of the dinner party but didn't want to seem too curious about her old beau, Tip Kent, so remained silent as she ate her peanut butter and blueberry toast.

"I guess it isn't hard to believe a woman as beautiful as Monica would have a stalker," said Cleo nibbling on a crispy piece of bacon.

"Eleanor, did Angus know about the abusive boyfriend Monica Fischer was allegedly hiding from?" asked Dede.

"No, he said it couldn't be verified since there was no record of it, no restraining order was ever issued, but there was a sexual harassment suit filed against one of her coworkers. Of course, now the investigation will look into that, but it could be a red herring."

"Why do you think Tip would spread a rumor like that?" asked Pearl.

"Perhaps he thinks Jesse Bomotti is a suspect and wants to throw them off his trail," Eleanor said. "Klara told me she's afraid the police are interested in Jesse since he was seeing her lately."

"That makes sense," said Dede.

"So, she was seeing Jesse romantically?" asked Josephine. "What else were you able to find out?"

"According to Klara, Jesse is still involved with his long-time lady friend, Molly Fiori, and just started getting to know Monica. I'm not even sure it was a romantic relationship, at least not yet anyway. Seems like Jesse is a lady's man, a confirmed bachelor."

"I looked into her personnel file," said Dede. "She came from a small town in southern Oregon, Jacksonville, where she worked for the city as an accounting clerk. She was hired here in December to work in the finance department under the director, Malcolm Manning."

"What do you know about him?" asked Cleo.

"He's been here about seven years, has a wife but no children. I haven't spent much time around him so I can't testify to his character, but he seems very charismatic."

"Do we know if Monica was divorced or separated? Does she have children?" asked Pearl.

"We're not allowed to ask those questions when we hire," said Dede, "so we have to find out that information in other ways. It seems she was very tight-lipped about her past."

"I Googled her," said Josephine. "She doesn't have any information out there. It totally makes sense if she's hiding from someone."

"Klara said she was from a small town in California," Eleanor said. "I suppose Klara could have gotten it wrong, or maybe Monica was in California before she moved to Jacksonville."

"This might be harder to crack than we think," said Cleo.

"There's more," Eleanor said, "Large footprints were discovered near the crime scene and evidence of pagan rituals were found nearby. Angus is meeting with a cryptozoologist this morning who can tell if the footprints are real or fake."

"Wow, this is getting more interesting by the minute," Dede said.

"I don't know anything about Bigfoot, nor do I know any witches. Are we still in Waterton or have we suddenly been transported to the land of Oz?" Pearl asked.

"Well, I don't believe in Bigfoot," said Josephine. "But there is obviously a mystery afoot."

What Eleanor didn't tell her friends was that Angus had invited her to meet Professor Harry Growth, the esteemed cryptozoologist, at the police station to view the plaster casts of the footprints that were found at the crime scene. Upon entering the building, she was escorted to a special room where a tall, thin, brown-haired man stooped over the items that lay on a long table. Eleanor immediately thought if Bill Nye the Science Guy and Miss Frizzle of the *Magic School Bus* married and had a child it would be Professor Harry Growth. Angus and a couple of policemen sat nearby but rose when they saw Eleanor.

"Professor Growth, this is Eleanor Penrose. Eleanor, this is Professor Growth from the International Society of Cryptid Studies (ISCS) Portland branch," Angus said.

As Professor Growth took Eleanor's hand, she noted his long dirty fingernails as well as his tousled curls and generally disheveled look. Of special interest was the red bow tie he sported printed with large yellow footprints.

"It's lovely to meet you, Eleanor. I understand you are interested in learning about the creature known in these parts as Sasquatch, or Bigfoot. You may not know that the first Sasquatch footprints were discovered as early as 1811 and hundreds have been adduced since then. Many of them false, of course. In 1924, five gold prospectors allegedly had a violent confrontation with what they described as "gorilla men" near Mount St. Helens, Washington. After the prospectors wounded one, the gorilla men ran off but later returned in the night and attacked the prospector's cabin with rocks until the prospectors fled. Even though none of this could be verified and the footprints found there were proved fake, the legend was spread far and wide and continues to be of interest to this very day.

"According to eyewitness reports, Sasquatch is an ape-like creature 6- to 15-feet-tall who stands upright and often emits a foul odor. The footprints discovered have measured up to 24 inches long and 8 inches wide. Some scientists speculate that it could be a remnant of Neanderthals, but most scientists believe it is a hoax, or possibly a bear. Now if you look over here at the casts of the footprints we found earlier in the woods, you can see they measure 20 inches in length and 6 inches in width. Interestingly, they are not flat like so many of the fake prints discovered in the past, but have a clear variation in depth with the heel and ball of the foot deeper than the arch. At first, I was excited by this but upon inspection of the many footprints on site I concluded that there is no variation in the prints and, although very good, they are in my estimation indeed fake.

"Now if you have questions or would like more information, please contact me at this number," he concluded by handing Eleanor his card.

Eleanor could only utter a polite, "Thank you, Professor," before Angus took her arm, nodded to the professor and led her toward the exit.

"I'll walk you out," he muttered to Eleanor.

As soon as the door closed behind them, Eleanor turned to Angus with wide eyes and said, "What was that?"

"I told him you were a famous author writing a book about Bigfoot," Angus explained. "I thought you would be interested in seeing the footprints firsthand."

"Thank you, I think," she said. "It's a good thing I didn't have any questions. The man never gave me a chance to speak."

"I know. Someone said he's on the spectrum, whatever that means. Fortunately, you got the condensed version. I, on the other hand, had to listen to him discuss reasons for and against believing in this creature, in detail I might add, on the way up to the crime scene, then during his measuring and casting, and again with much more minutia about various footprints on the way down. Do you want to go back to the scene of the crime and look around or go get pie?"

"What do you think?"

Angus only smiled. He knew how much Eleanor hated the drive to the crime scene and he was glad that her fear would keep her from nosing about.

Having just finished breakfast, Eleanor wasn't hungry but as they entered Sara Sota's Bakery, she knew she would order a piece of their lemon meringue pie. Then she remembered Professor Growth's long dirty nails and excused herself to wash her hands.

"I don't think I'll ever feel clean again," she said as she returned to Angus who sat patiently waiting for pie.

"Are you a believer?" he asked.

"Do I believe there is a big hairy ape roaming the forests? No, I definitely do not." Eleanor stated. After what seemed like a long pause, she looked at Angus and was surprised at his expression. "Don't tell me you do."

"I'm not ruling it out, but I don't believe the footprints at the crime scene are real," Angus clarified.

"Thank heavens for that. I was beginning to think you might be in the early stages of mental decline," Eleanor said.

"And here I thought you were a woman with an open mind," Angus teased. "I recall a poem by a very astute author:

    'What doors are closed to our humanity?
    Caused by indifference or apathy.
    Taught by others how to see
    What we're told is reality.'"

Eleanor was taken aback and touched all at once. Angus had memorized part of her poem and had called her out for her hypocrisy. Just when she thought she knew him, he surprised her with his insight.

"Doctor Growth had some very convincing facts about other footprints that have been discovered," Angus continued. He seemed quite pleased with himself for silencing Eleanor.

"And are you going to regale me with these facts in hopes of changing my mind about Bigfoot?" Eleanor asked just as the pie was delivered.

"As you wish," Angus replied and immediately filled his mouth with apple pie.

Eleanor delicately nibbled her meringue. She thought how much better it tasted than the crow she would be forced to eat if Angus presented proof that Bigfoot did exist.

"First, don't you agree that it may be possible that an apelike creature could exist in the forest?" Angus asked.

"Possible, but highly unlikely given the scientific information we have regarding such a creature. Most scientists think it's merely folklore or a hoax. Don't you believe in science?" Eleanor asked.

"Absolutely, but how many scientists have declared that this creature cannot exist, so it doesn't exist and they can't be bothered with the many eyewitness reports of native peoples, hunters, campers, forest rangers, and hikers. They dismiss it out of hand because they have already decided it doesn't fit with their reality. They even mock those who treat the topic seriously even as times have changed and new facts are brought to light. Dr. Growth has an open mind and actually studies the evidence that not only includes footprints but hair samples, scat, and signs of foraging."

"I'm listening," Eleanor prodded.

"I've had my own experience with the Troll of Horny Chessman, so I'm not willing to dismiss anyone else's account." Angus looked at his watch. "I've got a meeting to get to, so I'll have to continue this persuasive argument later. Are you available for dinner, or will you be busy brushing up on Bigfoot?"

"Dinner sounds good," she said. Eleanor watched him as he left Sara Sota's and wondered if he could be right. She did not have a recipe for crow.

After a quick trip to the Piggly Wiggly to pick up fresh ingredients for dinner, Eleanor drove home, poured a glass of red wine and sat in the living room to discuss matters with Feathers.

"Do you think it's possible that a large apelike creature could live in the forests for such a long time without being discovered?" Eleanor asked. Feathers rocked on the arm of the couch first on one foot and then the other and nodded emphatically.

"Oh, what do you know?" Eleanor snapped. She did not want to admit that she had doubts and now even her precious pet was on Angus' side. When did it become a competition anyway? It didn't have to be, but she picked up her wine and went directly to her computer to research Bigfoot. Angus was coming loaded with information to prove his point. She would be prepared to argue hers.

An hour later, Eleanor rubbed her tired eyes and stood up to stretch and came to the conclusion that there was no real proof that Bigfoot existed. On the other hand, it was like trying to prove the existence of God. There was no real proof that either one didn't exist. It was a matter of faith and wanting to believe, at least until someone brought forth a body that could be studied, and that hadn't happened. No one was going to win this argument.

She headed to the kitchen to prepare quail with tomato, anchovy, and fresh mint sauce. It was as close to crow as she could get and she wasn't going to eat it alone. As she worked with the tiny birds, Feathers watched suspiciously from a perch nearby.

"What do you know?" Feathers snapped in Eleanor's voice. "Bigfoot, Bigfoot, Bigfoot…" It sounded like the *Brady Bunch* chant of "Marcia, Marcia, Marcia".

"Silly bird," Eleanor said. "You're lucky I'm not cooking you tonight."

"Inky?" Feathers asked.

Eleanor was stunned. Inky was an unusually friendly crow that Feathers had grown fond of but had disappeared long ago.

"Good grief, Feathers, this isn't Inky! It's quail, not crow. I wouldn't make Angus eat crow."

"Eat crow, Angus," Feathers said scornfully and flew off in a snit.

"Humpf," Eleanor said and popped the birds into the oven.

When Angus arrived with a bottle of Pinot Noir, Feathers flew to greet him, landing on his shoulder, "Beware the jaws that bite, the claws that catch … Bigfoot, Bigfoot!" he warned. "One, two! One, two! Snicker-snack!"

"Calm down, Feathers," Angus said as he tried to pet the hysterical bird.

"Eat crow, Angus," Feathers said and flew off in a huff of gray feathers.

"Am I to assume you and Feathers spent the afternoon in pursuit of Bigfoot?" Angus said as he followed Eleanor into the kitchen and poured himself two fingers of Crown Royal.

"In a manner of speaking, yes," Eleanor answered, "but although Feathers agrees with you, I must remind you he has a bird brain, and I found no evidence to convince me of the existence of such a creature." She took the roasting pan from the oven.

"What smells so good?" Angus asked as he looked into the pan that contained the roasted quail. His eyes widened in surprise. "Eleanor Penrose, are you planning to make me eat crow?"

"Absolutely," she replied.

"Well, I am starving," he said poking a finger in the sauce and giving it a taste. "What are you planning to eat?"

"Angus, I really do have an open mind, so I've made enough for two. Excuse me while I close Feathers in the office. I don't want him to see us eating what he thinks is his friend, Inky." Angus watched her leave the kitchen and wondered where she could have gotten the crow. He knew it would taste delicious. Eleanor was a food magician after all.

Monica Fischer's murder was the reason the ladies sat around Dede's dining table drinking coffee. "So, what have we learned?" asked Josephine as she took out her notepad and pen.

"No luck yet on finding out anything about her personal life," Dede reported. "I asked some of the people she worked with and they said she was all work and no play. One even quoted her as saying she was there to do her job not to make friends. Malcolm Manning reluctantly admitted she was a hard worker but stopped short of giving her credit for finding more efficient ways to fund the city's newest renewal program. I won't go into detail here, but I know it was her plan and he tried to make me believe it was his."

"That in itself is not unusual," said Josephine who was an expert on toxic masculine behavior.

"I know someone who lives in Jacksonville and called her to see if she had heard any gossip about Monica Fischer. She told me she had a few close friends who might be able to shed some light on her personal life, but all she knew was that Monica was smart, efficient, and very stylish. There were men who tried to get close to her but she was very careful about forming relationships with them. They called her the Ice Witch. There was talk about her casting spells on them and most of the women there were jealous and fearful their husbands would stray if given a chance." Cleo stopped to take a bite of a cranberry scone.

"How very dramatic!" exclaimed Pearl. "I wonder if she was a witch. I learned that there is a group of women in Waterton who celebrate various natural events, like the vernal and autumnal equinoxes and the winter and summer solstices. As far as I know they just cast circles in the forest by the light of the moon and dance around. Nothing that involves human sacrifices."

"Did you actually talk to members of this coven?" asked Eleanor.

"No, it was gossip I heard while I was at the dentist. Dr. Babbity's walls are very thin. I really had no idea who was talking." Pearl said.

"I wonder if Madame Patruska would know anything about this," Eleanor said. "I'll give her a call."

"I tried calling her already, but she didn't answer her phone," said Pearl, "She was the first person I thought of, even though I don't believe she is a witch."

"It does seem to be right up her alley," said Dede.

"She's still not picking up," said Eleanor putting her phone down. "I'll try again later."

"I think she must be on vacation. Her shop wasn't open when I drove by the other day," said Dede.

"Yesterday I met Professor Harry Growth, a cryptozoologist who is here to verify the footprints found near the crime scene," Eleanor said. "According to him, the footprints are fake."

"How did you manage that?" asked Dede.

"Angus thought I would be interested," Eleanor said. "I never thought Angus would be a believer in something so unscientific."

"He believes Bigfoot is real?" Cleo asked incredulously.

"He believes in God, doesn't he?" Josephine said.

"I believe in God," said Dede, "but not in Bigfoot."

"I spent the afternoon researching evidence to prove that Bigfoot isn't real, thinking Angus would produce some overwhelming facts to prove me wrong. All I found was evidence of hoax after hoax, a lot of sightings and stories but no facts. It was a total waste of time. Come to think of it, Angus didn't add anything at all to convince me he was right," Eleanor said indignantly.

The ladies looked at one another and pondered this information as if it were the solution to the world's problems. "I think this is his way of keeping you off the case," said Josephine.

"Ah, you spent the entire afternoon researching a mythical creature instead of investigating the murder of Monica Fischer!" Pearl said nodding her head in agreement.

"Diabolical!" said Cleo.

Eleanor was speechless. She couldn't believe she didn't see through his plan. "I did discover the fact that the footprints were a hoax," she said. "So why would someone intentionally plant them near the crime scene?"

"As a diversion perhaps?" said Dede. "There seems to be a lot going on up there. Murder, Bigfoot, pagan rituals, and a hunt for a million dollars."

"I don't think the killer planted the footprints to make everyone think Bigfoot committed the crime," said Pearl. "That seems ridiculous."

"I agree," said Eleanor, "the body was dumped as though the killer wanted to be rid of it and be on his way."

"The way the murderer left her shows a deep disregard for her as a person," Josephine said. "I'd bet money on the killer being a man who hates women."

"If that's the case, the pagan rituals are probably not connected to the case either," said Cleo. "If Angus invites you to investigate that aspect, you'll know for sure what his intentions are."

"I don't believe the treasure hunters are involved either. Monica Fischer was dressed to the nines and wearing high heels. She wasn't after the treasure," said Pearl.

"We can't rule them out though because she wasn't killed up there," said Eleanor. "She was killed somewhere else and dumped there. Maybe to stop the hunt for the money or because she knew something."

"If she was randomly killed to deter the treasure hunters, it will be difficult to solve," Cleo said. "There are so many people from far and wide who are here to find that money. There may be sinister characters we don't know."

"I wonder if the Bigfoot prints were planted before or after the body was dumped. Angus would have seen them when he discovered the body if they were there already," Eleanor surmised.

"Do we know where the footprints were in respect to the body?" Dede asked. "Perhaps they were nearby but not in proximity to the body where Angus could see them until later in the investigation."

"Even so, I think they are not a factor in the murder," Josephine said. "Most likely they were planted there before the murder by some prankster maybe, or someone who wanted to scare away the treasure seekers."

"Someone who wanted to interfere with the murder investigation could have sneaked in after the body was discovered hoping to throw a lot of red herrings in the mix. So that person could be our killer," said Dede.

"Of course, we don't know if the prints were planted before or after the murder," said Cleo. "If they were there before it was probably someone who wanted to scare off the treasure hunters. The person who dumped the body wouldn't plan that far ahead. Monica Fischer was missing for days. Her body lay up there long enough for animals to feed on it. We know criminals often return to the scene of the crime, so maybe this person went back and planted the prints after he killed her but before she was discovered."

"I'm sure Angus would have seen them if they were near the body when he discovered it," said Eleanor. "I bet the killer simply dumped her from his vehicle and never went down to the place where she was found. We need to find out where these prints were in relation to the body."

"He may have seen them and not told you about them, Eleanor," Josephine said. "He's usually careful about disclosing information about a crime. The fact that he let you in on this makes me think the police believe it's not relevant to the case."

"So, should we focus our investigative snooping on finding the person who planted the prints?" Pearl asked.

"Only if we stumble onto it. We need to know who the last person to see her alive was," added Dede. "And what her activities were before her disappearance."

"And where is the missing shoe?" added Cleo.

"I'm going to look into the witch angle," said Josephine. "Women like Monica Fischer who were too pretty, too smart, and too successful were often accused of witchcraft during the women's holocaust. She may not have been involved in witchcraft but could have been killed by someone who thought she was."

"I'm exhausted," Pearl moaned as she put her head on the table.

Eleanor went immediately to her office to make a timeline of events leading up to the death of Monica Fischer. Her mind was spinning with questions after the meeting, and she needed to organize her thoughts. She set up her workspace and after what felt like hours decided a cup of tea would help in her endeavor. Feathers refused to acknowledge her presence and stayed in the corner window looking out over the restless ocean. As she moved through the living room, something caught her eye. On the end table sat a book she did not remember seeing before, *Big Foot-Prints: A Scientific Inquiry into the Reality of Sasquatch.*

Several of the pages were tagged with Post-it notes. Eleanor assumed Angus must have left it here last night but for some reason didn't pursue the argument. He must have decided she could not be swayed. How dare he try to sidetrack her attempts to solve a murder by inventing a bogus clue for her to investigate. He probably thought she would find the book and be so intrigued by the mystery that she would spend yet another day looking into it. Just who did he think he was dealing with here? She would walk over to his house and return the book. There would be no more time wasted on an obviously fabricated myth.

But curiosity temporarily got the best of her, and she couldn't resist taking a small peek at one of the tagged pages with pictures showing casts of footprints and the anatomy of a foot with each part labeled. Significant sounding measurements were documented and other diagrams of the foot showing fulcrum: axis of foot rotation, direction of pull by calf muscles, power arm of foot lever, load arm of foot lever, and pressure of foot against surface were noted. It was interesting, but none of it made sense to Eleanor and she didn't care. She gathered the book, put on her jacket, and walked to Angus' house like a woman on a mission.

All the way there, she practiced what she would say about deception, manipulation, and lack of trust, but as she drew close her attention was drawn to a Mini Cooper parked in Angus' drive. Angus had company and Eleanor suspected it was Helen Pence, a widow who had been pursuing Angus for years. Eleanor shook her head and knocked on the door. If Angus was surprised to see her, he didn't show it.

"Hi, Ellie," he said, "Come in. Helen Pence is here. She brought me a lovely casserole. Maybe you'd like to eat with us." Was that pleading she saw in his eyes?

Eleanor looked past Angus at Helen seated on his leather couch, the same couch where she and Angus had engaged in delightful acts in the name of love.

"Oh no," she said quickly waving to Helen who smiled smugly and raised her glass of wine in greeting. "I don't want to intrude. I'm just returning this book you obviously left at my house last night. One never knows when you might need to reference information about someone with big hairy feet, but I'm no longer interested in the subject."

With that, she turned and walked back to her house muttering the whole way about trust and deception but with a totally different focus. She couldn't believe how angry she was. The gall of the man; inviting Helen Pence in, drinking wine with her, letting her sit on their love seat. It was ridiculous.

Then she remembered *The Four Agreements*, a book she had recently read by Don Miguel Ruiz that promised to improve your life if you followed all four agreements. The third agreement was not to make assumptions, and that was exactly what Eleanor had done. She assumed Angus was interested in Helen Pence. She assumed he would praise her casserole, drink wine, and make love to her. Maybe Helen Pence had brought her own wine. Angus couldn't help it if Helen was attracted to him. He probably didn't ask her to sit on the couch. Maybe he had invited Eleanor to eat with them to show Helen how much he didn't want to be alone with her. These were all assumptions. She was ridiculous. She was jealous! Suddenly there was nothing more that Eleanor wanted than to kiss and hold Angus and tell him how much he meant to her and ask him if Helen Pence made a habit of bringing dinner. Eleanor was at odds with herself, so giving up on the idea of tea, she poured herself a glass of wine and turned her attention to her timeline regarding Monica Fischer's death.

Studying the timeline, Eleanor realized how little she actually knew about the sequence of events. She didn't know when Klara and Tip had arrived, when they had met Monica, how long before others realized Monica was missing, or the last time anyone had actually seen her or when she was killed. There was much to do. Tomorrow she would visit Klara at her rental and ask some defining questions.

Suddenly realizing she was hungry, Eleanor drifted into the kitchen noting on her way that Feathers was still sulking by the window. He opened up one eye, but didn't follow her. She opened the refrigerator and surveyed the contents looking for something quick and easy to eat. "Nothing in here," she said to herself, "at least nothing I want to eat." This was definitely a night for an ice cream dinner. Just as she was adding the cherry on top of her decadent ice cream concoction, the doorbell rang. Feathers flew to the door but seeing Angus there, he made a rude remark that sounded like a fart and flew back to his perch by the window.

"Hi Ellie," Angus greeted her in a somewhat reserved way eying the bowl she held. "I brought some of Helen's casserole, but I guess you've already eaten." He would have entered but Eleanor stood in the doorway. "May I come in?" he asked.

"Certainly," Eleanor moved out of the way.

"You're not mad, are you?"

"Why would you ask that?" she answered while filling her mouth with ice cream.

"No reason, I guess I was worried about what you might be thinking seeing Helen at my house." He was easing his way into the kitchen with the casserole.

"Not at all," she lied. "I'm sure Helen is an excellent cook and a marvelous conversationalist."

"Are you planning to eat that whole bowl of ice cream by yourself?" he asked as he got a spoon and dipped it into the vanilla bean covered with chocolate syrup and nuts. "Mmmmmm, this isn't your dinner, is it?"

"It's very healthy," Eleanor replied, "I put a banana at the bottom."

"I see," Angus said wiping his mustache with his hand and reading the signs that shouted Eleanor is really pissed. "You understand that Helen Pence wouldn't think of bringing me dinner if she thought I was a happily married man."

"Of course she wouldn't. You can add morals to her list of attributes," Eleanor said. "Just how often does she feed you?"

Angus pivoted back to the marriage part. "You know I'd like to be a happily married man, but only to you."

"Are you leading Helen on? I mean does she know you don't want to marry her? Are you just using her to get a home-cooked meal?" Eleanor asked.

"Maybe," Angus shrugged. "It's not just her."

"Good grief, Angus! How many women are feeding you?" Eleanor asked. Her disapproval was evident. "I can't believe it! All this time I thought you were a decent man and here you are using women in a way that is reprehensible."

"What can I say? I like to eat," Angus said in defense. "If you married me, I would never allow another woman to feed me."

"That won't work, Angus! You need to be honest with these women. If you don't intend to create meaningful relationships with them, you need to let them find someone who does. It's wrong to take advantage of them this way," Eleanor scolded.

"I do have meaningful relationships with them. I've told them I'm not looking to marry them. They aren't interested in getting married either. They're just friends who like to cook for me," Angus said. "You want me to have friends, don't you?"

"Oh, well in that case, I see no problem with it," Eleanor said knowing instinctively that wasn't true. "It's late, Angus, and I need to work on my writing," Eleanor said dismissively walking him to the door. "Thanks for the casserole. Good night."

Eleanor finished her ice cream, threw the offending casserole in the trash and reassessed her relationship with Angus.

In the morning, Eleanor walked to the house on Ocean Street where Klara was staying. She deliberately took the long way around so she wouldn't have to pass Angus' house. It was a rare spring day with blue skies and a gentle breeze that brought the fresh sea air with it, but Eleanor wasn't paying attention.

"Good morning!" Klara seemed delighted to see her.

"Sorry I didn't call first," said Eleanor, "but I didn't have your number."

"That's fine. Guess I'm living on the lucky side of the road this morning. Come in," Klara said and wiped her hands on a dish towel she was holding. "Sit a spell and I'll get us some coffee."

Klara sat across from Eleanor at a table with a view of the blue Pacific Ocean. "How are you doing Klara?" Eleanor asked.

"I'm not going to lie," Klara confessed. "It's been hard. One day you're the peacock, and the next day you're the feather duster."

"What's happened?" asked Eleanor.

"The police talked to Jesse about Monica's murder. They haven't arrested him or anything, but we don't know what's coming down the pike. It's just a worry. We've rented this house for the month, so we're here until May Day. Hopefully he'll be cleared of suspicion by then and we can go home."

"Did Jesse tell you what the police wanted to know?" Eleanor probed.

"Just what he knew about Monica's past: did he know of anyone who wanted to hurt her, if they were intimate, when he'd seen her last, and if he had an alibi for the night of April 5th?" Klara didn't hold anything back. It was obvious that she was sure of Jesse's innocence.

"I understand that Monica was a very private person. Did she confide in Jesse?" asked Eleanor.

"Jesse is a good man," Klara said. "He listened to Monica's concerns and was a friend to her. As far as I know they were not intimate sexually, but she did confide in him about men who treated her as less than an equal at work and hit on her when she was out alone. She hinted about someone in her past that she was avoiding. That's what Tip meant when he said she was running from an abusive relationship."

"Do you know who that was?"

"No, but I know it affected Tip in a positive way. He's a good man too, and a Southern gentleman in every sense of the word. Remember the day I met you on the beach? That night Tip went to the casino. It's not the first time he didn't come home at night. I don't like it but there it is. He told me about something he saw while he was playing the slots. There was a man yelling at a woman, saying awful derogatory things, calling her names. Then he pushed her and when she fell to the floor, he grabbed her by the hair and pulled her up. She was crying. Tip said they were both drunk. It made him angry to see it so he intervened and actually got between the man and woman trying to reason with the guy until security came and escorted him off the premises. Tip took the woman to a café in the casino and they drank coffee until she felt better. The whole time she defended the man who she said was her husband. Tip gave her his card with his number on it in case she ever needed help in the future. I know he would have helped Monica if he could have. Anyway, she reassured him that her husband would be waiting for her in the parking lot and she would be fine now that he'd had time to cool off. Tip walked her to the parking lot and watched as she got in her husband's car and they drove away. Then he rented a room at the casino since it was too late to drive home. I know what you might be thinking. How do I know Tip didn't take advantage of her? I don't, but I guess sometimes you have to give men the benefit of the doubt. Plus, he's too old for hanky-panky, and I've learned life is simpler when you plow 'round the stumps."

"I'm sure everything is going to work out for you, Klara. By the way, does Jesse have an alibi for April 5?"

"I wish I could say he was here with me, but he wasn't, of course. It was a Friday night. He told police he was at the Red Shed with Molly Fiori and I believe him," Klara said.

"Did you ever remember the name of the town in California where Monica lived?" Eleanor asked.

"Oh yes, Orick, California. She worked for the National Parks Service. Something to do with wildlife biology."

"I've enjoyed our visit, Klara. Take care and let me know if you want to walk together sometime," Eleanor said.

On her way back to her house, Eleanor pondered the subject of men. What makes a man a good man? She thought about the roles they were assigned to play in a patriarchal society and wondered if they were all taught to protect women and why some became abusers. Monica Fischer had met a bad man. Eleanor was sure of it. She hurried home to research misogyny.

12 Ways to Spot a Misogynist

He will zero in on a woman and choose her as his target. He may be flirtatious causing her to lower her defenses.

His personality may change alternating between irresistible and rude.

He will make promises to women and fail to keep them but almost always keep his word with men.

He will be late for dates with women but never with men.

His behavior toward women can be grandiose, controlling, and egocentric.

He is extremely competitive, mostly with women, and feels terrible if a woman does better than him.

He has a double standard for women in the workplace and socially. Allowing men to do things he criticizes women friends and coworkers for doing.

He will be prepared to make women feel terrible. He may demand sex or withhold sex in his relationships, make jokes or put them down in public, steal their ideas and credit himself with them, or borrow money from them and never pay it back.

On a date, he will treat a woman the opposite way of how she prefers. Taking control when she wants it or giving her control when she doesn't desire it.

He likes to control women and pays little or no attention to their pleasure. Foreplay is only a means to an end which is satisfying his own. He avoids looking her in the eyes during sex.

He will cheat because he doesn't feel he owes a woman monogamy.

He may leave a relationship suddenly and then come back months later with a story that is designed to lure her back into the relationship.

Eleanor thoughtfully ticked off any characteristics she thought Angus possessed. There were absolutely none. She was positive he was not a misogynist. She decided to invite the coffee group for afternoon tea to share her latest findings.

It was a twenty-minute drive from the small town of Waterton to Sand Beach where Eleanor lived in a house on the hill overlooking the Pacific Ocean. The blue skies had turned gloomy and the vast expanse of ocean churned angrily, leaving yellow foam on the beach below. Everything hinted of rain as the coffee group arrived in Dede's white SUV.

"It's gonna blow!" predicted Cleo as she took off her coat and hung it in the entryway.

"I'm dying of curiosity," said Pearl. "What have you discovered?"

"It's not that exciting," said Eleanor, who greeted her guests in her stockinged feet. "Please come in and sit down."

Eleanor's dining table was laden with petit fours, finger sandwiches, a fruit platter, and nuts. A pot in a colorful tea cozy sat next to lemon wedges and sugar. She knew no one took cream in their tea. Each friend chose their favorite among Eleanor's teacup collection and sat as ordered.

"I visited Klara this morning and she was very open about what has happened lately. It seems that Jesse has been questioned and is a person of interest but hasn't been arrested, suggesting the police haven't enough evidence to charge him. She and Tip are staying until the end of the month hoping Jesse will be cleared by then. That's not the interesting part. Klara claims Jesse did not have a sexual relationship with Monica, he may still be involved with Molly Fiori, and that Monica confided to him about men who treated her as less than an equal at work and hit on her when she was alone. She was avoiding a certain man which is why Tip said she was running from an abusive relationship. I believe she was involved with a misogynist. The police asked Jesse for an alibi for the night of April 5, so we know they think she was murdered that Friday. Jesse told them he was at the Red Shed with Molly. I also did some research on the subject of misogynists and thought we might be able to identify men we know who exhibit these traits." Eleanor stopped to sip her tea as the others studied the information that she had printed off the internet.

"Misogynists are everywhere," Josephine said, "but very hard to spot. They may have some of these traits, but not all of them and they are usually charming, at first anyway."

"Phooey!" Dede spat, "I think I can name at least ten of them who work in city government."

"Great!" Eleanor passed her a piece of paper and a pen. "Write down your suspects. We can start there."

"There are women misogynists too, you know," Josephine said.

"Now I can add three more," Dee said shaking her head as she added women to her list.

"There was something else," Eleanor said, "Klara told me Monica was originally from a small town in California… Orick where she worked for the National Parks as a wildlife biologist."

"That's interesting," said Cleo. "She left a good, high paying job to work as an accounting clerk in a small town."

"Sounds like she was running away from someone in Orick," said Pearl. "I'm not going all the way down there to investigate."

"I might know someone who knows someone down there," said Dede. "I'll give the mayor of Orick a call."

"Eleanor, I thought you would have some relevant information from Angus," said Cleo.

"No, we haven't talked about the case since the Bigfoot debacle. I'm sure we can solve it without his input," Eleanor said.

"Oh-oh, sounds like trouble in Paradise," said Dede.

Eleanor sighed, "Tell me what you think of this. I went to his house the other night and Helen Pence was there. Evidently, Helen, and a number of other women have been feeding him. She was sitting on his couch drinking a glass of wine."

The other ladies looked at each other and there was a deafening silence until Cleo spoke up, "We thought you knew."

Eleanor was flabbergasted, "Knew what?"

"Eleanor, a number of ladies at church take turns feeding Angus. They bake him cookies, take him casseroles, and invite him to dinner at their houses," said Dede. "It's been going on ever since his divorce from Margo."

"How come no one ever said anything about it to me?" Eleanor felt betrayed.

"Well, there didn't seem to be any reason to mention it," said Pearl. "I guess we assumed you knew."

"I didn't know and now I feel like a fool," Eleanor said. "I told Angus he needed to stop leading these women on because they must want something from him in return."

"I'm sure they're getting it," said Josephine who stopped suddenly when she realized how that must sound to Eleanor. "I mean, most of the women are widows and Angus does a few chores for them, you know, like mowing their yards, fixing a leaky faucet, that kind of thing."

"I see, but I thought I was the only one." Eleanor sighed again as tears flooded her eyes.

"Oh Eleanor, you are the only one in Angus' eyes," said Dede. "He would marry you in a heartbeat and spend the rest of his life with you, and no one else."

"So, you think it's fine that he allows these women to cook for him while he repays them with his handyman abilities?" she asked.

"I guess so, if both parties understand that there are no other expectations," Pearl said.

"Eleanor, it seems like you have other expectations," Josephine said. "Maybe you and Angus need to work out some wrinkles in your relationship."

"I see that," Eleanor said thoughtfully. "I can't expect him to give up his friends to suit me, especially if I refuse his offer to be my one and only."

"Let's help clean up and head out," said Dede. "I think we've done enough for today."

After the coffee ladies left, Eleanor reviewed the information about Angus and his lady friends with an open mind and decided she was a hypocrite. She would apologize to Angus immediately and reassess her own friendships with other men. Did she have dinner dates with other men? No. Did she want to? Maybe she did. If she wanted to invite someone to dinner, who would it be? She couldn't come up with anyone. It seems she had neglected to make male friends in favor of Angus. She picked up the *Fish Wrapper* and began to read about local events to focus on something else. When she got to the letters to the Editor she saw an interesting one:

Citizens of Waterton, wake up! We are being besieged by an evil force in our community. Witches are practicing their craft right under our very noses. Our children are in danger of falling prey to a group of women who actively observe the pagan rituals of solstice and equinox. I have actually witnessed them as they worshiped the devil by dancing naked in the moonlight. Our downtown has welcomed a shop that deals in the devil's toys: tarot cards, crystals, and the paraphernalia of magic used by witches to cast spells upon the innocent. We must act as a Christian community to dig this rot out and condemn those who would mock our celebrations of spirituality and godliness. The Bible says not to suffer a witch to live, and those of us who believe had better act for the goodness of all before it is too late.

– Helen Pence

Eleanor tossed the paper aside. It seemed as though the universe wanted her to dwell on Helen Pence.

As she pondered her situation inside her cozy home, outside the storm intensified. The wind threw a tantrum banging on doors and furiously pelting the windows with rain. Eleanor, deep in thought, ignored it all until Feathers flew by warning of intruders. It was then she realized the banging on the door was a person. Thinking it might be Angus she was surprised instead to find Tip Kent dripping wet on her doorstep.

"Tip, come in," Eleanor said taking his jacket and hanging it out of the way.

"Thank you," he drawled. "Sorry to drop in uninvited, but I wanted to clear up a few things with you."

"Please come in and sit down, I'll make us some tea," she offered.

"Oh no tea, thank you, but I wouldn't refuse something a little stronger," he said.

Eleanor looked at the clock and realized it was later than she thought. Tip was probably chilled to the bone and might benefit from a shot of Drambuie she had stowed away in the cupboard. Just a little of that would warm him from the inside out. She poured it in a brandy snifter and offered it to him.

"Now what's on your mind, Tip?" she asked as she watched him throw back the drink as though it were water.

"Boy, that's got some kick to it?" Tip sputtered. After he recovered, he began, "Klara told me you came to see her this morning asking a lot of questions about Monica and Jesse. Are you a detective or just plumb nosy?"

"Technically, I'm just nosy. I'd like to help if I can," Eleanor said sincerely. She didn't want Tip to think she was a gossip.

"My Klara is a good woman, but she dotes on that boy of hers. I don't know if he's guilty or not but Klara is positive he's innocent. I don't know your intentions, so if you hurt her, I'll cloud up and rain all over you. If you are really interested in proving he had nothing to do with this, I'd like to work with you."

"Trust me, I'm on your side, Tip. Do you know anything that might help? Klara said Jesse was at the Red Shed on the night Monica was murdered. Do you know anything about that?"

"I can't say that I do. Although, I was at the Red Shed that night too playing video poker in the back. I saw Jesse there with Molly, but I can't swear that they were there all night."

"What time did you see them?" Eleanor asked.

"Maybe around 9:00. I left around midnight and they were gone," he said. "I liked Monica. I'm sure Jesse did too, so I was surprised when I saw him with Molly. Guess I assumed they were history."

"I'm afraid assumptions don't pass muster as far as the law is concerned," Eleanor pointed out.

Feathers made a pass through the room announcing the arrival of another visitor at the same time as the doorbell rang. "I should be off." Tip said, "Klara will be wondering where I am. Thank you, dear lady, for your warmth and hospitality." He kissed her hand and walked with her to the door where Angus waited patiently.

"Come in, Angus," Eleanor said.

"It's a terrible night to be out in this weather," Tip said as he put on his coat and walked outside. "Good night, Angus." His greeting faded into the wind's din.

"I brought Chinese. Didn't want my girl eating ice cream for dinner again," Angus said as he hung up his raincoat and followed Eleanor with the food into the kitchen. "What was Tip doing here?"

"Thanks for dinner, Angus," Eleanor said. "I didn't realize how late it was or how hungry I am."

She dug out her chopsticks, opened a bottle of wine, and stuffed her mouth with almond chicken sub gum chow mien. Angus watched her eat. He sighed and waited for her to answer his question.

"What?" she asked.

"What was Tip doing here?" he repeated softly. Eleanor could tell he was on the verge of anger by the way his jaw muscles flexed and his brows descended.

"Are you jealous, or just nosy?" Eleanor couldn't help herself. She was still hurt by his secret harem of lady friends.

Angus took the chopsticks from her and asked, "Is this about Helen Pence? Because I told you she is a friend who likes to cook for me and that's all. I never asked any of those women for anything. It's harmless and I'm able to help them in return by doing odd jobs."

"Why not tell me about it then?" she asked. "I always thought you avoided Helen and her breathless way of speaking to you."

Angus sighed, "What do I need to do to make it right with you?"

"Nothing. I'm totally fine with it. Tip was here to discuss the case because I visited Klara this morning and he wanted to set some things straight."

"Set what things straight?"

"He wanted to know if I was a gossip or a friend," Eleanor said, "So forgive me if I don't share what she told me, because I told him I was a friend."

Angus studied Eleanor's face looking for some clue that would tell him how to proceed. "Are you okay?" he asked. "I'm feeling some animosity from you and I want to understand what's making you so angry. Let me have it. I can handle it."

Eleanor felt the anger leave her like air from a leaky balloon. "I feel like you are trying to sideline me with this bogus hunt for Bigfoot so that I won't interfere in the murder investigation."

"I see." Angus was busted. "So, this has nothing to do with Helen Pence? Honestly, I'm a little hurt that you don't care enough about me to be jealous. I love you, Ellie. That's why I don't want you mixed up in an investigation that deals with criminals, murder, and the ugly nature of men. I just want to protect you."

"Well, if it makes you feel better, I am jealous, but I'm not sure I have a right to be. I'm the one who won't marry you but I still want you all to myself. I realize I don't have a right to dictate who your friends are and I'm working through it. It's hard." A lone tear streaked her cheek and Angus cupped her chin and tenderly wiped it away with his thumb, pulling her close and holding her for what seemed an eternity.

"However," Eleanor said backing away, "I don't need protection from the ugliness of the world. I need to know I'm capable of finding my way in it, learning how to cope with it and if I can, doing something about it."

The storm passed, Angus headed for home and Eleanor felt adrift. The kitchen sparkled, floors were clean, and everything was back in its place. She noticed her woodcutting jacket had fallen from a hook onto the floor. That jacket needed to be washed, but as she picked it up, she felt something in the pocket and fished out the tarot card she found the day she and Angus had gone woodcutting, the day they discovered the body of Monica Fischer. Was this a clue? The Lovers suddenly had new meaning to her and she couldn't wait to learn what Madam Patruska could tell her about it. Even though it was getting late and Madam Patruska's shop of psychic necessities was certainly closed, Eleanor picked up the phone and called members of the coffee group. The only one she could reach was Cleo and it didn't take much to convince her that a visit to The Oracle was imperative. They decided to meet there as soon as possible.

"It's dark inside. I guess she's not in there," Cleo said peeking in the window.

Using her cell phone's flashlight, Eleanor illuminated the scene before her.

"The door has been forced, and the lock is broken," Eleanor said as she carefully pushed her way into what appeared to be the aftermath of a destructive storm.

"This doesn't look good," said Cleo moving quickly past the psychic books that spilled from shelves onto the floor and into Madam Patruska's private reading room. "There's no sign of her in here. Do you think it was a robbery?"

"It looks like someone was looking for something specific," said Eleanor as she noted the undisturbed tarot cards laid out on the table and the jar of dollar bills left on the counter.

"I'll call the police," said Cleo as she dug her phone from her purse.

"Wait," said Eleanor. "Let's look around first. Just don't touch anything."

"What are you hoping to find?" asked Cleo.

"I've always wondered how Madam Patruska could tell people their fortunes. How does she know the things she knows? Maybe we'll find her secret," Eleanor said as she pushed back the beaded curtain and stepped into the room where Patruska held her consultations.

"Maybe she's a psychic," Cleo said as she searched the room for hidden wires under the rug.

"You don't believe that, do you?" Eleanor asked checking the corners for sound devices.

Just then Cleo tripped on a corner of the rug and fell against the wall making a hollow-sounding thud.

"Are you okay?" asked Eleanor.

"Yes, but I think I broke through the wall," Cleo said righting herself.

Eleanor investigated the wall for damage. It appeared to be made of ordinary ridged paneling. "This is a very flimsy wall. My guess is it's false and there is something important hidden behind it." She continued to push on it until it folded like an accordion revealing a row of filing cabinets. "Eureka!"

"Must be something worth hiding in here," said Cleo.

"Maybe something worth breaking and entering for as well! Cleo, hold the light over here." Eleanor ordered and began to snoop in earnest, opening one of the file drawers and noting the names of various Waterton area residents stored in alphabetical order. "There's a dossier in here for several people in Waterton, and one on Josephine Flutter!"

"Oh great, what does it say? Is there information about Josephine's husbands?" Cleo was eager to learn more about Josephine's past loves.

"I don't think we should read these," said Eleanor.

Cleo snatched the file out of Eleanor's hands, ignoring Eleanor's words completely.

"It says here, Josephine has been married three times and her first husband, Biff Argyle, is dead. Her second husband, Harry Gilman, divorced, and her third, Richard Johnson, still married and extremely devoted to her. Did we know that about her first husband?" asked Cleo. "Do you think there was foul play involved?"

"Never mind that," Eleanor said. "I'm sure Josephine didn't break in and ransack Madam Patruska's shop looking for that information, let alone murder her husband, but somebody was definitely looking for something in here. We just don't know who or what. We need to find Madam Patruska, but I don't know where she lives and she hasn't been answering her phone."

"I thought she lived here," said Cleo. "I guess that's as juvenile as believing teachers live at school. Do you think she's in trouble? Maybe she's been kidnapped."

"Think, think, think," Eleanor chanted. "Maybe her home address is in here somewhere." Headlights from a passing car circled the room with an eerie glow causing both women to bury their lights and hide in darkness. "We have to get out of here and leave no trace behind."

"Right," agreed Cleo. She put Josephine's file back, wiped her prints off whatever she may have touched, and left the secret room. Just as Eleanor was ready to close the drawer an interesting file caught her eye—one labeled "The Witches."

"I'm taking this with me," she said.

"Fine with me," said Cleo reappearing behind Eleanor. "What should we do with this?" In her hand, she held a black velvet, high-heeled shoe with a red sole.

By the time Eleanor and Cleo erased all evidence of their presence at The Oracle and drove to Dede's house, it was almost midnight.

"I got your text," said Dede climbing into the backseat of Eleanor's car, "but you are not going to Patruska's house without me." Of course, Dede knew where Madame Patruska lived and she directed them to a cottage on the east side of town in short order. A yellow Kia Soul sat in the driveway of the orange house trimmed in blue.

"She must be home, since her car is here," said Cleo. But when they knocked on the cobalt blue door, there was no response. They peered in the window, afraid of what they might see.

"It doesn't look like things are disturbed inside," Eleanor observed shining her light in the window.

"Maybe she's asleep," said Cleo, "It's past *my* bedtime. Let's go around to the back."

"Don't you think it's strange that she hasn't closed her curtains?" asked Dede.

"Not as strange as seeing the mayor of Waterton in her pajamas roaming around town in the middle of the night," teased Cleo. Not one of the amateur detectives noticed a light come on in a window next door as they stood in awe of the garden.

Madam Patruska's backyard, lit by hundreds of twinkle lights, was alive with the colors of early spring blossoms. Purple and red rhododendrons, pink and white dogwood trees, and tulips of every hue filled the space and mingled with the rich scents of lavender and jasmine, all against the lush backdrop of Oregon green shrubbery. Eleanor opened the screen door and rapped loudly on the back door. There was no response. She turned the knob and entered the house calling out Madam Patruska's name. The empty house emanated an eerie silence revealing a tale of hurried departure, dishes in the sink, an unmade bed littered with discarded clothing, dresser drawers emptied, and a pile of unopened mail under the mail slot of the front door.

"Madam Patruska is missing," said Cleo.

"Yes," Eleanor replied holding up an envelope from the pile of mail, "But I think I know where she is."

The ladies of the coffee group had no time for breakfast or coffee. They were on a mission to locate the illusive Madame Patruska who evidently knew someone living on the golf course at Salishan, near Lincoln City.

"It might be a wild goose chase," warned Eleanor as she drove south on Highway 101 with the four other super-snoops all chattering at once. Cleo explained in great detail the break-in at The Oracle the night before and Dede added everything she knew about the contents of Madame Patruska's refrigerator.

"I wasn't surprised that she eats lots of fruits and vegetables," Dede revealed, "but there was vodka in her freezer, a bottle of Limoncello, and a great deal of tequila in her cupboard. I knew she was a kindred spirit."

"And why are we going to Salishan again?" asked Josephine who was still in shock at the early morning call that demanded her participation in an investigative trip.

"We discovered a personal letter from someone at this address. It must be someone close to her who may know of her whereabouts. It's important that we find her. The Oracle was ransacked, the incriminating shoe was found there, and she's missing. It all amounts to danger for her," Eleanor said.

"Plus, we steamed the letter open and found out she has a sister who lives there and sent her birthday wishes and an invitation to dinner," confessed Cleo.

"I had nothing to do with that," said Dede defensively. "Opening other people's mail is a criminal offense."

"Isn't breaking and entering also a criminal offense?" asked Josephine.

"It wasn't technically breaking and entering since the lock was already broken when we got there," explained Eleanor.

"I had nothing to do with that either," Dede said, imagining the headline: **Mayor Caught in Criminal Activities.**

"What did you do with the shoe?" asked Pearl.

"Cleo found it under the table in Patruska's consultation room. I can't believe she had anything to do with Monica's death," said Eleanor.

"We left it in the room behind the secret wall," Cleo replied. "It could be evidence and we didn't want to interfere with it, but didn't want it to be easy to find either."

"Do you think it was planted there by someone who wanted the police to think Madame Patruska killed Monica Fischer?" asked Josephine.

"Yes," said Eleanor, "But we left it there because we didn't want to incriminate ourselves. I mean what would we do with it?"

"Have you reported any of this to the police?" asked Pearl.

"Of course not!" said Eleanor. "Angus would be furious. I found that tarot card in the woods when we went woodcutting. He'll think I held back important information and this break-in at The Oracle will only prove that. Madame Patruska knows something and if we can find out what she knows maybe we can solve the case before the police arrest her. I don't believe she's a killer, but the evidence is piling up."

"Hasn't Angus given you any information about the case?" asked Dede.

"No, he said he's trying to protect me," Eleanor sighed.

"So that's why he put you on the trail of Bigfoot," Josephine said.

"Exactly," Eleanor said.

"So, what do you think the tarot card means?" asked Dede.

"It could have been planted at the scene to incriminate Patruska," said Cleo, "But why The Lovers?"

"Maybe to implicate Jesse Bomotti," said Eleanor.

"Only Madame Patruska will be able to help us with that," said Pearl.

"After we solve the case," Cleo began, "let's go shopping at the outlet stores in Lincoln City."

"I do need a new pair of walking shoes," said Dede.

"Maybe we could get lunch at Kylos," said Cleo, "I love their fish tacos."

"There may be a good movie at the Bijou," added Josephine. "I love that funky little theater and the organ player."

The directions to Madame Patruska's sister led them to a gated community armed with a special code necessary to activate the gate. Fortunately, the code was included in the letter that alluded to Patruska's absent-mindedness. They arrived at a lovely home on the fifth hole within view of the ocean.

"Do you think she'll be put off by five unfamiliar women at her door?" asked Josephine as they tumbled out of the car stretching their legs.

"I just can't sit anymore," Cleo complained. "I'm going in."

They all went to the door, knocked and waited politely on the welcome mat that spelled out BECKER. It wasn't long before a tall, beautiful woman with blond hair in a French roll peered out somewhat nervously.

"Yes, may I help you?" she asked.

"Are you Birdy Becker? We're friends of your sister, Madame Patruska. We are hoping to talk to her. Is she here?" asked Eleanor.

"Yes, my friends call me Birdy. Are you the witches?" she asked.

"No, but we have some information that may be of importance to her. May we come in?" Eleanor persisted.

"Of course," said Birdy, "Please sit down. Patricia is not here but maybe I can help you. Would you like a drink? I was just about to make a martini."

"No thank you," said Eleanor, "I'm driving."

"I'll take one," said Cleo.

The others shook their heads, shocked by the early offer of a martini. "Maybe a glass of water," suggested Josephine as she sat on the couch with the others.

"May I use your restroom?" Asked Dede who planned to scour the house for clues.

"Of course," said Birdy as she prepared the beverages. "Please make yourselves comfortable. Perhaps you would like a scone. My husband baked them this morning." She placed a plate of blueberry scones on the coffee table along with a pot of tea and a martini with extra olives for Cleo.

"They look delicious," Eleanor said noticing the browned scones cut into perfect triangles and drizzled with a delicate sugar glaze.

Cleo sipped her martini and silently wondered how Birdy knew she liked her martini dirty with extra olives. Maybe she was a psychic too.

"Is Madame Patruska here?" asked Pearl.

"No, she isn't." Birdy looked out the window as if in a trance.

"Do you know where she might be?" asked Cleo.

"I can't say that I do," responded Birdy mysteriously.

An uncomfortable silence hung in the air. Did she know or was she forbidden to say? They weren't getting the answers they wanted.

"I know she was here recently, but I don't remember if it was Sunday or Wednesday," Birdy said before sipping her martini and rolling her eyes at the ceiling. "Oh, I do remember now. She left an article about abused women here for me to read. Now where did I put it?" Birdy stood up and walked around the room in search of the missing article, stopping at several places to peer closely as if spotting it but then walking away. "Maybe it's in here," she said opening what looked to be an accordion case. She took an accordion out, sat on a chair, and began to play, but it quickly became obvious that she had absolutely no skill in the music department whatsoever. She squeezed the accordion and pushed the keys producing a discordant sound and then began to sing, "*And they called it puppy love…*"

Cleo began to giggle which caused Birdy to stop playing and break out in hysterical laughter and soon everyone was laughing and snorting. The whole bizarre thing lasted only minutes and ended with the coffee ladies clapping wildly as though Birdy had just finished, *La Cumparsita*, the most famous accordion tango ever played.

"That was fabulous," lied Dede, now appearing in the doorway, "But we really need to be going if we're to be on time for our next appointment." Suddenly, the coffee ladies were on their feet heading for the door. Dede's words conveyed the message that she had discovered something in her search for the restroom.

"It was so nice of you to visit. Please stop by anytime," Birdy said.

"Thank you for the martini, it was perfect!" said Cleo, stuffing the last of the olives into her mouth.

"Yes, I know," Birdy beamed.

"The scones were delicious too," said Pearl.

"My husband made them. Mine are much better," Birdy said, closing the door behind them.

Dede was already in the car when the others piled in. "What an unusual character," said Josephine, "I'm sure she was pretending to be forgetful because she didn't want to tell us where Madame Patruska was."

"We didn't learn anything from her, that's for sure," said Eleanor starting the car.

"Oh, yes we did," Dede said smugly. "I found an address scribbled on a piece of paper in the dining room. It's near Land's End and I'd bet my Sunday socks that it's where Patruska's hiding. By the way, Eleanor, there was a copy of your poetry book in the bathroom."

"Well, if Madame Patruska should ask how we found her, we can say a little birdy told us," Pearl said, and the super snoops were off.

Angus pulled out the chair with gentlemanly attentiveness, so that Helen Pence could sit at the luxurious table at Chez Pacifica, an elegant restaurant along the coast where he and Eleanor had never dined. He sat across from her and smiled pleasantly preparing himself for an hour of simple yet informative conversation. As she chatted away about her volunteer activities in the community, he noticed the large mole on her chin and the black hairs that protruded from her nose. Although he found these things unbecoming, they were nothing compared to the annoying exaggerated breathy way in which she spoke. He wondered if she thought this panting was sexy or if she actually had a medical condition that contributed to it. As she continued to regale him with her many charitable works, Angus lost focus and his mind envisioned her unable to breathe at all, and eventually falling off her chair in a total faint from lack of oxygen. He would rip open her polyester blouse, ignore her oversized breasts hanging flatly on her chest and provide CPR, or worse, administer mouth-to-mouth resuscitation. The mere thought of touching that thin mouth ringed with red lipstick bleeding into its creases made him visibly shudder and brought him back to the present.

"Oh Angus, you precious man," she wheezed, "It really wasn't necessary for you to take me to lunch."

"It's my pleasure, Helen," he lied. "You've provided me with many meals over the years."

"Not as many as I would like." She sighed heavily and reached out to touch his hand. She loved taking meals to him, but only once had he invited her inside his home and then that horrible feminist witch, Eleanor Penrose, had dropped by just when she was sure he was going to kiss her, totally destroying the mood.

"Are you sure you're alright?" Angus asked with genuine concern. "You seem to be winded."

"Well, I guess you take my breath away," she said with a little less drama. Perhaps she realized she had overplayed her part. "I so appreciate a man who takes charge. Perhaps you could order for me."

"Of course." Angus quickly scanned the menu and decided she should have the cob salad and a glass of white wine. He would have a burger and fries.

"It's so refreshing to enjoy the company of a man who treats a lady the way he should. The younger generation is so misguided with women who want to tell men what to do. A women should be submissive to her husband. It's written in the Bible, and you really can't blame them for acting in ungentlemanly ways when they are just trying to keep their wives in line. I really feel a woman should know her place in the order of things. My friend, Eva Blount, was telling me about a charming man she knows who agrees that our society is going to hell because women think they can take charge at work and in the home."

Angus didn't want to argue with Helen, so he merely nodded. "Now tell me about your latest project. I understand you are leading a group of women to look into the practice of witchcraft in the area," Angus said. He did not have to speak for the rest of the hour but what he heard concerned him greatly.

Eleanor drove to the address Dede had stored away in her magnificent brain. Outside, the building looked like any other beach house resting on the sand at Land's End; two story, gray shingles with white trim, driftwood and an anchor in the yard, a welcome mat on the porch, and a sign denoting the address. Cleo rang the bell and they all waited patiently to see who would open the door. Imagine their surprise when a kind, familiar face peeked out and cried with delight, "Cleo!" Sue Rawe, Cleo's friend from Portland flung the door open hugging Cleo as she pulled her inside. "Come in quickly," she said. Stunned by what was happening, the ladies stumbled into the house and Sue closed the door and locked it behind them.

"How in the world did you come to be here?" asked Sue.

"Mysterious machinations are at work," came a voice from another room.

"We're looking for a friend who might be in trouble," said Dede, her eyes searching for the owner of the voice. "Is Madame Patruska here?"

"Yes," Sue said. "Come into the living room and sit down and I'll tell you everything I know."

The ladies followed Sue into a very modern living room with windows that looked out over the ocean and flooded the room with light. They quickly found comfortable seating in a plush sectional that faced a fireplace whose embers glowed and chased away any morning chill.

"A few days ago," she began, "I was walking by the bus stop on the corner of 101 and Beach Street when I noticed this woman sitting on the bench with her head in her hands moaning. She looked as though she needed help so I stopped to talk with her. It was evident to me that she was in distress, so I asked her if I could assist her in some way."

Madame Patruska suddenly swept into the room; red frizzy hair floating around a pale face, the back of her thin hand pressed against her forehead as she began to dramatically add her perspective to the story. "It was as if the universe heard my plea and sent this angel in my harkest dour. I told her I was in teep drouble and needed a ride to my sister's house. I was so terribly afraid. I knew they would come after me and I had to weave Laterton before they realized I was involved. That poor girl …" Madame Patruska began to weep quietly.

The ladies of the coffee group were familiar with Madame Patruska's unusual manner of speaking which included spoonerisms that were simply word sounds or syllables switched around. Sometimes it made understanding her difficult, but if she concentrated, it happened with less frequency and sometimes not at all.

"She's had a bad time of it," Sue said. "She was terrified when I first met her so I took her to her sister's house as she asked, but she continued to say it wasn't safe there, so I offered to bring her here where I could hide her."

"Your background as a psychiatric nurse uniquely enabled you to help her," said Josephine. "How extraordinary that you would do such a thing for a stranger." Was Josephine questioning Sue's motives?

"It's not strange at all," Cleo said. "Sue is the kindest person I know so it's not unusual for her to help a stranger. It's baked into her DNA."

"I don't understand how you found us. We have been so careful not to be out and about and very few people know John and I bought this house, so how did you come to be here?" Sue asked.

Eleanor told them about finding the tarot card at the murder scene that led her to Madame Patruska's shop. "I thought you might be able to shed some light on how it came to be there. Do you remember the last reading you gave? Does The Lovers mean anything special to you?"

"No, I don't know what connection it has to the murder," Patruska said. "The Covers lard augers the necessity of choice of some sort but usually in love. Sometimes it means a love triangle, or a choice between love and career or some other creative outlet. It implies a leed to nook carefully at what your choices may lead to instead of just charging blindly ahead, but it must be evaluated in relation to other spards in the cread."

"Someone broke into your shop," Dede said. "Is that why you ran away?"

"No, that's a lack of pies. I ran away when I learned that Fonica Mischer was murdered. I believed whoever killed her would come after me next because of the letters. I didn't know they shoke into my brop." This news seemed to frazzle her even more. "I have to ball Cirdy and tell her you found me. If you can, they can too."

"We went to your house to look for you there," said Pearl, "And that's where Eleanor saw the letter from Birdy. Forgive us for opening it, but we were desperate to find you."

"Birdy was very hospitable and I found a note with this address scribbled on it. We took a chance and here we are," Dede added.

"I'll call her," said Sue kindly as she picked up her cell phone and left the room.

"Madame Patruska, what letters are you referring to exactly?" Josephine asked, "And how were you involved with Monica Fischer?"

"I'll show you," she answered, leaving the ladies to look at each other in wonderment, returning shortly with several sheets of paper, each with a simple message.

Saul died because he was unfaithful to the Lord; he did not keep the word of the Lord and even consulted a medium for guidance.

He sacrificed his children in the fire in the Valley of Ben Hinnom, practiced divination and witchcraft, sought omens, and consulted mediums and spiritists. He did much evil in the eyes of the Lord, arousing his anger.

A man or woman who is a medium or spiritist among you must be put to death. You are to stone them; their blood will be on their own heads.

I will destroy your witchcraft, and you will no longer cast spells.

Disaster will come upon you, and you will not know how to conjure it away.

"At first I didn't think much of them, but they became more threatening and then Fonica Mischer ... was she sturned or boned?"

"We don't know exactly what caused her death," Eleanor said. "I doubt she was burned."

"I'm pretty sure these are from the Old Testament of the Bible," said Dede. "Sounds like a fanatical religious person who takes the scriptures very literally. Do you have any idea who might have sent them?"

"Not really, there are so many people who think I'm a fake, or worse, doing the wevil's dork. Did they destroy my shop?" asked Patruska putting her head in her hands.

"No," Cleo said. "It was mostly messed up as though someone was searching for something. I accidentally fell against the false wall and discovered your files. We wouldn't know if anything was taken but something was left there. Monica's missing shoe was in your shop."

"That sakes no mense at all." Patruska said. "How would her shoe get in my shop? She's never been there, although she did celebrate the vernal equinox with a group of women I know. Oh, and she came to a pard yarty at my house recently, but as far as I know she was never at The Oracle."

"The shoe was from the pair she was wearing when she was killed," said Eleanor. "The other one was found at the crime scene."

"Perhaps the murderer planted it there to implicate Patricia," said Sue who returned with a tray filled with a teapot, cups, saucers, and a variety of little treats. She insisted on calling Madame Patruska by her given name.

"Maybe the tarot card was also planted at the scene for the same reason," Josephine said.

"Or maybe to throw suspicion on someone who was her lover," suggested Eleanor. The ladies pondered this information while laying out the tea items.

"Was Monica Fischer a witch?" asked Dede.

"That's a lirty die! I believe she was serely a meeker. She was looking for a safe place to belong and ground a froup of women who offered friendship in return for her help. I can't say for sure what she practiced, but most of the women at my parden garty were there to have fun."

"Well, Birdy has been alerted and promised to dispose of any items that might lead anyone else here. She claims she even destroyed the entire tablet the note was written on just in case they used that trick of rubbing on the embossed letters to read the blank page underneath," Sue reported while pouring tea into each lady's cup.

"Shall we have a reading of your lea teaves when you're finished?" asked Madame Patruska. Eying each person in the room for a nod of the head, she proceeded. "You shall be the querent and I the seer. Enjoy your tea while reflecting on what you would like to learn from the reading."

A comfortable silence descended over the room while everyone sipped their tea, nibbled on cookies, and contemplated what they wanted to learn. Even the musical rolling of the ocean's waves muffled by incoming fog encouraged meditation. After finishing the tea, each lady took her cup in her left hand by its handle, swirled it quickly three times from left to right and slowly turned it over into the saucer as Madame Patruska instructed. "We will leave the cup for a minute to let the moisture dissipate. When you curn your tups upright the tea leaves should be stuck in various shapes and clusters. Try to discern the major shapes, then curn your tups to view it from several angles."

Josephine held up her cup. "I see a small circle," she said, and maybe a bear." Madame Patruska peered into the cup and her face lit up. "A small circle like this is a very sortunate fymbol. It indicates marriage or a ring, but the bear brings obstacles from a previous bad decision."

Eleanor couldn't help but think of Klara's ring and Josephine's three marriages. She looked at her own cup and saw a nest and something that looked like a tiny alligator. What could they possibly mean. Madame Patruska nodded as she studied Eleanor's cup. "The nest is a symbol of emotional security and a wish to create a safe loving home. It could also signify a committed relationship, but the alligator means betrayal and rivalry. The fact that the nest is large and the alligator is small indicates its importance."

Of course, Cleo's chicken meant that her home would be a happy one and the bee confirmed a blissful busy life. Madame Patruska moved on to Pearl whose bull warned of slander by enemies and a broom predicted changes in life, perhaps a new home.

Finally, Dede showed her a gun and a goat. "This gun means discord, slander, and possibly injury," Madame Patruska said, "but the goat shows you will have success in any venture."

"That's politics for you," grumbled Dede. "Tell us what your tea leaves reveal."

"Sue and I read our leaves this morning. We only do one deading a ray," Madame Patruska said as she set the tea cups on the tray. Eleanor took this as a sign that they should leave and stood to go.

"Thank you for the refreshments," she began, "But we've completed our mission and should head back to Waterton. Now that you know about the break-in and the shoe, we'll let you decide how to handle that."

After they left, Madame Patruska eyed the large cross that looked like an 'X' near the top of her cup's handle. It was a warning: proceed with caution.

"Shall we go shopping?" asked Eleanor as they piled into her car once more.

"I'm hungry for real food," said Cleo. "All we've eaten today is cookies and scones."

"The urge to shop has passed for me," said Dede. "I just want to talk about everything we've heard today."

"For heaven's sake what is this file back here?" Pearl asked as she pulled something up that appeared to have slid under the car seat. "And who are the witches?"

"That's the file I took from The Oracle's secret room," said Eleanor. "I forgot it was back there."

"Let's go to Kylo's and grab a bite to eat," said Josephine. "It's not far." With everyone in favor, Eleanor easily found the restaurant despite the heavy fog that took the light from the day. It was as though some unseen force drove them. "Bring the file inside," said Eleanor.

They sat by the window facing the ocean waves that washed ashore under the restaurant and studied the menu.

"What's everybody having?" asked Pearl putting her menu down. "I'm having the clam chowder."

"It's fish and chips for me," said Josephine. "I'm starving."

"I love their crispy fish tacos," said Cleo.

"The hazelnut blue cheese salad looks good to me," said Eleanor.

"Hmmm," said Dede, "I guess I'll know when it comes out of my mouth." When the waitress came to take their orders, Ceasar salad and crème brûlé was what she chose.

While they waited for their meals, they munched on warm bread and fresh butter and finally turned their attention to the mystery at hand.

"Did anyone else notice how often the tea leaves told us of scandals and enemies?" asked Pearl.

"That was just you and Dede, Pearl. I told you to stop shopping at those resale stores. You know how people love to gossip," Cleo said. Dede and Pearl exchanged confused glances.

"I'm more interested in Josephine's ring," said Eleanor. "Were you thinking of Tip's ring while you were sipping your tea?"

"You don't believe in that, do you?" Josephine asked evasively. "I mean it's just for fun. Although I thought yours was spot on, Eleanor. Were you thinking of Helen Pence as a rival?"

"Actually, I was thinking of Angus," admitted Eleanor.

"Well, I was thinking about my thumbs," said Cleo, "and how much they hurt when I try to put on my bra. I like the bralettes because they don't have underwires or snaps in the back, but lately I can't seem to get them over my boobs. They roll up in back and I have trouble pulling them down. I'm sure I look hilarious getting everything in place. When Steve sees me struggling he always says, 'Corral those rascals!'"

"Why don't you step into your bra?" asked Dede.

Cleo pondered this before she said, "I can't believe I didn't think of that myself. Dede, you're a genius!"

No one knows what tipped the cup. It might have been the image conjured by Cleo stuffing herself into a bralette or the fact that they were even discussing it, but they all broke into hysterical laughter and there was snorting involved.

Josephine recovered first and turned the conversation back to more serious issues. "Do you think Madame Patruska is the killer?"

"The shoe and the tarot card might lead us to that conclusion," said Eleanor wiping tears of mirth from her eyes, "But how would the card end up at the murder scene? She wouldn't have a reason to take it from her deck. As for that, it may not even be hers. We never checked to see if The Lovers was missing from the spread on her table."

"As for the shoe," added Cleo, "Someone obviously broke into The Oracle perhaps with the intent of leaving the shoe where it could easily be found to incriminate the owner. I doubt Madame Patruska killed Monica Fischer in her shop, put her body in a car, and drove to a mountainous forest and dumped her over a cliff."

"I agree," said Josephine, "Monica Fischer's body was treated disrespectfully. It makes more sense that her killer was someone who had an intense dislike for her."

Pearl put the file on the table. "So maybe the answer is in here. Why did you take this file?"

"Remember Angus told me there were signs of pagan rituals near where the body was found. I was curious but didn't want to take the time to look through the file. Cleo and I didn't want to get caught there. Then I forgot about it." Eleanor explained.

"Well, what's in it for heaven's sake?" asked Dede impatiently.

Pearl opened the file that seemed to hold a single sheet of paper. "It's a list of names," she said.

"These must be the women who Madame Patruska was talking about who celebrated the vernal equinox." Josephine said.

"I don't think so," said Pearl slowly. "Our names are on this list."

It was all they could talk about on the way home. Who compiled this list of witches and how did their names end up on it. Each of them had their own opinions and each was disturbed by it. "I'm not a witch!" exclaimed Cleo.

"None of us are witches, but Monica Fischer's name is not on this list and she evidently participated in some witchy rituals." Dede said.

"I have danced naked under the moon on an equinox," admitted Josephine, "And some people might believe that makes me a witch, but I would rather call myself a goddess. There are all kinds of people and people who believe all kinds of things. It doesn't give them the right to judge and punish those who want to experience life in a different way."

"Maybe we got on the list because we hang out with someone who dances naked under the moon," said Cleo giving Josephine the side eye.

"If I'm going to be tarred with the same brush, I want to at least enjoy dancing naked under the moon too!" exclaimed Pearl who thought it sounded liberating.

"I'll be sure to invite all of you to the next seasonal celebration," said Josephine.

The fog was thick and Eleanor drove slower than usual but still had to slam on the brakes when something large darted out from the trees and ran across the road. The car zigged and zagged as Eleanor tried desperately to avoid hitting it. They ended up stopped along the shoulder of the road, shaken and amazed.

"What was that?" asked Pearl when she could speak.

"Did you get a good look at it?" asked Dede? "It was really big."

"It all happened so fast. It was just a furry blur to me," said Cleo.

"Is everyone all right?" asked Eleanor who tried to remain calm. "It must have been a bear."

"I'm sure it was running on two feet," said Josephine. "It might have been a man … or Bigfoot."

By the time Eleanor got home she was exhausted, both physically and mentally. She could not deny what she had witnessed, and she still felt the effects of the near collision with whatever it was. Feathers was glad to see her and showed his love by asking for kisses and flying around the house in parrot glee. After a warm soak in the tub, she got in her nightgown and settled in for the evening, but sleep would not come. Her mind replayed the events of the day over and over as she struggled to make some sense of it all. She tried reading the book club novel but gave up after reading the same page four times without comprehending a word. She tidied the kitchen, folded some laundry, and attempted a cryptogram but her brain refused to focus on anything other than the day's events. Finally, she turned on the television and fell asleep watching reruns of *Murder She Wrote*.

Angus heard an unusual sound coming from outside. It was dark and very late yet there was a crowd of twenty people or more walking up the hill by his house. They chanted loudly and carried torches that lit the night with a golden glow that might have been pleasing in another venue but emanated a hint of animosity. He listened carefully but couldn't make out the chant that filled the night like a dull roar, but he recognized the angry

tone. He stepped outside and heard, "Hang the witch, hang the witch!" repeated again and again in sync with the beat of their marching feet. He saw them dressed in their Sunday best, men and women, young and old. One with a noose in his hand. One that looked like Helen Pence carrying a crucifix. Understanding the power of a mob, he raced inside for his gun and ran to catch up with them hoping to avert an unfortunate tragedy. As he moved with them, he noticed their single-mindedness. They marched as one and chanted in unison only looking ahead. When he asked where they were going, no one answered because no one heard. Angus wondered if they were under the influence of some mind-altering drug. By the time he realized they were going to Eleanor's house, it was too late to get ahead of them to warn her. He cried out hoping the mob might hear him, but they could not be stopped. One man hit him with a torch, knocking him to the ground and sending his gun into the bushes. He watched helplessly as they beat down her door, dragged her out by her hair, barefoot, wearing only a thin nightgown, and then hanged her from the nearest tree. When he heard her neck snap …he woke up.

He knew it was a nightmare made up of fragments from his investigation, but his mind wouldn't let it go, so he got his gun, called Bones, his faithful dog, and together they drove to Eleanor's house in the dead of night.

Angus worried when he saw the lights seeping from Eleanor's windows. It was late. She should be safely asleep at this hour. "What do you think, Bones?" Angus ask, "Is our Ellie having a late-night snack?"

Eleanor heard the knocking on the door as in a dream, but woke surprised to find herself on the couch. She walked toward the sound, disoriented and still half asleep. Angus stood outside in his pajamas with Bones at his side.

"Angus, what's wrong?" Eleanor asked.

"I had a bad dream," he said, "Can I stay with you tonight?" He looked like a little boy looking for comfort and her heart melted.

"Of course," she replied, "Come inside."

"Just a minute," he said as he went back to his truck to get his gun. He saw himself as a strong protector of the woman he loved, but unable to keep her safe in his dream disturbed him more than he would admit.

"Ellie, every light in your house is on!" he said locking the door behind him and checking all the windows.

"I know, I couldn't sleep, but trust me I've already checked and rechecked every door and window. They're all locked."

"What are you afraid of?" he asked as he tried to smooth her bedhead hairdo.

"Promise you won't laugh?"

"Never!"

"Bigfoot," she admitted.

Angus tried but it was too hard to ignore the humor of the situation. It started as a smile and grew into a burst of uncontrolled hilarity. Once it started there was no stopping it.

Eleanor threw a pillow from the couch at him, "Liar!"

"I think that was my stomach growling," he said. "Do you have anything to eat?"

Dede called an informational meeting at her house the next morning. The ladies of the coffee club sat around her dining room table drinking coffee and eating pastries.

"You won't believe who I saw on my way over here," said Pearl. "It was the whitest man I've ever seen. He was wearing a black hoodie and sun glasses but his face was as pale as milk. I swear I thought it was a Halloween mask."

"Maybe he has albinism," Josephine said.

"That is just uncanny!" exclaimed Dede who suddenly plopped down on a chair and slapped the table. "I finally got a response from the mayor of Orick, you know the small town in California where Monica Fischer worked as a wildlife biologist. She told me that Monica grew up there, was well-known and respected by just about everyone until Andri Frost came to town and joined the National Parks as her boss. Evidently, he took an immediate dislike to Monica and made her life miserable in numerous ways, including promising promotions to her but then giving them to men beneath her, calling her stupid and taking credit for things that she did, and smearing her by saying she slept with him in an attempt to get ahead. Monica finally gave up and quit her job there and moved to Jacksonville."

"That's horrible," said Pearl.

"That's not all," Dede continued, "Monica filed a suit against him for sexual harassment and defamation of character, which she won, and he lost his job."

"Good for her!" said Cleo.

"I asked the mayor if she could describe this man and you'll never believe what she said." Dede paused for effect. "He's an albino."

"Do you think that's who Pearl saw?" asked Josephine.

"Possibly," Dede said, "And there's more. Andri, also known as 'Frosty', is a Bigfoot fanatic. He has been hunting the cryptid for years trying to prove its existence."

"I just got chills down my spine," Cleo said.

"That's a lot to consider. We'll have to do more investigating if we want to tie him to her murder," Eleanor said, "But I also learned something last night. Angus said there is a group of women looking into the practice of witchcraft in our area and our names are on the list. At least Dede, Cleo, and I are on the list for sure. Now we are on two separate lists as witches."

"So what?" asked Josephine. "I don't care if some women find me so powerful they think I'm a witch."

"Who are these women?" asked Cleo.

"Angus wouldn't say, but he's concerned about our safety," Eleanor said.

"I think I know who they are," said Dede thoughtfully. "Helen Pence lives next to Madame Patruska and can see right into her backyard. I bet she spies on the garden parties Patruska has there and even takes names. She probably sent the threatening letters to Patruska."

"Of course, she probably saw us go into Patruska's house the other night too," said Eleanor. "I wonder when she told Angus."

"I think we have to kill her," threatened Cleo.

Eleanor bit her lip and said, "We may have to kill them both."

Suzanna's bustled with tourists who had heard about the hunt for a million dollars and wanted to check out the sleepy village of Sand Beach overlooking the vast Pacific Ocean. Someone in the know had leaked the news about a murder and a Bigfoot sighting and it suddenly seemed there was something for everyone in Waterton County. Every hotel was booked and there were long lines at restaurants, gas stations, and grocery stores. Eleanor spied her Do Nothing friends, all retired professional women, and made her way to their table.

"This is incredibly inconvenient," complained Mattie, as someone passing her chair elbowed her in the head. "Please sit down, Eleanor, if you can."

"I don't think they'll allow us to sit here taking up space while we drink coffee and visit," Sybil warned.

"I'll order breakfast," said Eleanor, who was famished from her early morning walk on the beach.

"The whole of Waterton is bursting with people from out of town and now they're spilling over into our special spaces," Mavis said. "I can barely hear myself think in here."

"So, what do you know?" asked Eleanor. The Do Nothings were definitely not the Know Nothings and often fed Eleanor valuable information they learned from the street.

"Murder, money, and monsters are an incredible recipe for mayhem," said Mattie. "I don't believe any of it is real."

"It's all poppycock!" said Mavis, "Most likely a scheme hatched by the county commissioners to bring more tourist dollars into the economy."

"You should see what they're selling in town," said Sybil. "Sasquatch hats, T-shirts, keychains, and action figures. It's deplorable. They've even named a sandwich after the bigfooted creature. Look here. There's a bigfoot breakfast burrito on the menu."

Eleanor ordered a breakfast of bacon and eggs but the Do Nothings had little to offer in the way of information and left complaining about the noisy crowd. She was left alone at a table for four, so she thoughtfully moved to a seat at the bar. Sipping her coffee while she waited for her meal, she studied the people surrounding her. It was odd to see so many strange faces where locals used to fill the space with warm smiles and friendly greetings. Suddenly she became aware of the man sitting next to her when he turned to her and asked, "Your place or mine, sweetheart?"

"Excuse me, I must have misunderstood you," Eleanor said. "What did you say?"

"I saw you watching me from your table. I know what you want. Women always want to know what it's like to be with someone like me and I can tell you, I've never had any complaints," he said looking straight into Eleanor's startled blue eyes.

Eleanor looked straight back and saw her reflection in his wraparound sunglasses. What was he doing asking her a question like that? She must be twenty years his senior. Then Eleanor did the unthinkable. The thing every man fears a woman will do to him. Eleanor laughed.

"You may need your eyes checked if that's what you think you saw," she said, "As for the rest of it, Mr. Frost, my husband's home. Maybe he'd be interested in what you have to say." His pale face framed by a black hoodie was as white as the cream on the counter. Mr. Frost sat straighter and turned slowly away without a word. Eleanor ate her breakfast and crossed the street to the Post Office missing Angus as he entered Suzanna's. She had met the person with albinism, and she wasn't impressed.

Angus sat in the very chair Eleanor had just vacated. He ordered coffee and a breakfast of steak and eggs. Looking around he too was annoyed by the crowd that filled the normally peaceful restaurant. Mr. Frost glanced at Angus behind his shades and spotted Eleanor walking away up the hill.

"That bitch came on to me. Can you believe it?" Frost asked. "They're all the same, wanting something strange and never satisfied with what they have. She's a looker, I'll give her that even though she's older than I like. She said she'd be waiting for me."

Angus turned to look at the woman walking up the hill. The clenched muscle in his jaw, the only sign of his inner anger. "That's my wife," he spoke slowly, "And you are a liar."

Mr. Frost's face, like a stone sculpture, showed no emotion. He simply got up and walked away while Angus watched him climb into an older Ford pickup and drive away up the hill. Angus hurried to his own truck and drove in the direction of his house, searching for Eleanor along the way. There was no sign of her. Could she have already passed his house on the way to her own? Angus pulled over and called her on his cell. She picked up just as Frost rounded the corner on his way back down.

"Where are you?" he asked.

"I'm hiding in the bushes near your house," Eleanor whispered. "I think I'm being followed by Monica Fischer's killer."

"Stay put," Angus ordered, turning around to follow Frost who continued down the hill toward the main road. Angus called Eleanor back when he was sure Frost had left the village, then returned to Suzanna's just in time to receive his steak and eggs, but the meal didn't relieve the uneasy feeling in his gut.

Eleanor took off her shoes outside her door, went in and locked it. That man gave her the creeps and it wasn't because he was unusually pale. She knew as soon as she left that he would follow her. Maybe not to hurt her now, but to find out where she lived so he could come back later. She knew bad people did bad things in the dark. When she heard a truck coming up the hill, she got off the road and hid in the bushes until he passed but stayed hidden because she was afraid. Eleanor didn't like being scared to walk in her own neighborhood. Something would have to be done. Immediately she thought of buying a gun but dismissed the idea as more dangerous than safe. She didn't like to admit it, but she wasn't as young as she used to be and that came with limitations; not as quick, not as agile, not as strong. Not to mention she didn't think she could pull the trigger to kill anyone. She texted the coffee group for suggestions. Immediately Dede called her on the phone. She wanted details and Eleanor told her everything.

"There's a self-defense class for seniors being offered at the community college. I'll sign us up for it. In the meantime, get someone to stay with you. I think the class is tomorrow night," Dede said. "I'll see if Cleo, Josephine, and Pearl want to come." Eleanor hung up feeling better about the situation. She knew most worries were diminished with action and she decided not to spend one more minute thinking about that despicable man and jumped in the shower instead.

Eleanor answered Angus' knock clad only in her leopard printed fluffy robe, her entire head wrapped in a towel and bunny slippers on her feet.

"I tried to call, but now I'm glad I caught you in that robe," he growled reaching to pull her close and inhaling her fresh-from-the-shower scent. Could she be any more adorable? No wonder other men thought she was "a looker". Eleanor allowed him a kiss or two before breaking away to towel her wet hair.

"I wish I could wash that man out of mind," Eleanor sighed.

"Tell me what happened," Angus said. "I'm interested to hear why you think he's Monica Fischer's killer." And there it was … now Eleanor would have to tell him everything.

"I think I'm mad at you but I don't remember why," Eleanor began. "Oh yes, something to do with Helen Pence and witches." Because Eleanor could no longer keep track of what she had told him she assumed he knew nothing.

"I'll just start at the beginning. The day we went woodcutting."

"Wait, if you're going back that far, I may need to sit down," Angus said moving into the living room and taking a seat on the couch.

"Anyway, when I went to relieve myself, I found a tarot card in the weeds, put it in my pocket and forgot all about it until I rediscovered it the other day." Eleanor stopped when she realized Angus had begun to snore. "Angus, that's not funny."

"Well, get to the good part then," he said. "I want to know about the guy at the restaurant."

Eleanor sighed, "Okay, Dede did some digging about Monica's past and learned that she once worked for the National Parks as a wildlife biologist in Orick, California, where she met Andri Frost who harassed her until she left. They described him as having albinism, so it was easy enough to figure it was him at the restaurant, and he's obviously a misogynist. Monica filed a suit against him and he lost his job. Now he's here propositioning women and following them to their houses."

"He propositioned you?"

"His exact words were, 'Your place or mine, sweetheart?'"

"And what were your exact words?"

"Unfortunately, I laughed." Eleanor paused for effect. "It was funny considering our age difference. He also said some very insulting things about me wanting him because he was different. I really don't remember exactly, but he wasn't very nice. Then I told him my husband might like to hear what he had to say."

"That's all?" Angus asked. When Eleanor gave him her angry teacher look, he smiled and said, "Your husband, huh? Did you think your husband would protect you?" His tone was particularly annoying.

"Well, I thought *he* would think that," Eleanor said wondering how Angus knew to call her when he did and how he knew the coast was clear. "He gave off some very bad vibes. I just knew he would follow me, so I hid when I heard a truck coming up the hill."

"What makes you think he's Andri Frost?" Angus asked giving her no time to ask her own questions.

"He didn't react when I called him Mr. Frost. How many albinos can there be?" Eleanor said. Angus didn't answer.

"I'll be back tonight, Ellie. Keep your doors locked." And he was gone without giving her a single bit of information about anything.

Angus called Andy McGraw, a friend at the Waterton Police Department, and gave him information about the make, model, and license plate number of Andri Frost's gray pickup truck. If Andy confirmed his identity as Andri Frost, he had reason to pull him in for questioning regarding the Fischer case and his purpose for being in Waterton. Angus wanted to know how long he had been here and where he was staying. Mr. Frost had motive to kill Monica Fischer and now posed a threat to Eleanor. There was no doubt in Angus' mind that Andri Frost was a nasty man who didn't tolerate women who laughed at him.

While Angus was hunting down information about Frost, Eleanor was thinking about taking responsibility for her own protection. She liked the fact that she felt safe with Angus but she didn't want to rely on him, especially after her brave speech about not wanting protection from the ugliness of the world and finding her own way to cope with it. And she had to admit to herself she wasn't really prepared to protect herself. A self-defense class was a start, but maybe there was more she could do. She picked up her phone and called the number of a personal trainer she got from the internet, Molly Fiori. At the very least she could make herself as strong as a seventy-something woman could be, and also learn something about Jesse Bomotti and his relationship to two women.

When Angus returned later that evening they feasted on apricot glazed pork roast, rice and green salad. Bones waited patiently for something to drop on the floor while Feathers perched nearby silently watching for an opportunity to insult Angus. "That was delicious, Ellie," Angus said wiping his mustache with a napkin.

"There's strawberry shortcake," Eleanor offered.

"Maybe later," he replied.

"I could send some home with you for later, if you like," Eleanor said.

Angus thought a while before he spoke, "Don't you want me here, Ellie?"

"I just didn't want you to think you had to stay. I'm really okay here by myself," Eleanor stated with a bravado she didn't feel.

Angus sighed, "Andy McGraw checked the registration of the pickup the man at the restaurant was driving. You were right. It was Andri Frost, but when they searched for him, it seems he just disappeared. He's not staying at any of the hotels here and they're all booked. There's no sign of him."

"So, he's gone and we don't have to worry about him," Eleanor said. "He doesn't know where I live."

"No, he's not gone and could easily find you just by asking anyone in the village." Angus frowned. "When I followed him out of Sand Beach, I noticed he had camping gear in the back of his truck and a rifle mounted inside of his cab. He's gone into the woods most likely to hunt, but we can't be sure. He could be anywhere. I'd feel better being here with you just in case he comes back."

"What would he be hunting this time of year?" Eleanor asked but thought she already knew.

"Andy checked and Frost has a record for poaching and is a well-known Bigfoot hunter. My guess is he's heard about the footprints found at the crime scene and is up there looking to kill Sasquatch." When Eleanor didn't speak, Angus continued. "If you don't want me in your bed, I can sleep in the guest room but I'm staying." Angus wasn't sure what the underlying issue was that kept Eleanor so prickly. Could she still be mad about Helen Pence or was she just stubborn enough about her independence to put her life in jeopardy? Either way, she wasn't talking.

Eleanor spent the next day in her office writing.

I'm never upset for the reason I think
And I've been upset for a time.
I'm afraid and angry merely because…
I want who I want to be mine.
Midnight kisses, flowers and wine
Aren't enough for me anymore.
My heart doesn't race when I see your face
Or hear your knock at my door.
I'm sure there must be something more.
But I don't want someone new
I realize love is more than a word.
Love is something you do.
So, bring me every part of you,
Hold me while I cry,
Shield me from the pain I feel,
When I think romance must die.

Eleanor felt depleted. She suddenly knew why she was so
unhappy. She wanted the romance, but if what Oscar Wilde
said was true (*The essence of romance is uncertainty*) then she
wanted none of it. She only wanted Angus and she wanted
all of him; his love, his protection, and the certainty of him.
Her pride and fear of being dependent on him was getting in
the way of telling him how she felt. She stretched and made a
cup of tea. She had an appointment to meet Molly Fiori at her
pottery shop to discuss an exercise plan and hopefully much
more.

"You must be Eleanor," said Molly Fiori wiping her hands on
a rag and waving Eleanor in the direction of a small room off
to the side of her pottery showroom. "I don't usually have
a lot of customers on a weekday afternoon, so we won't be
disturbed. Please sit down." Molly was petite with red hair that
curled naturally down to her shoulders and a smile that radiated
warmth and the glow of good health. If Eleanor needed a

reference for a physical trainer, Molly's tight body was enough. Her arm muscles were firm and well defined and in perfect balance with the rest of her. They discussed Eleanor's age and issues that she might have in regard to completing an exercise program focusing on exactly what she hoped to achieve. Molly would create a specific plan for her that she could start in the morning by using her smart phone.

"I'm very interested in building muscles so I can protect myself," Eleanor began, "You must have heard about Monica Fischer by now."

"Yes, she was a friend. I'm so sorry about what happened to her," Molly said. "My boyfriend introduced me to her. It seems she didn't have many friends here and was having a tough time fitting into the community. He thought I could help."

Eleanor remained silent hoping Molly would say more.

"She was so pretty and smart, you'd think she'd have a lot of friends, but I guess when someone is that gorgeous women are jealous and men are … well you know how men can be. I know she was lonely so I did what I could to grow a circle of friends for her," Molly said.

"Did your friends welcome her?" asked Eleanor.

"I introduced her to some women I work with. I do some self-defense work with them and thought Monica could make friends there by sharing her stories and bonding with them. Sometimes when you're unhappy it lifts you up to help others. As far as I know they all loved her there. It's just so sad that when things were starting to look up for her, this awful thing happened." Molly stood when she heard a customer enter the shop and Eleanor thanked her and left. It would soon be time for the class and she was ready to learn to defend herself.

Eleanor arrived at the community college a little early and saw Dede and Cleo walking into the building. They waited for her and walked in together.

"Josephine had a conflict with a counseling session and Pearl said Cary was all the protection she needed," Dede reported. They were all wearing their black velvet stakeout uniforms which doubled as workout suits and made them look like a dance team from the senior center. As they passed a couple of staff from the college, they heard one of them say it was the biggest turnout they'd ever had for a self-defense class.

"I wonder why that could be," Eleanor said. "Do you think people are afraid because of the murder?"

Cleo snickered, "My guess is the instructor is hot and there are a lot of women who want him to get physical."

Dede said nothing.

"Do you know who the instructor is?" Eleanor asked as they entered the room where at least fifty chatting women sat on folding chairs in a double semicircle. Eleanor's eyes widened as she looked around the room. "I thought I was early." It wasn't until they took their seats near the back and chatted up some of the other participants that Eleanor noticed Angus who eventually walked to the front of the room, introduced himself, and welcomed them all to the class.

Eleanor gave Dede a withering look which she innocently shrugged off with a roll of her eyes as if to say, "I thought you knew."

While Angus laid out the benefits of self-dense training and gave a basic outline of what the course entailed, Eleanor looked around the room to see who was in attendance and wondered how many of these women offered meals to Angus in return for certain favors. When her eyes landed on Helen Pence, she observed the woman's rapt attention focused on the instructor. Eleanor sighed heavily in an attempt to cool the simmer inside. Then she noticed that all the women were glued to his every word, inflection, and movement. One was even fanning herself with a sheet of safety tips being passed around the circle. Finally focusing in on his lecture, Eleanor heard him say, "Be alert and aware of your surroundings. Make it a habit to scan the area around you. Look for exits if you need to escape, and potential threats so you can avoid them. Stand straight and keep your chin up and your shoulders back. Poor posture and a lowered gaze make you look fearful and weak.

"Walk with confidence, keeping the same pace as those around you if you can. Make brief eye contact with the people around you to show that you are aware of them. If a possible assailant knows you've seen him or her, the element of surprise is gone.

"Don't talk on your phone or look at a map while out walking. This shows you aren't paying attention to what's happening around you. Plan your route before you leave your point of origin. If you need help, go into a store and ask someone.

"Don't be distracted by a potential attacker. If a stranger asks for the time, don't look down at your watch. Bring it up to eye level and keep the person in your line of sight and keep walking. Stay in well-lit and populated areas at night. Keep a mini flashlight and whistle on your key ring and hold your keys in your hand with one sticking out of your fingers while you walk. The panic button on your key fob can also be used to scare off an attacker.

"Don't draw attention to yourself. Keep valuables out of sight and don't flash expensive jewelry or wads of cash. If you carry a purse, keep it close or conceal it under a jacket. Are there any questions, so far?"

All at once a multitude of hands flew up and as Angus tried to address them, Eleanor heard a bevy of women clamor for the attention of one man. Their questions bordered on the inane and ridiculous.

"How much money is a safe amount to carry in my purse?" asked one.

"Are you married?" asked another.

"Where do you work out?" asked one who was old enough to be his mother.

Angus answered each patiently and then moved on to how to fend off an attack "Your life is worth more than anything in your pockets, so if a thief demands your stuff, give it to him or her but if you can't avoid a confrontation make a lot of noise, use whatever is handy, poke with your car keys, throw dirt in their eyes or canned goods if you have them, swing a cane or umbrella. We'll try some cane defense moves later. Pepper spray works as well as stun guns which are legal in this state. A firearm can also be effective but I would advise against going that route because they can easily be turned against you.

If attacked aim for the most vulnerable areas such as the eyes, nose, neck, groin, and knees." Angus pulled a delighted lady from her chair to illustrate where to kick on the side of the knee or whack with a cane. Eleanor was almost ready to leave as she witnessed the women so transparently in awe of his masculine charms.

"Since there are so many here tonight, we'll have to break into smaller groups to practice a defense called Cane Fu," he said. Angus sorted the women into groups of ten and sent each group off with a police officer to another section of the room or a different space altogether. Dede, Cleo, and Eleanor went with Officer McGraw to the far corner just as Helen Pence hurried back from her group and demanded she stay with Angus. Now Eleanor could watch Helen Pence fawn over Angus. She glued herself to his side even reaching out to hold his arm while she pushed her large chest in his face. It was unbearable, but with clear determination and the help of her klutzy friends, Eleanor made it through with only a few glances their way and actually enjoyed the exercise and the company of those in her group. The highlight was when Cleo hooked her cane around Dede's leg and they both fell into Officer McGraw knocking him down on the mat in a dog pile that sent everyone in the group into hysterical laughter. The other members of their group rushed to help the three stooges get up and soon it was a free for all and everyone ended tangled up on the floor as though in a game of Twister. There was one man in the group who took an interest in Eleanor and held on a little longer than necessary when giving her a hand up. "Harry," he said.

On the way out after class was dismissed, Harry walked with the three ladies who were still laughing and snorting over their uncoordinated efforts to defend themselves.

"The only real danger I experienced tonight was a possible bone fracture," Cleo said.

"I thought Eleanor might have sprained her neck trying to observe Angus and Helen," teased Dede.

"Good night you two," Eleanor said, "I assure you my neck feels just fine." It was her heart that was sore. Harry continued to walk Eleanor to her car and gleaned a little information about her before she drove home. It was several miles before she realized Angus never acknowledged her in any way. She wondered if he even knew she was there.

Eleanor was just completing the last round in her workout when Feathers, who had been coaching her through the counting parts, flew to the door where Angus waited after ringing the bell. Slightly breathless and disheveled she greeted him with cool disinterest.

"Look at you!" he said, pleased and surprised to see her in revealing workout attire, sweaty, and her hair in wild disarray.

"What do you see exactly?" she asked thinking she had never looked so awful.

"I see what every man sees when he looks at you," he said closing in to hold her, "A beautiful woman."

"Angus, I'm all hot and sweaty," she said trying to extricate herself from him. "What happened to you? Did Helen feed you oysters?"

Angus dropped his arms and sighed. "Are you still stewing over Helen Pence? I swear to you I've never even entertained the idea of having sex with her."

"Do you think this is about sex?" Eleanor asked. "Is that all you see when you look at a woman?"

Angus hung his head and shook it knowing part of what Eleanor thought was true. He did look at women that way before he got to know them. Helen Pence was not a woman he wanted to have an intimate relationship with because she wasn't Eleanor. "I see all of you, Ellie, not just your outer perfection, but your light and kindness, how you think, and the way you make others feel—the way you make me feel. I'm happy when I'm with you and I miss you when I'm not. I can't sleep or think straight when you're troubled, especially if I might be the cause."

Eleanor's heart softened a little. "Well, I realize I haven't been honest with you Angus."

Angus' heart sank. Was she breaking up with him? Was there someone else? Had he screwed up the best thing in his life over a casserole? "Is it Harry Stone?" he asked, "I saw you two together last night, Ellie. He's not who you think. He's a retired security guard who is just looking to pick up women at places like that self-defense class. I've seen him do that number on women at the gym."

"No," Eleanor said, "I haven't been honest about how much it bothers me that there are other women in your life who bring you food in return for your favors. I hate it! Watching those women drool all over you last night made me angry and I'm not going to apologize for it. You can't have Helen Pence's meatloaf and eat my apple pie too. I love you and I want all of you."

Angus let out an enormous sigh, wrapped Eleanor in his arms, and whispered into her messy hair, "I love you, Eleanor Penrose."

The coffee group met at the Boat House as usual. They had a great deal to discuss about the murder case. Eleanor's focus on Angus and his harem took her out of the game. She could hardly remember what clues had been discovered and felt she had nothing to offer. After her make-up session with Angus, she had only one thing on her mind, and it wasn't murder.

"Just remind me of what we know for sure," Eleanor said.

"Monica Fischer is dead," Cleo reported. "Killed Friday, April 5, and dumped in a wooded area up in the coast range and found by Angus and Eleanor. We know for sure that Eleanor found a tarot card at the scene and Madame Patruska's shop was broken into and Monica's shoe was found there."

"We know there were fake footprints in the area and pagan ritual paraphernalia," Pearl said.

"There's a man with albinism connected some way and he may be in town," said Dede.

"Oh, I can confirm that the man in question is Andri Frost who harassed Monica when she worked in Orick and who drives an older gray pickup and may be hunting for Bigfoot in the area where the body was discovered," Eleanor remembered. "Also, I talked to Molly Fiori and she claims to have been a friend of Monica's. She tried to help her make connections with other women in some helpful capacity, but didn't say what it was."

"That's interesting," said Josephine. "I wonder what those women know and if there could be a connection to the killer there?"

"Who are our main suspects?" asked Dede.

"Andri Frost tops my list," said Pearl.

"I just wonder why he would still be here then," said Eleanor.

"Well, there's Jesse Bomotti, Molly Fiori, and Klara Kent, but none of those people seem to fit the profile. Klara couldn't possibly have done it by herself. She's not strong enough to deal with a body," said Dede.

"What about the misogynists on your list, Dede?" asked Cleo.

"I don't know, they all seem pretty harmless, and Malcolm Manning is the only one who worked closely with her," Dede said.

"Are we giving up on the witch hunters? Helen Pence did it!" said Cleo. "Or maybe it was a woman who was jealous of her. Someone whose husband worked with her. Does Manning have a wife?"

Eleanor shrugged. "I don't know. It could be a serial killer who saw an opportunity and killed her at random. The woods are so full of strangers we may never know."

"We need to know how she died," said Josephine. "Eleanor, Angus knows. Find out."

Angus would take care of the problem with Helen Pence. Helen was not a bad person, and Angus didn't want to hurt her feelings in any way, but she was the kind of woman who believed in the superiority of men and traditional roles for women which made her rather boring in Angus' view. She would make a fine wife for someone who wanted to make all the decisions in a relationship but Angus liked the clever banter Eleanor and he enjoyed. He liked listening to her ideas which offered him a different perspective. Even when they disagreed and he grew frustrated, he respected her opinions, her independence and willingness to follow through on her convictions. Eleanor was also a far better cook.

If he had to choose between hurting one or the other, he knew he would cut Helen loose to spare Eleanor heartache. After struggling with a solution for several minutes, he came up with what he thought was a brilliant idea. Whether Eleanor would like the plan or not, Angus wasn't sure, but he decided to go with it before running it by her because he felt Eleanor had given him signals that indicated she might be receptive to a marriage of sorts.

He may not have thought it through as well as he should, but he was certain as he walked into Diamond Dan's Jewelry store that the problem could be solved as he began to browse the selection of wedding rings. He knew her size because he'd bought her a ring before and he knew she preferred yellow gold. Angus wanted to give Eleanor a spectacular band with big sparkly diamonds that made a statement about how much he loved her. When other men saw it on her finger, they wouldn't dare make a pass at her, so it had to be something incredible that no one could miss. When he saw it, he knew it.

"Hi, Angus," Diamond Dan said. "Are you looking for something special today?"

"I want that one," he said pointing to the biggest and brightest ring in the showcase.

"Someone's going to be very happy with that choice," Diamond Dan said as he took the ring out and let Angus look at it more closely giving him all the details of cut, carat, color, and clarity. "I can give you a good deal," Diamond Dan offered. Angus wrote a check and while Diamond Dan was completing the necessary paperwork, Helen Pence entered the store.

"Hello Angus," she said in her breathless way. Suddenly Angus felt uncomfortable. Why did she have to come in now when he only wanted to think of Eleanor? "Hi Dan," she continued as she heaved her breasts in Angus' direction. "I need this watch repaired."

"I'll be with you in a minute," Dan replied tearing his eyes away from Helen's ample bosom to finish Angus' transaction. "Good luck, Angus. I hope she says yes."

"Thanks Dan," Angus nodded to Helen and left the store as if it were on fire. He didn't hear Dan tell Helen he thought someone finally snared Angus McBride, Waterton's most eligible senior bachelor. He didn't see Helen's face when she thought it might be her.

"Do we know anything more about Andri Frost?" asked Cleo.

"Is Angus still staying with you, Eleanor?" asked Dede.

Eleanor sat with her friends at the Blue Moon Café enjoying a late lunch. "Angus thinks Mr. Frost is camping somewhere in the coast range and won't come back to civilization until he runs low on supplies. He's an avid hunter and a fanatical believer in Bigfoot, so I'm not worried about him. He's probably forgotten all about me," she said.

"This isn't for public consumption." Dede lowered her voice and the ladies leaned in to hear what promised to be a confidential fact. "Rumor has it that Monica Fischer died of strangulation and a noose was found around her neck. I think the police are keeping this information on the down-low. But someone leaked it."

"Does this mean she was hanged in the woods?" asked Pearl.

"I'm not sure," Dede said.

"You know during the women's holocaust, women believed to be witches were burned in Europe but in America they were hanged," Josephine said.

"Do you think someone hanged her because they thought she was a witch?" asked Pearl.

"She wasn't found hanging from a tree," said Eleanor. "I suppose animals may have drug her to the spot where Angus and I discovered her."

"I'm having a problem piecing this all together," said Pearl. "Are we to believe someone is hunting women as witches and hanging them, or that witches are performing some horrible spell that involves human sacrifice?"

"I don't think Helen Pence and her committee to stop witchcraft would do anything like that," said Cleo. "Maybe it's just another misdirection to lead us to the wrong conclusion."

"Yes," said Eleanor. "Someone wants us to believe other forces are at work here. First the tarot card, then the Bigfoot prints, and Monica's shoe found at The Oracle … maybe to divert us from the treasure seekers."

"Maybe just to divert us from an old-fashioned murder and throw suspicion on Madame Patruska," said Josephine.

"We need some solid evidence," said Eleanor. "We need to go back to Madame Patruska's shop and do some real digging in her files. I'm certain whoever planted that shoe there killed Monica."

"Have the police been there?" asked Cleo.

"They know Madame Patruska is out of town and think this was a crime of opportunity. I'm sure they didn't connect it to the murder case or search for a secret room," Dede said. "The door to The Oracle has been boarded up, but I think you all know there is another way in."

"Are we going to be in trouble for interfering with an investigation?" asked Pearl.

"We're beyond that now," said Dede. "We have to solve this case before the powers that be find out what we've done."

"I don't know if I can get away from Angus. He's protecting me to death," said Eleanor.

"Easy," said Dede, "We'll plan a girls' overnight getaway. He won't worry about you if we're all together."

Eleanor caught sight of Helen Pence entering the café with two other women. They sat at a nearby table talking and laughing loudly. What the coffee ladies heard was bits and pieces that disturbed them all.

According to Helen Pence, she was so happy because there was going to be a wedding. There were glances at Eleanor, and Helen even waved at one point causing Cleo to suspect an evil plan was in the works. She lowered her voice and hissed, "What are they so happy about? If Helen gets married, you won't have to worry about her stalking Angus anymore."

The words witchcraft and broken spell were heard with more sinister looks cast in their direction. "Do you think that's the committee to research the practice of witchcraft in Waterton?" asked Pearl.

"Maybe," said Josephine. "I wonder what they plan to do if they find any witches. It's not against the law."

"I can't believe they're serious," said Eleanor. "Are we back in the dark ages when women were accused of witchcraft for being too intelligent, too pretty, or too anything?"

"It may be a backlash. Women are coming into their own and there are men who don't like it. They feel threatened by their success. If I had to guess, it wouldn't be a committee of women searching for witches, but of men."

"Speaking of successful women, are any of you planning to attend the celebration of life for Monica Fischer tomorrow?" Dede asked.

"Of course," said Eleanor trying not to overhear anything else from Helen's table. "We might learn a great deal from the people who show up, and I'm sure Klara would welcome our support."

"I wonder how many people will be there. The short time she was here didn't give her much opportunity to make many friends and I hear her family is having their own memorial in her hometown," said Dede.

"I bet the murderer will be there," said Josephine. "I'll bring my phone to take pictures of all the attendees.

"Oh, I just thought of something. Andri Frost might be there. I'm not looking forward to seeing him again," said Eleanor emphatically.

"Members from the local association of artists will be there. I'm helping display some of her work in the reception area," Cleo said.

The discussion changed from what to wear to the memorial to what to wear to break into The Oracle. After their plans were made, they each left to go their separate ways ignoring the witch hunting committee on their way out which annoyed Helen Pence who thought she knew something Eleanor didn't.

"Monica Ann Fischer was an amazing woman," said Jesse Bomotti as he stood in a circle of acquaintances in the reception hall of the church following the memorial service. "She had a great deal to offer and someone robbed us all by putting an end to her unfinished life. I was just getting to know her, and I can say she was the real deal."

Eleanor and Angus listened attentively as they took note of those in attendance. Despite the short time Monica spent in Waterton she had made a big impression on the small town. The number of people there was a testament to her contributions to the city. There were people from the church, the artists' association, the women's crisis center, city hall, and others who she befriended in various ways. Some were just curious and hoped to gather information about the gruesome murder of a beautiful woman. Josephine flitted around the room taking photos of everyone in the most inconspicuous manner she could devise, fooling no one.

The large room was graced with purple and white lilacs, which Cleo determined were Monica's favorite flowers and the walls were covered with her paintings, mostly landscapes and forest animals, attesting to her love of wildlife. Banquet tables were loaded with bread, salads, deli plates, fruit, and rich desserts, all donated by the church ladies.

"There's nothing like a funeral to reveal a person's strengths," whispered Cleo in Eleanor's ear, "Unless people lie, of course. No one wants to speak ill of the dead."

"Have you seen Andri Frost?" asked Pearl who swept in like a bird of prey.

"No," Angus responded quickly. He'd been searching the crowd for Frost since the event began and there was no sign of him. Pearl flew off to photograph the guest pages, acting every bit like a secret agent.

Klara and Tip stayed close to Jesse's side, along with Molly Fiori who frequently chatted with several women who formed a close circle. Many were red eyed from crying. It wasn't unusual to see groups of people gathering together with those they knew or shared a common interest. Dede mixed among those from city hall. Eleanor noticed Tip glancing frequently at a woman talking to Dede who was unfamiliar to Eleanor. She didn't know the people who worked at city hall and wondered if Tip was a player trying to catch the eye of an attractive woman. It wasn't long before an ordinary looking middle-aged man appeared and whispered something in the woman's ear. She immediately went to the banquet table, filled a plate with food and brought it to a table where the man and another couple sat. Eleanor sighed audibly, thinking how stereotypical the entire scene had been. She didn't know who the woman was, his secretary, coworker, or maybe his wife, but definitely his gofer. People were beginning to sit down to enjoy the buffet. She watched Tip pull out a chair for Klara at the table where the object of Tip's attention had placed her plate. Such a gentleman she thought, but what were his motives. Tip sat next to the man who Eleanor now assumed was the attractive woman's husband. Angus touched her gently on the arm and asked, "Will you be all right if I mingle over there among that group of men?"

Eleanor nodded and watched him cross the room where Officer McGraw sat at a table with three others Eleanor recognized from the police force. She wondered if they were there for Monica or to observe the attendees the same way she and her friends were and if they were all just wasting their time. Could the murderer be in this room? Andri Frost wasn't here. Maybe the absence of someone was just as incriminating. She didn't see Helen Pence and her committee here. Madame Pastruska wasn't here. Eleanor decided to introduce herself to the ladies who gathered around Molly Fiori like disciples around their leader. Eleanor smiled warmly at Molly and Molly made room for her by widening the circle and drawing her inside.

"Mary Cambell, Joan Floyd, Erin Hart, this is Eleanor Penrose," she said. "She and Angus found Monica's body." If Eleanor thought the women looked sad and forlorn before she was surprised at the stricken look that replaced that expression after they learned of her involvement.

"That must have been so horrible for you," said Mary, tears leaking from a blackened eye. "I've never seen a dead person before."

"Please don't feel sorry for me," said Eleanor, "I didn't know her, so even though it was indeed unfortunate, I'm sorrier for your loss. She must have been a friend to you when you needed one."

"Isn't that the truth?" said Joan, "She took me to the doctor when my husband broke my arm and stayed with me until she knew I was safe."

"She was an angel for sure," said Erin. "When things seemed so hopeless, she listened and offered a path to make things better. She brought me clothes so I could go to a job interview. I just don't know what we'll do without her."

"You still have me," said Molly. Eleanor realized these must be women from the women's crisis center. Molly and Monica must have been advocates for them.

"Now you have even more reason to take back your power and live the lives that Monica would want for you," Eleanor said.

"I never thought of it that way," said Joan as new tears filled her eyes.

"Do you know anyone who would want to harm Monica?" asked Eleanor.

"Men," said Mary. "All the men who hurt us would want to hurt Monica too, because she was strong and stood up for us in ways we didn't. She wasn't afraid of them. That's the only reason I'm here. I don't want to be afraid anymore. I want to be like her. There are women at the crisis center afraid to come here today to honor Monica, because they might see the men who beat them, raped them, and gaslighted them. I'm tired of being afraid." Suddenly there was a loud crash, gasps, and a flurry of movement over near the banquet table. Eleanor saw Angus moving quickly in that direction. When she maneuvered through the crowd, she saw Tip Kent lying on the floor covered by the tablecloth and Dede's devil's food chocolate cake.

Eleanor immediately called 911 as Angus knelt by Tip and loosened his tie. Tip's body arched in spasm. His face red as he struggled to breath, his hand clenched around the tablecloth in a death grip. Klara appeared beside Eleanor, her hand covering her mouth as she watched her husband's distress.

"Is it a heart attack?" she asked. Eleanor's only response was to reach out and take her hand. By the time the ambulance arrived, Tip Kent was dead.

"There should be one more," said Cleo, "Bad things come in threes." The five friends sat at Dede's dining room table trying to make sense of the events of the afternoon.

"If that's the case, let's hope the bad thing happens to Monica's killer," said Josephine.

"A bad thing happened to Dede's cake," said Cleo, "What a waste!"

"Are we still on for tonight?" asked Dede.

"I'm in," said Eleanor. "Klara is staying with Jesse so there's nothing we can do for her tonight."

"Do you think she killed Tip?" asked Josephine.

"Why would you think such a thing?" asked Pearl. "That poor woman just lost her husband."

"Yes, Josephine, why would you think he was murdered? Do you think you can get your hands on that ring if Klara goes to prison?" Cleo teased.

"Don't be silly," Josephine chided. "I just think the way he died is odd. It didn't look like a heart attack."

"I have to agree," said Eleanor. "It looked like strychnine poisoning to me and I said as much to Angus before we left the church."

"Do you think it may be connected to Monica's murder?" asked Pearl.

"I don't know," Eleanor said. "It's usually women who use poison to commit murder and I think Monica was killed by a man."

"The spouse is usually the number one suspect, and Klara is now a very wealthy woman," said Josephine.

"How do you know that?" asked Pearl.

"Remember, I was engaged to marry that man, so I know he had family money," Josephine said.

"I guess you never know what happens in a marriage," said Dede. "People put on a front, post happy pictures on social media, hold hands in public and then go home, shut the doors and make each other miserable."

"We need to look at the guest list," said Eleanor. "If it was strychnine poisoning, the murderer had to be at Monica's memorial."

"I'll email you the pictures I took of the guest book. It's a shame they let everyone go home before they realized it could be poison," said Pearl. "Now the killer can get rid of the evidence."

"What evidence are you talking about?" asked Cleo.

"The poison, of course," said Pearl.

"I suppose it could have been in the food, but we don't know what Tip ate or drank," Dede said.

"Why aren't we all dead then?" asked Cleo. "We all ate the food there. Someone must have slipped it into his food."

"I bet the police will test the food on his plate for poison if that's the determined cause of death," Eleanor said. "It will take time before there are results from an autopsy."

"Have they taped off the church as a crime scene?" asked Josephine. "Those church ladies can be very quick to clean up; important evidence could be destroyed."

"We don't know for sure what killed Tip," said Eleanor. "Maybe we should focus on Monica Fischer's case. After her memorial, I feel she's in need of serious justice."

On the drive home Eleanor became more and more enraged. The thought of those women at the mercy of the men who were supposed to love them touched something deep within her. Broken bones, black eyes, women made dependent on men by sex, pregnancies, children, fooled by what they thought was love. In her mind, Monica Fischer became a martyr for battered women and her killer had to be a man. Maybe one of the husbands of the women she met today. By the time she reached her house a deep rage seeped out of her eyes in the form of tears. She had never been so angry at the unfairness or injustice of it—the power men held over women. Even if she never experienced it in her own relationships, she wasn't immune to it. Some might say it's the choices you make and blame the victims for such misery, but she knew falling for a charming man was an easy thing, finding a good one was luck. Eleanor wiped her tears away when she heard Angus at her door. Angus saw Eleanor's face and felt the ring in his pocket. Now was not the time.

The super-sleuths met at Dede's house that night dressed in their usual stakeout outfits. Black everything—no stocking hats, mustaches, or other silliness this time. It was serious business and they knew it. Their plan was to go to city hall, find the trapdoor that led down into the underground tunnel and follow it until they arrived beneath The Oracle. Once there, they would climb the metal ladder, go through the trapdoor and enter the back room of the shop where they intended to search for more evidence.

It was an ordeal from start to finish. "I can't seem to turn the key in the lock," said Dede as she struggled with the key that unlocked the trapdoor leading to the tunnel.

"Let me try," said Eleanor who finally managed it. "It helps if you don't suffer from arthritis in your fingers."

"I don't remember it being so dark," said Josephine missing a step going down the metal ladder, her legs kicking out wildly as she tried to keep from sliding to the ground and unfortunately kicking Pearl in the head.

"Ouch," Pearl screamed.

"Shhhhh, we can't afford to be caught here," warned Dede.

"There's something in my hair," Cleo insisted. "I think it's a spider. Somebody, help me get it out!" An extensive inspection followed with all the flashlights turned on Cleo's head. After several minutes, Pearl simply tousled Cleo's hair and stomped on the ground claiming to have killed the spider. Of course, it was difficult to prove with the absence of a body in the darkness of the tunnel, and the ladies were now blinded by the flashlights on their phones. Eleanor led the way and missed the ladder that went up to The Oracle giving everyone anxiety about never finding their way back, and finally when they did, no one was strong enough to push the trapdoor open.

"Maybe someone put something heavy on top of the door," suggested Dede who stood on the topmost rung.

"Let me try," said Cleo who stood at the bottom of the ladder. "I've been lifting weights." Eleanor and Dede got down and Cleo went up but couldn't make the door budge.

"Maybe I can do it," said Pearl who thought her daily yoga routine made her the right one for the job. Cleo got down and Pearl went up but after several tries resigned herself to failure and backed down.

"Are you sure you unlocked it?" asked Eleanor.

Dede and Eleanor climbed back up the ladder.

"I'll try the lock again. Here, hold the flashlight …" Dede didn't get a chance to finish because stomping and banging from above startled the snoops and suddenly the door flew open revealing a dark shape wielding a wooden bat silhouetted against a bright light. There was horrific screaming from both sides. Pearl and Cleo scurried down into the tunnel, knocking Josephine down in a mad rush to hide in the darkness. Dede and Eleanor finally realized it was none other than Madame Patruska herself who thought they were intruders on a mission to make good on their promise to kill her.

"Well," Madame Patruska finally spoke when things calmed down and both parties recognized the other. "If I knew you were coming, I'd have caked a bake." She helped each of them into the back room of The Oracle before asking politely, "What are you doing here?"

"We came to search for evidence," Pearl said.

"There are some questions that need answers," said Eleanor. "I'm so glad you are here. When did you get back?"

"I came back today and I've been cleaning up this mess." She pointed to the front room that looked fairly good compared to the disorder they had discovered before. Books were back on shelves, magical paraphernalia was on display, crystals found homes on countertops next to mood rings and pendants. "The shop needed a dood gusting any way. What questions?" Patruska led them to a table draped in black with silver stars and they sat down. The consultation room was cozy, and a lamp gave off a warm, hazy glow.

"Is The Lovers card missing from your tarot deck?" Asked Eleanor.

"No," answered Patruska, "but I don't remember doing this one. It's very strange the way the cards were laid out on the table. It sakes no mense. I think someone else just placed them there nilly-willy. I usually put the cards away when I'm done and no, The Lovers card was not missing. Many people own carot tards."

"Great," said Dede. "Now all we have to do is find a tarot deck missing The Lovers card."

"That would point to premeditation," said Josephine. "Someone would have to buy a tarot deck, take the card to the murder scene and plant it there, knowing they were going to commit murder."

"Then there's the issue of this list we found in your files," said Cleo. "The file titled The Witches includes our names. What does that mean?"

"You went frough my thiles?" Patruska was shocked. "There is very confidential information in there." She didn't mention the information that gave weight to her readings.

"Well, we didn't have time to go through them," Cleo confessed.

"I took the file labeled The Witches because I learned there was a group investigating witchcraft in Waterton," said Eleanor. "I was curious."

"I was alarmed," said Cleo. "I'm not a witch!"

"Of course you're not, the title is a lack of pies. Didn't you read the entire list?" Patruska got up and went to the secret wall that hid her files. She returned with several loose pages. "The gile is fone and these pages were on the floor." Patruska laid them on the table.

"Sorry," Eleanor said, "I didn't have time to look at the file so I took it hoping to read it later, but I forgot it in my car."

"Well, in your haste it seems you spilled the contents of the file on the floor," Patruska said. "The Witches are a loup of gradies I work with from the crisis center. They aren't witches. They are abused and battered women. Fonica Mischer and Molly Fiori came to me for help getting these women away from their abusers and into a protective home. I use my skills to work with them. Mostly we have fun. Sometimes I'm able to help them see options through my readings. It's a kind of therapy."

"But why are our names on the list?" asked Eleanor.

"That is the last page of a list of possible sponsors for our cause. We were hoping you would tonate dime or money," Patruska explained, "It's critical to keep the names of these women secret, we don't want their abusers to know anything about us." There was silence while the group processed this new information.

"There seems to be a link connecting Monica Fischer's death and the break-in at The Oracle, and it's the women's crisis center," said Eleanor.

"Okay then," said Cleo, "how did that shoe get in here and what do you plan to do with it?"

By the time they figured out a plan, it was midnight, but they all knew what to do with the shoe.

Eleanor slept late but woke feeling refreshed and eager to start her day. The sunlight hit the water and a fresh breeze blew gently off the ocean while the ever-present gulls offered their morning hymn. It promised to be a beautiful day. Eleanor walked toward the beach. When she came to Angus' house, she noticed Helen Pence's Mini Cooper parked in his driveway. Eleanor's heart sank and the sky suddenly darkened behind a nonexistent cloud. She no longer heard the joyful song of gulls, only their discordant cries of complaint. She hurried by, hoping to avoid being seen and continued her walk along the shore so into her head she neglected to enjoy the beauty that surrounded her. What could possibly explain Helen's car parked there at this time of day? Had she come to deliver a breakfast casserole? Had she stayed all night? Angus thought she was spending the night with her coffee friends. Was he enjoying more than Helen's cooking? Jealousy is a terrible thing. Angus didn't belong to her. She loved him, and she wanted him to be happy, so if Helen Pence made him happy, she would deal with it. There really was no other choice. She told Angus that he couldn't have Helen's casserole and eat her cake too. She knew that jealousy was the death of love, but unrequited love hurt. Maybe it was time to step back before things hurt more than she could bear. Feeling that she had worked the whole drama out in her mind and resigning herself to a different relationship with Angus, she started home.

Angus came over later, while Eleanor was working on a project in her office. He stood in the doorway looking very handsome in his flannel shirt and blue jeans and smiled wickedly as though he hadn't done anything wrong. When he pulled her into his arms, she could smell Helen Pence on him and it sickened her. "I saw Helen's car at your house," she said as she pushed him away.

"I'm sure you didn't. You must be mistaken," he said. "Weren't you gone overnight?"

"I came home early," Eleanor said, "I saw her car there this morning."

"She's just a friend with benefits, like you," Angus replied shrugging his shoulders.

"I don't like it," Eleanor responded as her face turned into a rich carrot cake covered in buttercream frosting.

"Oh, I think you do," he said as he grabbed her and began licking the frosting and biting into her face.

This time when she tried to pulled away, he became angry, held her tightly and continued his advances.

"Angus, you're hurting me," she cried.

"Love doesn't hurt, Eleanor," Angus said, "But I can hurt you if you want me to." Then he slapped her, again and again causing her cake face to fly off in different directions.

"Angus, you're hurting me, you're hurting me, you're hurting me…" Eleanor cried. She had never felt so helpless, so powerless, so heartbroken. It was more than she could stand … she took charge and woke up.

Eleanor was shocked by the dream that was merely the remnants of her experience with Monica Fischer's story, the violent drama of the women from the crisis center and the presence of Helen's car at Angus'. Never would the Angus she knew behave in such an awful way! She wondered if the women at the crisis center felt the same shock when the men who professed to love them treated them with such disrespect. She imagined how it would start; first a romance with a charming man filled with compliments, flowers and candy, then an argument ending in an insult and verbal abuse, next the contrition and begging of forgiveness, a vow to never treat her that way again, more flowers and make-up sex, then another argument ending with a push or a slap, and a repeating cycle that escalated in violence until she either left or ended up dead. She made herself a cup of tea while Feathers watched her every move. "Ellie, you're a bad girl, he said, "Give me a kiss."

"Give me a break," she said, "I'm not a fan of men right now!"

It wasn't surprising that when Angus showed up at Eleanor's door, she was less than welcoming. One look at her stony glare caused him to ask, "Still grumpy? What's wrong? Did something happen last night?"

"Maybe you should answer that." Eleanor hated the way she sounded. "What do you need?" she quickly added in an attempt to lighten her tone.

Angus wasn't sure how to proceed so he just plowed through. "I need your help. Helen Pence is becoming a nuisance. Last night she arrived at my house with enough lasagna to feed the entire village of Sand Beach. Then her car wouldn't start, so I promised to fix it and drove her home. I've been working on it all day and now I need to drive it back to her so I need a ride home. Can you meet me at her house?"

Eleanor was still hearing the words 'Helen Pence is becoming a nuisance.'

"Ellie, did you hear me?" Angus said as he studied her face with concern.

"Yes," Eleanor smiled and threw her arms around Angus and buried her nose in his shirt, happy it smelled like car grease.

Members of the coffee group and Madame Patruska donned gloves, typed and put notes in shoeboxes, wrapped them in brown paper, tied them with string, and separately took them to the post office. They met that evening at the Red Shed sure that the packages would not be delivered until the following day.

"This may be the last night of our lives," moaned Cleo, who remembered their last fiasco at the Red Shed when they had done something equally dangerous.

"I'm going to play KENO," said Pearl and she disappeared into the back room with a pack of cigarettes.

"Why are we here?" asked Josephine who didn't drink alcohol and sat sipping a glass of ginger beer.

"It may be the last time we see each other," said Cleo who remained awash in gloom even after finishing her dirty martini.

"Our plaster man is in effect. There's no going back," said Madame Patruska, who drank her whiskey neat.

"Yes, but why the Red Shed for heaven's sake?" persisted Josephine who didn't like the sawdust on the floor or the rough crowd of men who hung out here with their overly made-up girlfriends.

"Don't be a snob, Josephine," warned Dede. "Although I agree, it would be slumming for Jesse Bomotti to bring a date here, but maybe he just wanted an alibi."

"It seems unlikely Tip Kent would frequent a place like this either," Josephine added. "Unless he's changed a great deal, he prefers a pickup bar with a more refined setting."

"I'm sure he'd rather be here now, than where he is," said Eleanor.

"Do you think we've made a mistake?" asked Dede, "Perhaps it isn't one of the abusive men."

"We'll find out soon enough," said Madame Patruska. "If none of them respond we'll work out another master plan."

"Oh crap," said Dede, "Don't look now, but the snowman just walked in."

Eleanor's heart froze. She turned her face to the wall afraid he might recognize her and felt a shiver from her head to her toes as his icy gaze passed over the group of women at the table, finally being able to relax a little when he turned and sat at the bar.

"He's drinking whiskey," said Cleo who watched without fear, "If only I had a little rat poison."

It was as if the entire group had an epiphany at the exact same time. It was Dede who said it out loud, "What if someone felt that way about Tip?"

"It would have to be Klara," said Josephine. "Who else would want him dead?"

"Klara told me about a woman Tip met at the casino. Someone he rescued from a drunk who was violent with her. Maybe he took her to his room and took advantage of her," Eleanor said. "Maybe that woman was at the memorial. We don't know who he's been in contact with and Klara admitted he sometimes doesn't come home all night."

"Are you suggesting one of the women from the crisis center poisoned Tip?" asked Pearl.

"Do you think someone just happened to have rat poison on them just in case they met someone they wanted to kill?" asked Cleo.

"The rat poison could have been in a cupboard at the church. I know they've had an infestation there before," said Dede.

"Seems strike a letch to me," said Madame Patruska, "Unless this Tip guy killed Monica and the crisis ladies knew it. Could he have any reason to kill Monica? Do we know for certain he was poisoned?"

"I think our list of suspects just got bigger," said Eleanor. "I need to go home and organize my thoughts before I forget."

The friends slipped out the back taking Pearl with them against her will. She had lost twenty dollars.

Eleanor was so engrossed in her thoughts about organizing the suspects she didn't notice the pickup truck tailgating her until the bright headlights flashed in her rearview mirror. Had that truck been there the whole time? Had they been driving without lights? Were they trying to sneak up on her? Her first thought was to pull over to let them pass but instead she listened to that little voice in her head that told her something wasn't right and sped up. The pickup seemed to fall back but then raced forward ramming her rear bumper causing Eleanor's car to swerve as she tried to stay in control. Suddenly Eleanor was afraid.

There was evil intent, Eleanor could feel it. She knew it was Frost. Don't panic, stay calm, she told herself. You know this road even in the dark, you can go faster around the curves than that truck. If she could get a little distance between them, she could pull off onto a side road and hide. She stepped on the gas maneuvering deftly around the tight curves with sand hills to the right and a drop to the ocean on the left. Eleanor felt the abyss and heard the waves crashing below. This was not the place to lose control.

Then all hell broke loose when another car behind the truck appeared flashing its headlights from dim to bright and honking its horn nonstop. Eleanor slowed down trying to understand the drama behind her. Almost immediately, the pickup passed Eleanor recklessly on a blind curve and disappeared into the dark. Eleanor pulled to the shoulder of the road her hands too shaky to open her door. In her rearview mirror she watched as Dede and Cleo scrambled out of the car with Josephine and Pearl right behind them.

"Are you alright?" asked Dede.

"Yes, just a little shaken," Eleanor said getting out of her car. "How did you know to come?"

"As soon as you left, we saw Frost get in his truck and follow you," Cleo said. "I had a bad feeling, so I called Angus and he called Officer McGraw."

"We knew they couldn't get here as fast as we could," said Pearl, "especially with Dede driving."

Eleanor began to cry from shock and gratitude. They had saved her. Angus drove up and knew everything was under control when he witnessed the big group hug on the side of the road.

Officer McGraw came later and drove after Frost hoping to see his truck somewhere nearby. Angus refused to leave Eleanor and insisted the ladies go back to town.

"Are you okay to drive?" he asked after checking her bumper for damage.

"Yes, I'm fine," Eleanor said and bravely got behind the wheel, knowing that Angus would follow her home.

"Red or white," Angus asked as he studied Eleanor's wine selection, and twisted the ring in his pocket around his pinky finger. Once again, he decided it wasn't the right time.

"Whiskey straight up," Eleanor responded as she followed him into the kitchen wearing only her bathrobe. "Never mind that. I'll have a shot of Drambuie." They took their remedies into the living room and sat on the couch. Eleanor gazed blankly as she relived the night's scary event.

"Lie down and tell me what happened," he said taking her feet in his hands and massaging the stress away.

"We went to the Red Shed and he must have seen me when he came in. We left out the back and when I drove off, he followed me. Dede and the others saw it all and chased after us after they called you. I didn't notice him until I was almost home. He sped up and bumped me from behind. I managed to stay on the road but I was afraid he was going to keep doing it until I crashed. Then my friends came on the scene, lights flashing, horn blaring, and he passed me. Oh, Angus, he could have killed someone passing like that. He could have killed you."

"I never saw his truck. He must have pulled off the road before I got there. Did you see who it was?" asked Angus.

"No, but Dede, Pearl, Cleo, and Josephine did. It was Andri Frost." Eleanor said sitting up. "Have you heard anything from Officer McGraw?"

"He called while you were in the shower. There was no trace of him. The man's a ghost. I don't think he went to the village, but most likely circled back to town on the loop road. There are a number of side roads he could have taken to hide." Angus reached for Eleanor, holding her tight. There was no resistance in her body.

"What were you doing at the Red Shed?" Angus asked. "You know that's not a safe place."

"We were having drinks there," Eleanor said.

"Were you checking out Jesse Bomotti's alibi?" Angus asked, already knowing the answer.

"Maybe we hoped to hear something, but we didn't," Eleanor said. There was a long silence as Angus waited for Eleanor to tell him more, but she didn't.

"I'm worried, Ellie," Angus began, "Every time you and your band of amateur detectives go there, trouble follows."

"That may be," Eleanor admitted, "It's not my favorite place, but going there did remind us it's a place men go to pick up women. It made us wonder why Tip and Jesse, two high-brows, would go there, with Molly no less."

"So, you think they were lying?" asked Angus.

"Klara told me that was Jesse's alibi for the night Monica was killed. She said he was there with Molly, and Tip repeated that the night he visited me."

"The bartender remembered them there that night, at least until eleven," Angus said. "Monica could have been killed after they left, so they're not in the clear."

"Do you think Tip was involved?" asked Eleanor. Angus shrugged. He had other things on his mind.

"I can't shake the feeling that you're up to something, Ellie," Angus said. "Tell me you're not doing something dangerous."

"Oh, look what I got," she said, changing the subject and rushing to the closet, returning with a cane. "I'm taking this wherever I go. Do you want to practice some Cane Fu moves?"

"I think you've had enough drama for one day." Angus stood and walked to the kitchen. "Let's make popcorn and watch a movie." Eleanor followed poking his back with her cane. "I'm warning you, Ellie. Don't make me hurt you." The words reminded Eleanor of her dream. Maybe Angus would hurt her if the circumstances were right. Something in her wanted to know how far she could push him. She poked him again, harder this time, even harder than she intended. She thought about catching his leg with the hook of the cane, but before she could act, he turned around, grabbed her cane and pushed her to the floor using a technique unfamiliar to her. She stared up into his eyes with the realization that she was helpless. He was bigger, stronger, and far more experienced in physical combat than she was. "Uncle," she whispered.

Angus got off her and offered his hand to help her off the floor. Feathers watched from his perch in the kitchen window and offered his own opinion of the matter. "Ellie, you're a bad girl."

"You definitely need more practice," Angus said taking the cane. "Want to go again?"

"Maybe later," she said as her robe fell open. She had powers of her own if she chose to use them.

Eleanor walked to Klara's house carrying a basket of muffins fresh from the oven. When Klara opened the door, Eleanor thought it was Klara's mother standing in front of her. Everything about her sagged as if her entire body was frowning. "Eleanor, please come in," she said.

"How are you?" Eleanor asked even though she could see she wasn't doing well.

"I'd have to be better just to die," Klara said taking the offered muffins. "Thank you so much for coming. I haven't seen a friendly face for days. I'll make some tea."

They sat at the dining table and chatted about unimportant things until the teakettle whistled. When Klara came back to the table, she began to talk. "I didn't know how much I cared for that man, but now that he's gone, I miss the old fool."

"I didn't know him well, but he seemed like a gentleman and he obviously adored you," Eleanor said.

"Don't pee down my leg and tell me it's raining. I know he had flaws; drank, chewed tobacco, chased plenty of skirts in his day. There may have been snow on the roof, but there was fire in the hearth. Now I even miss his spittoon."

"Sorry, Klara, is there anything I can do to help, besides chewing tobacco?" Eleanor asked. Klara smiled and her entire face changed.

"Yes, tell me something about you that will take my mind off my troubles," Klara said. "You do realize I'm a suspect in Tip's murder."

"No, I didn't know," Eleanor said.

"Strychnine poison in his nicotine pouch. They found it in the one he had in his jaw although they never found the tin. I didn't even know he was using a nicotine pouch. He must have been trying to quit that nasty habit. They've searched this place high and low for poison, but there's nothing here, of course, because I didn't kill him, although there were plenty of times I've been tempted."

"Sometimes I think men are an entirely different species." Eleanor thought about Angus and his harem of women, his obsession with protecting her, and his failure to understand her need for independence. She shared the part about Helen Pence's infatuation with Angus and his inability to see the harm in it.

"You have a relationship with Angus McBride. He's that tall hunk with a full head of hair and deep dimples, and isn't Helen Pence that pretty woman with asthma? You know the one with big boobs and a wheezy voice?" asked Klara.

"I wouldn't call her pretty," said Eleanor, "but big breasted yes, and definitely breathless."

"Oh, she's nothing compared to you," Klara said, "You're prettier than a store-bought doll. I saw Helen just yesterday at the grocery store. She was telling another woman she was getting married to Angus McBride. Sorry, Eleanor, but that woman has enough mouth for ten rows of teeth. You better tell Angus he's getting married before the whole town hears what he doesn't know."

Eleanor stewed over Helen Pence's gossip and Angus' failure to address the situation she had warned him about. Helen assumed Angus loved her and wanted to marry her. What did he do to make her feel that way? Fix her car, drink her wine, bring her flowers? Was there more to it than that? Was he nibbling on more than her casseroles? The day she picked him up at Helen's house, she hadn't asked him what he intended to do about the nuisance Helen had become. Evidently, he had done nothing. Maybe he was fine with leaving everything the way it was. What if he was planning to marry Helen and didn't know how to cut Eleanor loose. Eleanor realized she wasn't focusing on her coffee friends, Andri Frost, the murder cases, or the dangerous plan to flush out the killer—only this ridiculous situation that was spiraling out of control. She needed to address it as soon as possible, but she also needed to be there for Madame Patruska in case their plan paid off.

Madame Patruska opened a box of psychic jewelry that included amulets, mood rings, crystal bracelets, pendants and earrings as Eleanor dusted around the already crowded shelves. The front door had been replaced with a solid oak one with a beautiful stained-glass window of brilliant rainbow colors and sported a new lock and dead bolt. Madame Patruska had sprung for a camera that recorded everyone who came to the door for the benefit of her own safety and at the urging of her crystal ball. They were ready and waiting for the killer to come for the shoe.

"Eleanor, let's do a tarot reading for you while we wait. It will make the time go faster," Patruska offered.

Eleanor sat across the table from the seer who shuffled the cards and fanned them out on the table. Eleanor chose ten cards and Patruska laid them out in the Celtic Cross in order of Eleanor's picks and began to read them with great concentration. "The Six of Pentacles augers a situation where there is money to be shared. Be open to offer generosity or be the recipient of another's generosity. The Wheel of Fortune suggests a change of fortune—good or bad—and brings growth and a new phase of life. The Moon indicates a time of confusion, fluctuation, and uncertainty. The Queen of Swords says it is time to cast away immovable faith in high ideals and live life to the fullest. Stop pit-nicking and looking for perfection in yourself and others and live.

"The Nine of Pentacles shows a past of strong identity based on solid achievements and unique abilities and the worth of one's work. A strong belief in self and an appreciation of the finer gifts based on independence has provided pleasure and seep datisfaction.

"The Three of Pentacles heralds a time of early success in a material endeavor. A project may earn profits (from the billy sook sales perhaps) but it is not a final resolution.

"The Lovers is the necessity of choice, it could mean a love triangle, or a hasty marriage, the choice between career or love. Look carefully at the implications of your choice and don't be driven into something blindly.

"The King of Swords appears when it is time to meet the ambivalence of intellect and strategy. This fart smeller may be striking by their mental gifts and ability to initiate change in the world and be a catalyst for you.

"The King of Cups signals a time to experience the ambivalent side of yourself. You are someone who can help others yet can't lust trife enough to take its course. You must be in control to protect from being hurt again. If the King of Cups enters a person's life in this form it indicates a time to meet this dimension of yourself."

"That's a lot to take in," said Eleanor as she struggled to understand it. Deep down she knew it had everything to do with her relationship with Angus and why she couldn't commit to him. Was she afraid of being hurt? Was Walter's memory keeping her from living her best life? The tinkle of the bell over Patruska's door ended her thought processes as the fortune teller stood to attend to business. Eleanor peeked out from behind the beaded curtain and saw Helen Pence standing at the counter.

"Mow hay I help you?" Patruska asked.

"I was wondering if it was possible to buy a love potion," Helen asked casually.

"No, I have nothing like that here," Patruska answered.

"How about something to cancel a spell that a witch has cast over a man?" she continued.

"No, nothing like that," Patruska said shaking her head.

"Well for heaven's sake what *do* you have in this shop?" Helen asked impatiently.

"You can find things like that on the internet," advised Madame Patruska. "Also, I have these crystals over here. Some are good for attracting love, but there are many kinds of love. What kind of love do you seek?"

Helen moved to the display of crystals and picked up one. "That is malachite, a stone that fosters self-love," Patruska said.

"That's not what I had in mind," Helen murmured. "I want something more for romantic love."

"Sunstone is an excellent one for the libido, and carnelian promotes a healthy sex life along with joy and creativity," Patruska said. "Oh, just in today are these bracelets made of starious vones. Let me see, yes, this is sunstone and here is carnelian."

"Oh, how pretty," Helen put the sunstone bracelet on her wrist and admired it from all angles. "I'll take both. One for him and one for me."

"Perfect," Patruska said and rang up the sale.

"Do you know Eleanor Penrose?" Helen asked out of the blue.

"Yes, a lovely woman," Patruska said putting the bracelets in a bag.

"Does she buy love crystals here?"

"No, Eleanor doesn't need help in that department; she buys charms to ward off evil gossips and keep men away. I understand she has many suitors." Patruska offered a sly smile and handed the bag to Helen who left in a huff.

Madame Patruska couldn't hold her laughter in a second longer. Pushing through the beaded curtain where Eleanor hid, they both had a good giggle. Before Eleanor left The Oracle, Madame Patruska pressed a gift into her hand. It was a hat pin with the eye of Horus on it to protect her from those who would cause her harm by looking at her with evil intent. Eleanor didn't believe in such things but stuck the cobalt blue onto her sweater to please Patruska. What harm could it do? Eleanor liked blue.

Later that evening after The Oracle closed its doors for the day, the coffee group met at Madame Patruska's house to share information about the murder case. Patruska's kitchen looked like any other kitchen although more colorful than most with turquoise appliances and purple accents. There was nothing to indicate she was a psychic. Evidently, she kept those things at The Oracle.

Eleanor and Patruska shared their experience about Helen Pence's visit. "Do you think she's gathering information about witches for her committee?" asked Cleo.

"I'm sure that's what she'll say if asked, but I think she honestly wanted a love potion for Angus," Eleanor said.

"Has he told her he's not interested in her romantically?" asked Josephine.

"I don't know," Eleanor admitted. "Klara told me Helen is telling everyone Angus is going to marry her, so I don't think he's said anything that would cause her to believe otherwise."

"What are you going to do about that?" asked Dede.

"I'm going to talk to him tonight. He's clueless about Helen's assumptions and much too kind to hurt her feelings," Eleanor said with more conviction than she felt and was ready to change the topic. "I've listed the suspects and their motives here." Eleanor placed a sheet of paper on the table. "Let's look at each one and assess what we know about them and what we still need to learn."

"**Jesse Bomotti** befriended Monica but not sure if their relationship was more than that." Eleanor said. "He has an alibi of sorts, both Molly Fiori and Tip Kent saw him at the Red Shed between 9:00 and 11:00 p.m. on the night Monica was killed. The bartender remembers them there.

"**Klara Kent** has no alibi and may or may not have motive. She told us she liked Monica but may be an overprotective mother.

"**Molly Fiori** is Jesse's long-term girlfriend who befriended Monica and may have worked with her at the crisis center for abused women but could have been jealous of Monica's friendship with Jesse.

"Tip Kent, known womanizer, who may have liked Monica too much.

"Malcolm Manning worked with Monica at city hall, misogynist, might have resented her skills at work.

"Andri Frost, big-time misogynist who worked with Monica in Orick, lost his job because of her, and is here in town now tracking Bigfoot.

"Madame Patruska, who may have been implicated by a tarot card found at the scene, although The Lovers card from her deck was not missing. Monica's shoe was found in her shop and she also worked at the crisis center.

"Husbands of crisis center victims who believed Monica helped their wives leave them. Don't know anything about them except their names and addresses.

"Members of the witchcraft committee who thought Monica was a witch and hanged her.

"There's too many!" said Pearl. "Let's eliminate some."

"Let's start with Jesse, who has no motive and Molly who is a sweetheart and Tip who is dead. They all have alibis and I don't think they are guilty," said Dede.

"We know Madame Patruska is innocent and the evidence against her looks like a setup," said Cleo.

"Thank you," said Madame Patruska.

"So, we're left with Klara, Malcolm, Andri, husbands of the crisis center women, and the witchcraft hunters," Eleanor said. "I made this list of suspects for killing Tip." She laid out another sheet. "Klara told me Tip was poisoned with strychnine laced in his nicotine pouch. She's the number one suspect since she inherits a large sum of money upon his death, but I'd like to eliminate her from killing Monica because I don't think she's physically capable of putting a body in her car, driving up that road in the dark, and dumping the body."

"Maybe Jesse and Tip helped her with the body after she killed Monica," suggested Josephine. "Then Jesse killed Tip. If

Tip was dead, Jesse could share the inheritance. Money can be a powerful motive."

"Jesse has more money than God," said Dede, "and what motive did Tip have to kill Monica?"

"Perhaps Klara accidently killed her and Tip just helped her get rid of the body and then Klara killed him to tie up loose ends," Cleo said.

"My bet's on Andri Frost," said Eleanor, "but I can't connect him to Tip."

"There is nothing more deceptive than the obvious fact," Pearl said, quoting Sir Arthur Conan Doyle.

"Well, no one showed up at The Oracle today except Pelen Hence," said Madame Patruska. "She must be the killer."

"I'll go over to her house right now and ask her," said Cleo.

"Don't forget Monica was hanged, so it's not far-fetched that someone who believed she was a witch would kill her," said Josephine.

"Monica was strong and healthy. It would take the entire witchcraft hunting committee to kill her and dispose of her body. Let's wait a few days to see if our plan turns up anything," said Eleanor. "I don't think we have enough facts to implicate anyone at this point."

"There are no practicing witches in Waterton," said Madame Patruska, "And even if there were, they wouldn't go that far up in the woods to cast a circle. I believe someone wants to make it look like this murder was committed by a woven of kitches—the noose, the candles, the circle; all that information can be found on the internet. Witches are to blame, all women are warned not to be too loud, too smart, too independent or they will be wabeled as litches and punished for it. I suspect Monica was murdered by a man or many men who feel they have lost control over their women. I suggest we focus on the husbands of the abused."

"I agree, said Dede, "Someone has gone to a great deal of trouble to make Madame Patruska look guilty."

"Possibly someone who believes all women are witches and resents them," said Pearl. "The hanging part is a warning to all women to obey their men."

"I wonder if and how the murder of Tip is connected. Maybe someone from his past was afraid of a secret he knew," said Cleo. "You didn't kill him did you, Josephine?"

Josephine rolled her eyes.

Eleanor was making smothered chicken for dinner. Ever since the Andri Frost incident Angus insisted on staying with her every night and Eleanor felt exactly as smothered as the chicken she was cooking. She would smash some potatoes and toss a green salad for some relief. She opened a bottle of pinot gris and waited uneasily for Angus to make his appearance. Their evenings together felt off somehow as if some obstacle sat between them and kept them from enjoying the comfort they used to feel in each other's company. Tonight, she would find out what was going on with Helen Pence. Feathers flew to her shoulder and spoke in Walter's voice, "I love you, Ellie. Give me a kiss." For some reason it made her cry. "*The essence of romance is uncertainty.*" She had been certain with Walter all through their marriage until she wasn't, but by then the romance was gone anyway. Walter was gone. Eleanor wiped the tears away. Those tears belonged to the past. Her future was ringing the doorbell.

Angus stood in the entryway with a bouquet of red roses. There must have been two dozen. Suddenly Eleanor worried such a gesture might be Angus' way to buffer a harsh truth. "Come in," she said. Angus seemed ill at ease and offered no kiss or comment about the magical aroma emanating from the kitchen. "These are beautiful," Eleanor said. "Help yourself to a drink while I put these in a vase."

Angus poured three fingers into a glass and took in the comfortable aura of Eleanor's kitchen, the delicious smell, the warm glow of the lights, the accent color of red that contrasted against the white, the extraordinary organization of the room. The only off-putting thing was the parrot by the window. Feathers looked at Angus sideways and squawked, "You're a bum!" It made him anxious and Angus wasn't a man who ever felt that way. Lately Eleanor seemed angry with him. He knew it was about the ladies who brought him meals and he knew she was right. He hadn't addressed the issue properly and Eleanor had every right to kick him to the curb. He would have been furious if the shoe were on the other foot.

"There," she said placing the roses on the table. "Dinner's ready." They sat at opposite ends of the table barely speaking while they ate. Eleanor picked at the food and took no pleasure in Angus' company. In the silence she could hear him chewing and it annoyed her. Angus cut his chicken with such force that it sounded like nails scrapping on a chalkboard. Eleanor glared at him causing Angus to shift uneasily in his chair and notice for the first time her judgmental attitude and overall displeasure directed at him. The grandfather clock chimed the half hour breaking the silence while each of them wondered whether the other wanted to continue this relationship.

"That was delicious," Angus said wiping his mustache on a napkin, "What do you call it?"

"Smothered chicken," Eleanor said. "Do you want the recipe for Helen? Klara said she's telling everyone you two are getting married." There it was. Eleanor was angry. "Does she know where you are tonight? Are you here to tell me it's true?"

Angus didn't know what to say and then it took too long to say it. "No, no, no, Ellie," he sputtered. "I know you're right. I didn't mean to lead her on but it's become clear to me now. I swear, I didn't do anything more than I thought was appropriate in the way a man might help a widow."

"A widow like me?" she asked.

"Ellie, you know what you are to me. I've asked you more than once to marry me. You're the one that won't have me. I can't help that Helen got the wrong idea or that she's telling people things that aren't true." Angus paused. "Well, maybe it is my fault. I took her to lunch to find out about the committee she's on to look into witchcraft. I guess she misinterpreted that as romantic interest. She's been pestering me ever since."

"Really, what did you find out?" Eleanor said, suddenly intrigued.

"I already told you. You and your friends are on the list as witches, based on something she witnessed in Madame Patruska's yard. She said she saw you go into Patruska's house. There have been several gatherings in the backyard where women meet and dance around under the moon, drink wine, and have sex with the devil." Angus flashed his dimples.

"You never told me that," Eleanor objected. "You're making that up."

"I'm sure I told you about the list," Angus said. "Listen Ellie, I think I know what happened. I came up with a solution to our problem." He reached into his pocket and pulled out the ring. "I was buying this ring for you at Diamond Dan's when Helen came in to get her watch repaired. She must have seen it and assumed it was for her."

Eleanor took a long look at the ring, "This is a beautiful ring, Angus."

"Try it on," he slipped it on her ring finger. "It fits. I thought we could each wear a ring to lead people to believe we're married and then they'd leave us alone. We don't have to actually get married or even explain it to anyone."

Eleanor looked at the ring on her finger. She loved it. There were five sizable diamonds that threw flashes of light in every direction all set in a gold band. "I don't know Angus, that seems dishonest somehow."

"It doesn't have to be," he said. "Think of it as an engagement ring. I'm willing to promise my fidelity to you. There's no one else."

"I'll have to buy you a ring too," Eleanor said warming to the idea.

"I've still got the one Margo gave me," Angus said.

"No, you can't wear that!" Eleanor was adamant. "I'll get one tomorrow. Until then you'll just have to wear this." She slipped a gold napkin ring on his finger. Surprisingly it fit.

Eleanor was filled with unexpected joy. She was in love with the idea of a never-ending engagement that promised commitment but held no legal responsibilities. Knowing either of them could walk away lent the necessary uncertainty to the relationship that let romance endure. Eager to put a real ring on Angus' finger, she walked into Diamond Dan's jewelry store and looked over the possibilities. It would have to be gold, simple yet beautiful and expensive. Angus worked with his hands so the ring couldn't have sharp edges or protrusions. If it complimented her ring, that would be perfect. Diamond Dan watched Eleanor and waited silently until he thought she might be ready for his assistance. It was his gift to know when someone was ready to make a purchase or just wanted to window shop. He immediately thought about the day Angus McBride bought the ring he now saw on Eleanor's hand and knew exactly what Eleanor wanted.

"Good morning, Eleanor," he said stretching his obligatory smile so it showed every one of his gold crowns, "May I help you find something to match the beauty of the ring on your finger?"

"Oh, you noticed," she said.

"Hard not to see that one. Congratulations," he said. "There will be lots of tears shed when Waterton society learns of this."

Eleanor wasn't sure what that meant. "You don't think people will be happy for us?"

"You must realize that ever since Angus' divorce, he's been the object of desire among all the single ladies in the county. Probably married ones as well."

"No, I didn't." Eleanor was miffed. "What a gossip you are! I just want a gold band."

Diamond Dan had been chastised and felt it like a slap across his face. He struggled with something to say to appease Eleanor whom he considered a real peach.

"I guess I am a gossip," he confessed, but recovered by adding, "It's hard not to see that you and Angus are a perfect match, so let me show you a ring that complements yours perfectly." He took a tray from the showcase and plucked from it a narrow, gold-channeled band filled with diamonds.

"Lovely, Dan," Eleanor said as she studied it carefully, "but it seems a bit flashy for Angus. I'd like to see this one." Eleanor pointed to a wider band with one diamond embedded in the gold.

Dan handed it to Eleanor knowing it was less expensive than the one he selected but more suited to Angus. "Are you sure you don't want the flashy one that will show all those widows he's taken?"

"The ring is for Angus," she said, "My only concern is that *he* likes it." Eleanor put her card on the counter and smiled at Diamond Dan. Next time she bought jewelry, she'd go to Costco.

Meanwhile Angus and Bones returned home after a long walk on the beach where Angus plotted to make this extended engagement end in matrimony. Ellie surprised him when she agreed to enter into it at all. The moment she began to talk about dishonesty, he thought it was over. She had high ideals and he loved that about her. It was what kept her in the light and brightened his dark days when he thought the worst of people. Ellie made him see the best. The idea of a long engagement came to him out of panic, but it appealed to her. The worm was turning. Ellie was leaning in the direction of marriage and he wasn't going to screw this up. He'd refuse any more meals from the ladies who brought casseroles and find ways to avoid doing things to help them. He'd continue to court Ellie with flowers and wine, maybe take her on a romantic trip. He touched the napkin ring on his finger and smiled at how happy it made him and how that happiness would grow as he imagined waking up beside her every morning, sharing the simple day-to-day pleasures like walks and cups of coffee, making love in the afternoon, coming home to a house filled with warmth and good food, and kissing her goodnight every night. The ringing of his phone interrupted his revery and he answered before he knew who it was. If only he'd looked beforehand, he wouldn't have been at a loss to make an excuse. He would have let it go to voicemail. "Hello," he said and listened to the breathy voice almost hysterically crying on the other end.

"Helen, slow down, I can barely understand you," and then the line went dead. He tried to call back but the call went to voicemail and Angus, being the good guy, went to Helen's aid.

He parked in front of Helen's house, and rang the bell. The fact that she came to the door in her robe didn't go unnoticed. "What's wrong, Helen? What's happened?" he asked.

"Oh, Angus, I'm so glad you're here. You have to see this for yourself." Helen led him upstairs to her bedroom and pointed to her bed.

"What am I supposed to see?" The words fell away as he felt a sharp pain and everything went dark.

Helen Pence went to work, knowing he could awaken any minute. Fortunately, he fell onto the bed and she didn't have to lift him. She turned him over, stripped him, and tied him to her bedposts with silk scarves. She took off her robe and crawled into bed beside him. Afterward, she took selfies of them together so she would always have the memory of their time together. Helen Pence, church lady and witch hunter, had snapped.

When Angus began to stir, Helen slipped back into her robe and sat down at her vanity where the pink candle had been burning for two days. She checked the paper where she had written their names and circled them. In her fantasy, she imagined them together. Angus at her door with flowers and candy, swooping her into his arms, and carrying her to the bed where he now lay moaning in pain. She pretended it was ecstasy as she repeated the chant "For the highest good of all, may this bring me his love," three times. When she turned to the bed, she saw Angus was awake and watching her.

"Helen, what the hell are you doing?" Angus shouted, wincing at the pain it caused.

"Don't worry, darling, the spell only takes five more days to work and then I'll untie you," Helen said. "In the meantime, just rest."

"My head hurts. Can you get me some aspirin?" Angus asked.

"Of course, dear heart, I'll be right back," Helen went into the bathroom. Angus tried sitting up. He pulled at the scarves holding him to the bedposts but the more he pulled the tighter they got and silk was much stronger than its weight suggested. He looked around for something he could use to free himself but Helen came back with aspirin and water before he could do more. She helped him take the pills and then cozied up to him again.

"Helen, I'm naked and cold," he said.

"I know, isn't it great? I like looking at you and touching you. I think you're hot," she said as she snuggled up to him and ran her fingers over his chest. "Are you hungry? I can whip up something fabulous. Maybe something with whipped cream."

Angus didn't answer. He closed his eyes and thought about the movie *Misery* where the kidnapper held her favorite author tied to a bed and broke his ankles so he couldn't escape. His head was throbbing and he couldn't think. He closed his eyes. When he woke Helen was next to him and it was dark except for the glow of a single candle that burned on her vanity. She had covered them with a blanket but he still felt cold and sick to his stomach. "Helen, wake up, I'm going to be sick."

Helen awoke immediately and ran downstairs to the kitchen for a bowl. She held it under his chin as he heaved and vomited into it. "That wasn't very romantic, Angus," she said as she took the bowl away. When she returned, she washed his face and put pillows behind his head.

"It wasn't very romantic of you to hit me on the head, Helen," he said, "Now I've got a concussion and you know what that means…"

"What does that mean?" she asked.

"I've got a headache. What do you think it means?" Helen was elated. The spell must be working if Angus was thinking about making love to her.

"Well, go back to sleep. Maybe you'll feel better in the morning." She laid her head on his chest and soon began to snore.

"Helen, wake up, I need to pee." Angus was growing more uncomfortable by the minute.

"For heaven's sake, Angus, you're just like a baby. How am I supposed to get my beauty sleep with you waking me up every other minute?" Helen complained. She made another trip to the bathroom and finally returned with a pint jar.

"I can't go if you touch me," he said. "Untie me or I'll soil your bed." In Helen's groggy state, she untied one scarf which could have been her undoing.

While Angus was relieving himself, someone was pounding on the door. Helen went to peek out the window and when she saw who it was, she laughed with glee, stumbled down the stairs and threw the door open revealing her nakedness to Eleanor and Dede who immediately jumped into action with their unique interpretation of Cane Fu. Dede hooked Helen's leg pulling her to the floor while Eleanor twirled her cane in a flurry, and sat on Helen pressing her cane to Helen's throat. "What have you done to Angus?" she cried. Helen wriggled and clawed at Eleanor in an attempt to get free. Realizing that Helen couldn't speak due to the cane choking her, Eleanor released her hold on the cane but continued to sit on her.

"He came here of his own free will," Helen said between coughs. "We made love and then he left."

"Liar," Dede said, "His truck is still parked outside."

"Where is he, Helen? You better tell me before I put this stick up your smelly freckle," Eleanor threatened.

"You wouldn't dare," Helen said as she began to buck like a rodeo bull in an attempt to throw Eleanor off. Eleanor held on until Helen lashed out and hit Eleanor in the eye giving her just enough time to escape into the downstairs bathroom.

"Eleanor, are you alright?" asked Dede who was stunned by the violent events unfolding before her.

"She poked me in the eye and it hurts like the devil." Eleanor sat on the floor holding her eye. "I guess Helen learned something from the self-defense class in spite of all her flirting."

"I'll go to the kitchen and get some ice," Dede said. It wasn't long before she returned with several ice cubes wrapped in a kitchen towel and gave it to Eleanor. "I'm surprised to learn that Helen cheats at cooking. Her freezer is full of frozen dinners and desserts. The only food in her refrigerator is some sour milk and a few boxes of food from the Chinese Garden."

"Where do you think Angus is?" Eleanor said.

"Helen's locked herself in the downstairs bathroom. We may as well search the house for him before she comes out," said Dede.

"Surely, he would have appeared by now after all the noise we made. What if she's hurt him?" Eleanor imagined Angus lying in a pool of blood or locked in some tiny trunk in the attic.

Dede looked around the first level. It was an open floor plan with the dinning room off the living room and connected to the kitchen. Not a huge space, but done with high-end finishes and decorated in neutral colors of tans and blues.

"He's not down here. I'll look for him in the garden shed and you check out the upstairs." With that, Dede left through the back door and Eleanor began her one-eyed search by climbing up the stairs. Just as she reached mid-way Helen flew up the stairs screeching like a banshee and grabbed Eleanor by the leg causing both of them to tumble down the stairs. Eleanor landed on top of Helen who appeared to be lights out. Amazed that she survived the fall without apparent injury, Eleanor continued up the stairs calling out Angus' name.

"I'm in here," Angus called out weakly. He sat naked on the edge of Helen's bed with a jar of urine in one hand and the other tied with a scarf to the bed post. "It's not what it looks like," he said.

Eleanor insisted on Angus moving into her guest room where she could care for him and he could rest quietly until the concussion was resolved.

"How did you find me?" he asked when he had settled into her luxurious bed with fluffy pillows and fresh linen sheets.

"It didn't take much detective work. When you didn't come over for dinner, I went to your house and found Bones eager to go out. Your car was gone but you left your phone on the table so I couldn't call you. Bones and I came back home and waited. Dede was visiting Madame Patruska and noticed your truck parked outside Helen's house, which seemed odd because it was so late and she knew you were staying with me because of Andri Frost, so she called me. I drove over to Patruska's house and the rest is history.

"But what made you knock on the door?" Angus asked. "You must have thought I was a two-timing jerk."

"Honestly? I was going to kill you," Eleanor said, "but after your proposal the other night I decided to give you a chance to explain. I knew something was wrong and I really wanted to keep the ring."

"I'm sure I could have escaped. She'd already untied one of my hands but my head hurt, my brain was foggy, and I didn't want to spill the contents of that jar," Angus said.

"You're safe now," said Eleanor planting a kiss on his forehead. "Officer McGraw took Helen to a psychiatric facility in Portland for evaluation. She was pretty incoherent when he asked her what happened and totally lost it when Dede blew out the candle in the bedroom. It looks like she was trying to cast some sort of love spell on you, Angus."

"How'd you get that black eye?" he asked.

"Caught an elbow in a friendly scrimmage." Eleanor would have winked but it hurt too much.

Bones jumped on the bed and Eleanor left the two alone to rest. She noticed Angus was still wearing the napkin ring.

Eleanor's world was in chaos! Angus was in the guest room with his dog, Bones. Andri Frost was still at large, Madame Patruska and the coffee group were engaged in a master plan to lure the killer out because of a missing shoe, and Helen Pence was driven to insanity by witchcraft. What next? Maybe Bigfoot would show up for dinner. Eleanor went to the kitchen to make a cup of tea. What she really needed was a nap, but she had some serious thinking to do. That wasn't going to happen either because just as she sat down in her office to study her notes on Monica's case, someone came to the door. Eleanor was more than surprised to see Professor Growth looking very dapper and holding a bouquet of pink lilies.

"Professor Growth, please come in," Eleanor said. "What an unexpected pleasure to see you again. I was just having a cup of tea. Would you like some?"

The professor nodded slightly. "That would be lovely, thank you. Ahh these flowers are for you. I hope you don't mind my dropping in unannounced. I didn't have your number but an acquaintance at the police department told me where you lived."

"Thank you. Please sit down." Eleanor pointed to the living room sofa and went to get the pot of tea, dropping the lilies in the kitchen sink.

"I'm sure you're wondering why I'm here," said Professor Growth, "so I'll be perfectly clear with my intentions. I find you to be quite beautiful and enchanting. I did some research on you and feel that you may be the perfect mate for me. You are mature but healthy, intelligent, and a clever cook. You don't seem too opinionated or talkative and that suits me. I'm here to offer you a proposal that we see each other on a regular basis for a period of time and enter into a legal union if we are compatible."

Eleanor wasn't sure how to respond to the professor's rather abrupt declaration so busied herself with pouring the tea, studying him for a moment before speaking. He was not an unattractive man, tall, younger than she was, but his fingernails were dirty.

"I see you are considering my proposal in a thoughtful manner and that excites me and emboldens me," he remarked. "You have a lovely home with an extraordinary view. It would make an excellent vacation rental that would provide added income."

Eleanor remembered her first encounter with Andri Frost. She had laughed at him and this made him want to hurt her. She had no intention of repeating that mistake. She sipped her tea and finally said, "I understand the benefits a marriage would bring to you, but what do you have to offer me?" She sat back and waited. Professor dirty digits seemed to be struck dumb. Perhaps the reasons were all too clear in his opinion.

"How rude of me not to consider your needs, but of course, I assumed my attributes were obvious. I'm a man of great intelligence and could - ah - provide you with - ah — a wealth of knowledge for your writing. I know a great deal about the study of cryptids ah -I could give you social status in the academic world possibly and …" he began to squirm. "Well, what are your needs exactly?"

"How kind of you to ask," Eleanor said. "I'm a widow and frankly I have no unmet needs at this time. I think you may want to seek a younger woman for a mate, Professor Growth, someone who won't become a burden on you as time often takes a great toll on someone my age. I really am flattered that you even considered me."

"Well then," he said standing to leave. "I guess that's that. I will definitely take your advice to heart and will look forward to reading your publication on Bigfoot. Perhaps I may offer a foreword or a review."

"How very kind of you to offer," Eleanor said as she led him to the door and closed it behind him. Good lord, what could possibly happen next? She didn't have to wait long to find out because next Diamond Dan arrived just as she was finishing with tidying up the tea things and putting the lilies in a vase.

"Oh dear," she said as she opened her door again to a surprising visitor. "Did my check bounce?" she asked.

Dan laughed, "No Eleanor this is a social call."

"Well come in then," she said. "Have a seat."

"I heard about Helen Pence and I just wanted to tell you how sorry I am to hear of the scandal," he said. "If it helps, I'm here to console you and let you know that you can return the rings for a full refund."

"Really, what have you heard?" asked Eleanor.

"Well, it's all rather sordid." Dan smiled a smarmy smile and raised his eyebrows. "But as I understand it, Angus and Helen were caught with their pants down. Sorry, that's a very crude way to put it, but you discovered them, so you know the nasty details. Just so you also know, Helen came into my store minutes after you left and I may have told her you had just bought a ring for Angus. When pressed I admit I told her you were wearing the beautiful three-carat diamond ring Angus bought. I knew she was upset because she left without her watch. I'm sorry if it caused her to go all sex-crazed, but Angus really should have been able to control himself. Eleanor if you want a little payback, I'm here to provide it. Sometimes it's healthy and I'm certain I can make you forget that two-timing scoundrel."

Eleanor was in shock. She remembered that she needed to be impeccable with her words. Dan was a horrible gossip. "I really want to tell you, Dan that I appreciate you coming to me with your version of the drama so I could set things straight." She paused and continued, "but it didn't happen quite that way. Helen isn't well. She's in the hospital, so in all fairness, let's not spread the story of her being sex crazed. She hit Angus on the head and knocked him unconscious, but he's recovering. There was no hanky-panky as you seem to think, and Angus and I are solid."

"Oh, so I guess you don't want to seek revenge with a roll in the hay," he said with a chuckle.

"No."

"Forgive me, dear Eleanor," he continued, "My line of work puts me in a position to see the inside workings of many relationships. Like those men who feel compelled to buy expensive trinkets for their pets whenever they stray, if you know what I mean. Mrs. Manning has many jewels and every time she's gifted, I've been able to comfort her as well, so I'd like to offer you the same service if you should need it in the future."

Eleanor was dumbfounded by Diamond Dan's kiss-and-tell information but said nothing.

"Well, I'll be going then, Eleanor. Please don't tell Angus I was here. I'll let myself out."

Eleanor went to the mirror and studied her reflection, normal except for the black eye. No magic had reversed time to make her young again or turned her into a great beauty. Feathers flew to her and whistled, "Pretty woman." She sighed and then quietly peeked in on Angus who was sleeping peacefully in the guest room. Bones gave her a mournful look but didn't move from Angus' side. At least there was one male loyal to Angus.

Eleanor worked on her murder board until her eyes were blurry. So much had happened and it was difficult to determine if any of it was relevant to either case. The only sure thing was Monica Fischer and Tip Kent were dead and the link was Klara who couldn't possibly have carried out the crime alone. She searched the internet for photos of the husbands who might want to take revenge on Monica for helping their wives escape them. Mary Cambell was married to Aaron Cambell, a logger for the Eastham Logging Co. Eleanor printed his photo and hung it on her wall. Joan and Howard Floyd were still newlyweds. He was a salesman at the Chevy dealership and a handsome man. Eleanor added his picture to her list of suspects. Erin and Scot Hart had their own janitorial business. Scot obviously worked out and proudly showed off his bulging biceps in the photo she pinned next to the others. Eleanor noted that all three men were very fit and credited it to their line of work or at least their vanity. No wonder they were able to overpower their wives physically. They weren't the only women at the crisis center, but these were the ones who felt the need to come to Monica's memorial, probably because she had helped them the most. It was a place to start and good to know who to look out for if one of their husbands showed up at The Oracle.

Eleanor caught movement out of the corner of her eye and turned to see Angus standing at the door. He moved to the murder board studying it closely.

"Are you feeling better?" Eleanor asked.

"I only ran into the wall three times on my way here," Angus said touching his head. "Still a little wobbly."

"Are you hungry?" Eleanor asked.

"Always."

"I'll heat up some soup," she offered, making her way to the kitchen.

"I can heat up some soup myself. I'm sure Bones is hungry too."

"If I can pry your loyal friend away from you, I'll walk him to your place and get some food for him," Eleanor said as she grabbed her sweater. Bones was more than willing to go out and Eleanor realized she needed the fresh air too. The sky was overcast with a patch of blue promising clear skies but Eleanor knew it couldn't be trusted. She walked briskly breathing in the moist ocean air and enjoying the sounds of nesting murres on three arch rocks and the unexpected brown pelicans that appeared along the shore. Bones stopped several times to check out interesting smells and mark his territory but never went out of view. He had matured and wasn't that wild puppy any longer. Eleanor stood on Angus' deck and looked down over the village. She loved this peaceful paradise, especially before summer tourists invaded, when it seemed almost deserted as it did now. Most of the treasure hunters must have gone up in the coast range to seek the treasure, or found lodging in the nearby town of Waterton. Eleanor enjoyed the moment that she knew wouldn't last.

A sudden chill ran down her spine when she spotted a hooded figure leaving Suzanna's. He turned his head to look up and she saw the white skin of Andri Frost. If she could see him, it was possible he could see her too. She slowly stepped back and made her way inside where she quickly gathered a couple of cans of food and a bag of kibble. She knew where Angus kept his gun and was tempted to take it. A little voice told her it was dangerous to even touch his gun, but she wasn't a child and if Andri Frost came for her it might make a difference. She'd watched Angus take his gun from the locked safe built into his headboard. She bargained with the little voice," If I can't remember the code, I'll just leave it, but if I can open it on the first try, I'm taking it." Of course, Eleanor opened the safe, took the gun and put it in the bag of kibble, locked Angus' door, and hurried up the hill. As she walked, she kept a look out for Andri Frost and listened for his truck on the narrow lane. Maybe it wasn't him she thought. Maybe he didn't see her. Why was he here if not to find and punish her for laughing at him. Bones sensed her fear and stuck close to her. By the time Eleanor reached her house she was sweaty and out of breath. Angus sat at the dining table with his bowl of soup and a toasted cheese sandwich.

"You did that in record time," he said. "I made you a sandwich too."

"Yeah, I was afraid it was going to rain," Eleanor said. She didn't want to worry Angus about news of Andri Frost in the village. She didn't want to tell him she didn't think he could protect her in his current state. She locked the door. If Andri Frost was coming, he would come in the dark and Eleanor would be ready.

Angus woke from a nap and ached from his enforced confinement in Eleanor's guest bed. He was a man of action and his muscles cried out to be useful. He still had a headache but when he stood up the dizzy feeling was gone. He wandered into the office where Eleanor seemed to spend most of her time. Strange how he never wondered how Eleanor spent her daytime hours. He just assumed she was having coffee with her friends, shopping for fresh vegetables, and cooking up delectable dinners for him. He knew she was a writer but he didn't realize how much time it took to create a poem. Eleanor wasn't in the office. Only Feathers sat looking out the window and when he saw Angus flew from his perch crying, "Two-timing scoundrel!"

He looked at Eleanor's desk, covered with notes on paper scraps. A quote from Oscar Wilde about romance. Pieces of poems with lines crossed out, words circled and arrows indicating a change of place. She was writing poems about women, for women. He accidentally brushed her mouse and a poem popped up on her computer screen, neatly typed without corrections.

Born a Woman

I was born a woman,
"It's a girl," they cried, before they said, She's white, or she's black, or she's mine." Sealing my fate as wife, mother, and less than divine.

I was born a woman
In a world where misogyny hides
And man decides
The choices that should be mine.

I was born a woman
Possessed
Repressed
Undressed
Pampered at best
Put to the test and finally blessed.

I was born a woman
Whose struggle has made her strong
Opened her eyes to see the hate
That portrayed her as vile and wrong
Who demanded fairness as her fate.

I was born a woman
Whose strength before was unheard of
A being whose power is love.

Angus was looking into Eleanor's mind and saddened by what she experienced as a woman. He thought he was the only one who saw the ugly side of men and he wondered what had happened to her to make her feel such anger toward them. Why hadn't she shared her pain with him? Was it because he was a man? Was he a good man? He began to question his own actions toward women. Had he taken advantage of Helen and caused her to lose her mind? *Possessed, repressed, undressed, pampered at best.* No wonder Eleanor didn't want to be married, or even protected. Suddenly his head began to ache. He needed some air.

Eleanor stood on the deck outside with Bones. She turned when she heard him behind her. "You look better," she said, "Are you feeling it?"

"Yeah, I want a drink. I want pizza and a movie," he said wrapping Eleanor in his arms like a blanket.

"No drink, no movie, but maybe pizza." Eleanor knew that a concussion needed time to heal without the stimulus of alcohol or screen time. "I called Officer McGraw to tell him I saw Andri Frost coming out of Suzanna's when I went to your house. I think he saw me on your deck."

Angus sighed deeply. "If he saw you there, he'll think that's where you live, but he's the kind of man who does his work in the dark. I'll go get my gun. If he comes it will be at night."

"No need, I brought your gun here in the bag of dog food. Officer McGraw is coming over with pizza." Eleanor said.

Angus didn't know why he was surprised. Eleanor was a woman.

Officer McGraw didn't stay long. He checked in with Angus and Eleanor, ate pizza, and searched for Andri Frost in and around the village, but found no sign of him. Eventually he went home. Eleanor knew she wouldn't be able to pull the trigger and was relieved when Angus took the gun and put it within arm's reach of him in his bed.

"I'm bored," he stated with conviction.

"I know just the thing to lift your spirits," Eleanor said. Angus thought he knew what she meant and was elated, but it wasn't that. That would have been considered too stressful, like running a race or some other sports activity. "I'll read to you. I have just the book." She disappeared into the office and returned with a copy of Ernest Hemingway's *The Old Man and the Sea*. She propped Angus up on several fluffy pillows, pulled up a chair, and began, "He was an old man who fished alone in a skiff in the Gulf Stream and he had gone eighty-four days now without taking a fish." It wasn't long before Angus nodded off dreaming of what Hemingway thought it took to be a real man. Eleanor turned off the light. She had work to do.

A Woman's Wish

I am not your enemy
I do not belong to you
I'm unfettered, I am free
I do what I want to do.

I am not your competition
I don't want to displace you
I just want the recognition
I can do what I can do.

I am not your enemy
I do not belong to you
I'm unfettered, I am free
I do what I want to do.

I am not your incubator
I'm not just for giving birth
I'm more than a spectator
I want to know my worth.

I am not your enemy
I do not belong to you
I'm unfettered, I am free
I do what I want to do.

I'm not a man or brother
I'm a woman, not a fool
I know we need each other
I wish that love could rule.

I am not your enemy
I do not belong to you
I'm unfettered, I am free
I do what I want to do.

Eleanor turned out the light.

Angus slept well and deeply the entire night. When he woke, his headache was gone and he felt like a man who could catch a huge marlin and keep a dozen sharks at bay. Eleanor sat on the sofa, drinking coffee and working the crossword puzzle, surrounded by assistants of fowl and canine persuasion. "Five down, five down," Feathers repeated. Bones snuggled by her side.

"Good morning, beautiful," Angus said as he bent to kiss her.

"Wow, what happened to you?" Eleanor said, noticing that the twinkle in his eye had returned as well as the color in his cheeks.

"I feel great!" he said and went to the kitchen to grab a cup of coffee.

"Glad to hear it. I'm planning to have breakfast with the coffee group after I go for a walk and do my workout."

"Are you saying you don't want to babysit me anymore?" Angus returned with cup in hand. "You aren't planning to make breakfast?"

"Yes, that's exactly right." Eleanor rushed off to get dressed.

"I'd like to go for a walk with you," he said following her and wondering if Eleanor was happy to see him feeling better. Had he been a burden? Was she having second thoughts about marriage? Maybe her first thoughts were returning. He hurried to dress, finished his coffee, and grabbed a banana so she wouldn't have to wait for him. When she returned in her workout attire, Angus and Bones were ready to go.

"What a glorious day!" Angus said, stretching his arms out to the sky, a brilliant blue sky, cloudless, and promising a rare dry occasion for outdoor adventure. The early morning breeze fresh from the ocean revived and exhilarated him as he breathed it in deeply. "Let's plan something we can do together this afternoon. Maybe hike the Cape Lookout trail, or hang glide off Maxwell Point." Eleanor smiled to see him so happy and well.

"I'd love to hike the spit out to the jetty," she said, thinking this would be the perfect place to give Angus the ring. "I'll try to get away early so we can pack a late lunch to eat on the beach."

"Perfect," Angus said. Bones ran ahead to Angus' house and began to race from door to deck with his nose to the ground. "I wonder what's got Bones in a tizzy." As they neared the house Angus could see the broken glass in the front door. He pushed the unlocked door open as he signaled for Eleanor to stay back. He returned within minutes with his phone in hand and a scowl on his face. "Someone's broken in, but they're gone now. I've called McGraw. Come in but don't touch anything."

Eleanor walked through the house and noted the mess in the kitchen where someone had helped themselves to a can of beans, made a sandwich, and drank half a bottle of Crown Royal. In the bathroom there was evidence that someone took a shower and a dump in the toilet they did not flush. "It was Andri Frost," Eleanor said without a doubt.

"Whoever it was they weren't concerned about leaving their DNA behind," Angus pointed to his unmade bed where white hairs lay on the pillow. "Now I know how the three bears felt when they found Goldilocks in their house."

"Did he take anything?" Eleanor asked.

"Only my peace of mind."

The coffee group met at the Boat House prepared to discuss any new developments in the case of Monica Fischer's murder but ended up discussing the break-in at Angus' house instead. It was clear to them that Eleanor was upset by the way she babbled. "I told Angus I would stay to help clean up, but he insisted it was a crime scene and I should come here while the police took evidence. It could take hours. He knows someone who cleans up crime scenes, so I'm really no help at all. I can't believe Andri Frost would act this way just because I laughed at him. I feel like it's all my fault and now Angus has to pay."

"Well, it isn't your fault," said Josephine. "You did nothing wrong. The man is obviously disturbed. Now tell us about the beautiful piece of jewelry on your finger."

Eleanor had forgotten all about the ring and the plan behind it. She wasn't sure what to say. "Angus and I are engaged to be engaged. It's going to be a very long engagement so don't go planning anything."

"I see," said Dede, "It certainly will have all the church ladies talking."

"They won't be inviting him to dinner or bringing him casseroles anymore," said Cleo with a wink.

"You, clever girl!" said Pearl, "Was it your idea or did Angus come up with it?"

"It was Angus' idea," she said, "And it's made me wonder about how men think." Eleanor related the proposal of Dr. Growth and Diamond Dan. "Dan is such a gossip too. He heard all about the scandal of Angus and Helen being 'caught with their pants down.' Then he told me that some men buy their wives expensive gifts after cheating on them and then Dan takes advantage of the wives. He mentioned Mrs. Manning and said she's often taken him up on his offer for a roll in the hay as revenge."

"What! You mean Malady Manning?" asked Dede. "That's Malcolm Manning's wife. He's on our list of misogynists and he worked closely with Monica. I guess I'm not surprised.

Misogynists don't feel the need to be monogamists, but I'm surprised Malady knows what he does and acts that way. She seems so sweet."

"Do we know how Helen is doing?" asked Pearl.

"Oh, about Helen," Dede continued, "It seems she was the only member of the witchcraft research committee. None of her friends or other women that I talked to knew anything about it. At least they're denying it now."

"She must have created it to stir up trouble between Eleanor and Angus," said Cleo.

"I don't think she's coming back to Waterton. She must be totally humiliated," said Dede. "Her friends admitted she was spouting nonsense about Eleanor casting a spell over Angus and how she was going to save him."

"It sounds like she has some type of dementia, or possibly a psychotic break," said Josephine, "And doesn't even know what she's done."

"How can we find out if Andri Frost has an alibi for the night Monica was killed?" Eleanor said. "I'm certain he's the one."

"Madame Patruska hasn't had any of our suspects visit her shop since we sent the shoeboxes," Cleo reported. "I think she's given up on that angle. Only the guilty party would come to The Oracle knowing that was where he planted the shoe."

"Just when we let down our guard, that's when they'll strike," Josephine said. "It's not safe yet."

"I'll talk to Molly Fiori about other men whose wives are at the crisis center," said Eleanor. "It could be we sent the boxes with the note saying we know what they did to the wrong ones."

"I haven't been able to find any covens that cast circles that far from town," said Josephine.

"Does that mean there are covens practicing in Waterton?" asked Cleo.

"If there are, I'm sure they are very secretive," said Josephine. "The women I know who celebrate the pagan rituals of equinox and solstice do it out of the joy of nature. They don't practice witchcraft."

"I think we should drive to the crime scene and check things out for ourselves," said Dede. "We still haven't ruled out the treasure hunters, and I'd like to see those Bigfoot prints for myself." There was total silence.

"I have to go to the grocery store. Let me know what you decide about that," said Eleanor and she got up to leave. Suddenly everyone was gathering their things and disappeared leaving Dede sitting alone.

At the grocery store, Eleanor picked up some roast beef and warm deli bread for sandwiches, fresh strawberries, potato chips, and two bottles of fancy bottled water. Knowing there wasn't time to bake, she stopped at Sara Sota's for cupcakes. Before she went home to Angus, she popped in at Molly's pottery shop.

Entering the shop, Eleanor noticed only one customer leaving as she came in and Molly was busy rolling out clay. "Do you have a minute to talk?" asked Eleanor.

"Of course." Molly wiped her hands on a towel and led Eleanor into the back room. "What is it?"

"I was just wondering if there were other women at the crisis center that Monica helped," Eleanor said.

"Oh, I'm sure there were several," Molly said. "You mean besides the ones that came to her service. I couldn't tell you everyone she helped, but there were at least two others who found themselves in horrible situations that owe their lives to her. I can't give out names. That is confidential. Unfortunately, one went back to her husband, but I'd bet money we'll see her again, if we can stay afloat, that is."

"Are you hurting for funds?" Eleanor asked.

"Yes, we are always looking for donors, but our resources are drying up for some reason."

"Let me donate," said Eleanor as she took out her checkbook, wrote a check, and handed it to Molly.

"Thank you, Eleanor. That's very generous," said Molly. "Why are you so interested in these women?"

"I'm interested in finding Monica's killer and curious about the men who abused their wives," Eleanor said, "Do any of these husbands seem like the type that would want to get revenge on Monica? Someone angry enough to blame her, to kill her?"

"All of them I suppose," Molly said, "But they wouldn't know it was Monica who helped them."

Eleanor drove by Angus' house and noticed there was a cleaning van in the driveway. She continued up the hill to put together the sandwiches and packed a picnic for an afternoon hike. When she finished, she put the ring around the neck of a water bottle and called Angus.

"How's it going?" she asked.

"I'm almost done replacing the window. I think you'll like it. Found some pretty glass at the Building Supply Company. It sure does add a bit of class, "Angus said proudly.

"Do you still want to go for a hike?"

"Absolutely, I'll pick you up in a few minutes. The cleaning crew is still working here, but I don't need to stay." Angus said, "I'm already hungry, that banana didn't last."

Eleanor tossed in a bag of trail mix to the lunch and changed into something more suitable for hiking the Bay Ocean spit.

The day continued to be sunny and warm with not a cloud on the horizon. Sounds of surf and bird song filled the air and three deer made their way across the trail within feet of the hikers causing them to stop to watch as they meandered into the brush. Angus reached to take Eleanor's hand in his as they continued on their way filling their senses with the beauty of nature.

After hiking the two miles to the jetty, Angus and Eleanor found an excellent piece of driftwood where they could sit and enjoy their lunch. Angus reached for the bottle of water and immediately spotted the gold band with the diamond embedded in it. Eleanor watched his expression to see if he really liked it and wasn't disappointed. "I'm going to need my napkin ring back," she said when he fell short of words.

He slipped the old ring off and replaced it with the new. His eyes never leaving Eleanor's face. "I promise to always pursue you, Eleanor, to fight for you and love only you as long as I wear this ring." And then he kissed her.

"Does that mean I should worry if you take it off," Eleanor asked suspiciously.

"I'm just keeping it romantic," he said. "Now let's eat. I'm starving."

"We need to focus on Andri Frost or the treasure hunters, because the women at the crisis center are sworn to secrecy to protect each other by keeping their presence there confidential," Eleanor told the coffee group.

"Madame Patruska hasn't had any nibbles on our bait, either," said Pearl.

"That means we must engage in this treasure hunt," Dede said. "I'm sure Mark won't mind if I drive our pickup to the crime scene. It has four-wheel drive and I'm sure I can get us there safely."

"I don't think there will be enough room for all of us to fit in a pickup, so I volunteer to stay behind," offered Josephine.

"I'm sure I have an appointment whenever you decide to make that excursion," said Pearl.

"Pearl and I will research the treasure hunt clues," Josephine said.

"I'm in," said Cleo., "Steve and I used to drive up there all the time to get wood. It will be exciting and we might even find the treasure."

"I know exactly where the crime scene is since I've driven it before, so I'll go," Eleanor said with a hint of trepidation in her voice.

"Let's do it right away before we lose our nerve," said Dede. "I'll gather some necessary tools: shovel, gloves, rope, evidence bags, camera, what else?"

"We'll need to dress appropriately, so dress in layers and boots," said Eleanor.

"Maybe a weapon of some kind," said Pearl, "In case you meet Bigfoot or Andri Frost up there."

"Lunch," said Cleo.

"We ride at dawn," Dede said, "Our pickup has a crew cab, so there's room for everyone."

There was a sad sigh from somewhere, but no one knew from whom.

When Eleanor got home, the first thing she did was Google the Gerald Park Challenge. What came up surprised her because it was a poem filled with clues to find the treasure.

Lush and green the Beaver State
In coastal range where Bigfoot mates
Follow narrow roads up high
Where wild things live, and eagles fly.

Leave the highway three and three
Cross the bridge so you can see
Where hunters take their arrows
The path goes up and narrows.

Climb to the sky and find the sea
Among the living one dead tree
In whose heart you will find
A message that will blow your mind.

Eleanor was excited. She knew this place. At least she thought she did. It had to be the same place Angus had taken her to cut wood. Turn onto Jordan Creek Road and take every left turn going in and every right turn coming out. She could hardly wait to tell the others. It was possible they could comb the crime scene and find the treasure at the same time.

Then came the doubt. The coastal range extended vertically along most of the state, but highway three and three had to be Highway 6 and where hunters take their arrows must be Archer's Road. Oregon was covered in trees. Finding one dead tree among them would be a fool's errand! Oh well, she would be a fool on an adventure no matter the outcome, and Eleanor would enjoy the company of other fools. She packed the necessary items and went to bed early. Tomorrow would be a test of her physical and mental strength. No fear. She had been working out after all.

It wasn't surprising that everyone showed up bright and early bringing all sorts of items necessary to complete a major investigation as well as a hunt for a million dollars. Dede drove while Eleanor sat in the navigator's seat and the others squeezed in the crew cab. They traveled down Highway 6 and took the turn onto Jordan Creek Road. It was the first sign of what was to come. Cars were everywhere. Several parked along the narrow road, some coming, others going. "Good grief," said Dede, "It's a traffic jam!"

"Do you want to turn around?" asked Eleanor as several four-wheelers passed them.

"They can't all be going where we're going," said Cleo.

"No, but it's going to be slow going anywhere," said Pearl.

"Especially if we have to pull off to the side to let them pass," said Dede pulling over to let a big blue truck go by.

"I don't know if there is another way to get where we want to go," said Eleanor checking her map. "Wait, turn around up here in this wide spot. There's another road that leaves the highway and goes to Archer's Road, but it's farther down the highway."

Dede managed to maneuver to turn around and she followed Eleanor's directions. They had the next narrow road all to themselves and began the adventure again. No one knew Eleanor feared they were heading into unknown territory and possibly lost forever. The simple directions of take every left going in and every right going out were of no use now. She would definitely need to pay close attention to turns along the way. When they came to a fork in the road, Eleanor chose the one that climbed up and left the creek below as they rose higher and higher. It was ominously quiet in the crew cab as Dede focused on shifting into 4-wheel drive and keeping the truck on the gravel road. "Do you know where we are?" asked Josephine looking down into a deep gully.

"Absolutely not," said Eleanor who had given up trying to keep track of the turns they had taken.

"Well, no one else seems to be interested in this road," said Dede. "We haven't seen a vehicle since we got on it."

"I have to go to the bathroom," said Pearl.

"Great," said Dede pulling into a wide spot. "I need to stretch my legs." They all tumbled out moaning and grumbling about a variety of aches and pains while Pearl hunted for some toilet paper before disappearing into the bushes.

"It really is beautiful up here," said Josephine.

"Look at this!" cried Cleo pointing at a patch of dirt. "What animal made that?"

"Oh, my lord," said Dede. "We've stumbled into Bigfoot's neighborhood." Pearl took that moment to break from the bushes in wide-eyed terror.

"Come quick," she said, "Someone is living in there!" The ladies hurried to see whatever it was that Pearl had discovered. Beyond the bushes was a clearing where they saw a tent, an area with a camp table covered by a blue tarp, and a campfire pit circled by stones.

"Whoever lives here isn't here now or we'd have seen a vehicle of some kind," said Eleanor. "Let's see what's inside." She quickly lifted the flap of the tent and peered in while the others followed closely behind. Inside was a sleeping bag on a cot, a duffle bag full of men's underwear, a black hoodie, and two large rubber feet attached to the bottom of a pair of boots. Eleanor's hair stood on end and ice shivered down her spine.

"We have to leave," said Dede, "This doesn't feel right." Cleo was already out of the bushes before the rest of them appeared.

"I found the vehicle," she whispered. On the other side of the bushes, just feet away from Dede's truck was a gray Ford pickup covered by a camo net and broken branches.

Not another word was spoken as the snoops loaded their old bones into Dede's truck in record time and drove away. Ten minutes later, Pearl said, "I didn't get a chance to pee."

Everyone broke out in pent-up nervous laughter. It sputtered out and then started again when Cleo began to giggle and Josephine snorted. Finally, when everyone was in control Eleanor said what each had been thinking, "That was Andri Frost's camp."

"Why is he planting fake footprints with those special boots?" asked Cleo.

"I don't know, but I won't be happy until we are far away from wherever he is," said Dede.

"I bet he's looking for the treasure and wants to scare everyone else away," said Pearl.

"Does that mean we're close to where the treasure is hidden?" asked Josephine.

"I'm not sure where we are anymore," said Eleanor, "but there's a sign that says Archer's Road. I think we need to go that way." Dede turned on the road and followed it to the highest point where they stopped once more to let Pearl find relief at last. The road had ended at an old clear cut that opened to a view that was awe inspiring with valleys and mountains all covered by thick forests of evergreen trees.

Several clouds floated below and between each ridge like moving glaciers while the cry of a red-tailed hawk could be heard above. Newly leafed alder trees flanked a short turnout and dappled the path with sunlight and shadows as a gentle breeze blew through the branches.

"I never want to leave here," said Cleo as the breeze lifted her hair.

"It's like we're part of it all," said Eleanor.

"Even if we go home empty-handed, we certainly found this treasure," said Josephine gazing off in the distance.

"I think I can see the ocean," said Peal looking to the west.

"'Climb to the sky and find the sea,'" quoted Eleanor. "I wonder how many places like this are up here."

"Probably hundreds," said Cleo, "But I can see one dead tree from this place." She pointed to a tall bare evergreen down below them. "Looks like an old spar tree to me."

"How would we get down there?" asked Josephine.

"We could hike down that slope," said Dede, "or we could drive down that logging road." She pointed to a steep dirt road that led in the direction of the tree. The choice was easy.

Dede fearlessly but slowly drove down the slope to where an old, weathered tree loomed over a clear cut that was overgrown with brush and replanted saplings.

"We're going to the tree, but remember, we can't afford any sprained ankles or broken legs, so go slow and use a walking stick. The ground is uneven and there are briars and tripping hazards," cautioned Cleo who had brought a walking stick for everyone complements of her husband whose hobby was making them out of tree branches. They began their cautious descent. After several minutes, Pearl called out, "How are we ever going to get back up there with a treasure?"

Everyone was slowly making progress with the intention of getting there without mishap and not thinking about a million dollars and how much that would weigh. Eleanor was wishing she had brought a rope to tie on the treasure and pull it up the slope when she suddenly realized she was at the tree. Looking up, she saw several nesting cavities and her heart sank. Some of them were very high. All the ladies stood looking up at the tall, dead tree filled with dozens of holes that might lead to its heart and each felt the same hopelessness.

"I'm hungry," said Cleo. "Let's find this treasure and eat lunch."

"Okay," said Dede. "I wonder how tall Gerald Park is. I hope he's very short."

"If I stand on Josephine's shoulders, I can reach two of those holes," said Pearl.

"It would be better if I stood on *your* shoulders," said Josephine.

"What a great idea!" Cleo said forgetting her hunger. "We should at least give it a try since we didn't think to bring a ladder."

Pearl felt the pressure of her peers, and being taller than the others, stepped close to the tree and grabbed two broken branches while Dede got on all fours to provide a step for Josephine and Cleo as Eleanor pushed her up far enough to maneuver onto Pearl's somewhat fragile shoulders. There was moaning, some wobbling, and gasps of fear mostly from Cleo who stood safely on the ground. Eventually, Josephine reached into one of the holes and retrieved a handful of dried leaves.

"Oh phooy!" said Eleanor, "Can you reach the hole to the left of you?"

Pearl moved to her left, causing Josephine to teeter perilously before she regained her balance and reached into a larger hole that provided her with an empty nest of twigs and feathers.

"I think you need to come down before you fall and break something," said Eleanor.

"Excellent idea," Pearl grunted, "I'm sure I'm much shorter now." Getting Josephine down proved to be even more difficult than getting her up. When she looked down, she became frozen and indecisive about which foot to put down first. She put her hands on Pearl's head and her knees on her shoulders making Pearl cry out. Dede rushed to provide the necessary step and finally Josephine touched down much to the relief of everyone on the ground who clapped and cheered.

"Let's never do that again," said Pearl.

"I don't think Gerald Park could stuff a million dollars into any of these holes," said Josephine.

"But maybe he could put a message into this one that looks like a heart," Eleanor said reaching into a cavity about five feet off the ground. There was a flurry of movement as they all rushed to Eleanor and watched her pull out a small gold capsule sealed with shrink-wrap. "Did anyone think to bring scissors?"

"I hate shrink-wrap," said Pearl.

"This has to be it!" said Dede. "We met the challenge and found the treasure!"

"Shhhhhh," hushed Josephine, "we can't be sure there aren't others around who would kill for a million dollars. Let's go back to the truck and get out of here. We can do our happy dance later."

"Right, the forest is swarming with treasure hunters who may have binoculars or spotting scopes just waiting for us to lead them to it," said Pearl. The idea of their success gave them the fortitude they needed to climb back to the truck without any broken bones, although there were a few trips, slips, and lots of swearing.

"Let's get out of this open area before we even try opening that capsule," said Dede, "Put it in the glove box." And away they sped. "Where do we go from here?"

"We need to go down. Take every road that leads down but let's don't go back the way we came. There's no way I want to run in to Andri Frost," Eleanor said.

"Roger that," said Dede as she headed down.

It seemed like forever as they bumped along one dirt road that turned into a graveled one and then another. "I'm beginning to feel like I'm in the Twilight Zone," said Cleo. "We'll just keep driving and never get out of the forest."

"What should we do with the money?" asked Pearl.

"If we split it five ways, we'd each get $200,000," said Dede. "I'd buy a condo in the city so I could stay over and see concerts, plays, and art exhibits."

"I want a new luxury car, home improvements, and a swimming pool," said Cleo.

"Traveling would be nice," said Josephine.

"I think we should donate it to the women's crisis center," said Eleanor.

"Aww, what a buzzkill, Eleanor!" Cleo moaned. "Now I could never enjoy my luxury car."

"How much gas do we have?" asked Josephine. "Did anyone think to bring sleeping bags in case we're stuck here all night?"

"Maybe we should stop and study the map, eat lunch, and walk around for a while. It worked last time," said Pearl.

"Wait, I think this road looks familiar," Eleanor said.

"Right, it looks just like the last ten roads we've been on," said Dede.

"No, I recognize that stand of trees. Stop. I'm sure this is where Angus and I had lunch the day we found Monica's body," Eleanor said, "There should be a clear cut just around that bend."

Dede drove round the bend and they all saw the clear cut. "Yay, we're saved!" cried Cleo. Dede pulled over and they piled out once more moaning and grumbling. On a distant ridge they could see several 4-wheelers. "Civilization," said Dede.

"This is a moveable feast!" said Pearl as they laid out the food each had brought for lunch. Eleanor had even included a red and white checkered table cloth that she used to cover a large tree stump. There were ham and cheese sandwiches, turkey sandwiches, apple slices, celery sticks, Cheetos, grapes, chocolate chip cookies, carrot sticks, pita chips and humus, bottles of water, Orange Crush soda, and toothpicks.

"I'm almost too tired to eat," said Pearl.

"Wait until tomorrow when your muscles catch up and are angry," said Cleo. There was a period of silence while bodies refueled and hydrated.

"I almost forgot about the treasure," said Dede quietly.

"We don't know what the capsule contains," said Eleanor.

"Right, it may be just another clue," said Josephine forlornly.

"But the fact that we found it before anyone else means no one else will have this clue," said Cleo. "The treasure is as good as ours."

"What if the whole thing is a bad joke?" asked Pearl. "What if there is more than one gold capsule?"

"It hasn't cost us anything except a day out of our lives," said Dede.

"I can't believe we are sitting here with nothing sharp enough to cut through the shrink wrap," said Josephine.

"Patience, Grasshopper," said Eleanor, "Good things come to those who wait."

"Exactly like this delicious lunch," said Cleo wiping cookie crumbs from her chest.

"Eleanor, where exactly was the body?" asked Dede. "There isn't any crime scene tape that I can see."

"I'm sure it was taken down by now, if not by the police, by the treasure hunters. Just look at all the garbage they've left behind," said Josephine.

"Angus and I drove up the road a bit and ate under a grove of trees. The body was downhill on the other side of the road," Eleanor said.

"Let's clean up our mess and go back there," Dede said as she stood and began to pack up what was left of the lunch. "Is it very far?"

"I need to walk," said Cleo, "Sitting too long makes me stiff and sore."

"I'll walk with you," said Pearl, "I need to pee."

"We'll drive up there and start looking for clues," said Dede. "You can meet us at the truck." The last of her words were drowned out by two motorcycles that passed by kicking up a cloud of dust.

"This is it," said Eleanor looking over the side of the road. Josephine and Dede stood beside her weighing the risks of sliding down the slope.

"I'm not going down there," said Josephine. "It's too steep."

"I didn't go down there. Angus told me to stay up here," said Eleanor. "He didn't want me to see her or disturb the crime scene."

"Let's just look around up here," suggested Dede. "Maybe we'll find something they missed."

"That works for me," said Eleanor. "I found the tarot card up here. If animals drug her down there, we probably won't find any evidence of the person who killed her there anyway."

"I wonder where the witches cast their circle," said Josephine wandering off.

"It might be a good idea to put on gloves and take some plastic bags to collect evidence," said Eleanor.

"Let's meet back here in twenty minutes," said Dede locking her truck.

Thirty minutes later, the coffee group gathered by Dede's truck sharing the evidence they found.

"I think the police must have taken all the evidence that proved witches were here," said Josephine. "All I found were a few cigarette butts and some broken glass."

"I took these pictures of Bigfoot prints that were crossing the road," said Dede, "and I found a black button."

"I went back to the place where I found the tarot card and found this piece of fabric caught in a sticker bush," said Eleanor. "It looks familiar. It might be from the shirt I was wearing when we were cutting wood."

"Pearl spotted a bird nest in one of those trees," said Cleo pointing to the stand of trees Angus and Eleanor had picnicked under. "We knocked it down with one of the walking sticks and found this gold earring and some hair along with broken egg shells. Oh, I also picked up this snuff tin along the road."

"Walking along the road, I discovered this oddity that looks like chewing gum," said Pearl, "I didn't want to touch it because who knows what it is, so I rolled it up in this leaf."

"Let's bag all this and go home," said Eleanor. "I know exactly how to get there from here. It's as easy as it is right."

It seemed like it took hours. The narrow gravel road was busy with motorcycles, 4-wheelers, pick-ups, and pedestrians. Dede must have pulled off the road a hundred times to let one vehicle or another pass on the narrow road. There were absolutely no animals, other than the human kind, anywhere in the area. Campsites were everywhere as well as the litter that went along with a population explosion. It was like a circus. By the time they drove up to Dede's house it was way past dinner time. They all trooped inside looking for a sharp object to open the covering on the capsule.

Angus and Mark stood in the kitchen looking like guardians of the galaxy, arms across chests and disapproval written all over their faces. "Where have you girls been with my truck?" Mark demanded.

"We're not girls, we are tired and dirty women looking for a sharp tool," said Dede. "Since neither of you meet that definition, you'd better move out of our way." Mark dug a knife out of his pocket and handed it to Dede who held the capsule.

"What is that?" asked Angus moving in for a closer look.

"It just may be the treasure from the Gerald Park Challenge," said Josephine.

"Why are you here?" asked Eleanor whose hair stuck up in wild disarray and her face smudged with dirt.

"Mark called me. He was worried because you were gone so long. We were just formulating a plan," Angus said, all the time watching as Dede sliced through the plastic coating and opened the golden capsule.

Inside was a was a note that read:

QKAG K OLLA VC RF WKXLTVQG MLLA
"VW PLN KTG K HTGKRGT, HLRG VU,
VW PLN KTG K HTGKRGT, K ZVMIGT, K FVKR,
K ILYG-GT, K YTKF-GT, K RKCVN MGKU MNP-
GT..."

-BIGF BVFXGTBQGYC
**KBA K FVMTKTVKC*

"What language is that?" asked Mark.

"It's a cryptogram," said Cleo, "a message in code like the ones in the Sunday paper."

"Can you decode it?" asked Angus.

"Of course," Eleanor said confidently.

"I just want to go home, take a shower and go to bed," said Josephine.

"Me too," said Pearl. "I hope Cary made dinner."

Cleo was busy breaking the code while Dede tried in vain to take off her boots. Eleanor looked on and offered her two cents. "The K has to be an A, and the G is E," she said. It wasn't long before they had it solved.

TAKE A LOOK IN MY FAVORITE BOOK
"IF YOU ARE A DREAMER, COME IN,
IF YOU ARE A DREAMER, A WISHER, A LIAR,
A HOPE-ER, A PRAY-ER, A MAGIC BEAN BUY-ER..."
                                  ___ SHEL SILVERSTEIN
**ASK A LIBRARIAN*

"Well, it's obviously *Where the Sidewalk Ends*," said Cleo and Eleanor at the same time.

"But what does it mean?" asked Mark.

"I guess we have to ask a librarian," said Dede finally getting her boot off.

"We are very close, but I'm going home," said Josephine.

"Let's go to the library tomorrow," said Cleo.

"We're not quitting, just going home to rest," said Eleanor walking out the door.

"Mark, I guess we still need to formulate that plan for dinner," whispered Angus.

"Oh crap," said Dede, "In all the excitement about finding the treasure, we forgot to tell you that we found Andri Frost's camp."

"I better follow Ellie home." Angus was out the door behind Eleanor before Mark could protest.

The coffee group met early the next morning for breakfast at the Boat House before the library opened. "It's too bad we couldn't have planted that shoe in Andri Frost's tent," said Cleo. "We would have rid Eleanor of her stalker and solved the murder of Monica Fischer in one act."

"Diabolical!" said Josephine. "You have a criminal mind, Cleo. What if he isn't guilty?"

"He's guilty of something. People like him shouldn't be allowed to harass innocent citizens," Cleo said.

"Lock up Frost and the killer might still be out there," said Eleanor.

"We need a new plan to flush out the killer," said Pearl. "Madame Patruska thinks it's someone other than the angry husbands."

"Well, I can't wait to announce that the treasure has been found, so all these people will go home, and our peaceful little town can get back to normal," said Dede.

"Did you get a chance to show Angus the evidence we found?" asked Josephine.

"I was so tired last night. I fell asleep soon after Angus came over. He was mostly interested in where Andri Frost's camp was and when I woke up this morning he was already gone," Eleanor said.

"Were you able to give him directions to the camp?" asked Dede.

"I did the best I could," Eleanor admitted. "I showed him the map and told him about the hidden truck. He'll have to use his professional detecting skills to find it."

"Why do you think Frost is making the fake footprints?" asked Pearl.

"Maybe he wants to keep the legend alive," said Cleo, "We should investigate him more deeply. He might have a financial reason."

"Like trying to find a million dollars?" asked Dede. "News of the footprints just brought more people to the area. It certainly didn't scare them away."

"Speaking of a million dollars," said Eleanor, "It's time to go to the library."

"I've decided not to go," said Dede. "How would it look if the Mayor of Waterton found the treasure?" She could already see the headlines: **Mayor Finds Treasure and Collects Million Dollars, Investigation Follows**

"Maybe I shouldn't go either," said Pearl. "I'm on the library board of directors. If the library is involved it might look sketchy."

"I certainly don't want any additional attention," said Eleanor. "I'm already being stalked."

"Cleo should go," said Josephine. "I could be accused of knowing something confidentially told to me by a client."

"Sure, I'll go," said Cleo, "but just remember I have a criminal mind and you may never see me again. Give me the note and capsule."

"We'll wait for you at my house," said Dede. "If she's not back before lunch, I have a big pot of hamburger soup in the Crock-Pot we can eat."

Cleo had the important information in a huge leather tote. She had no idea what to expect when she entered the library. Perhaps there would be a large suitcase full of money that she would have to carry out to her car. Maybe it would be another puzzle that needed solving or just a big disappointment. She was mentally prepared for anything. She climbed the stairs that led to the librarian's desk and approached the man who sat there.

"Hello, I'm looking for Shel Silverstein's *Where the Sidewalk Ends* and was told to ask a librarian for it," Cleo whispered. The librarian studied her closely and smiled. "Can you show me the note?" he asked.

Cleo pulled the note from her tote and watched as he read it. Then he reached under his desk and handed her a copy of the book. She thanked him, put it in her tote and left. When she got to her car, she opened the book and found a key taped to the back cover. Great! What lock did the key open? She drove to Dede's house feeling every bit like a secret agent in a spy film.

"I can't believe this," said Dede. "Is this the hunt that never ends? I might have to have a word with this man."

"Maybe there is no treasure," said Josephine, "and he's just stringing us along hoping we give up."

"I need more time to recover from yesterday's adventure," said Pearl whose shoulders were sore from carrying Josephine. "I'm going home to take an ice bath."

"This is a book cipher," said Eleanor studying a group of numbers she found on a thin sheet of paper wedged between the pages of the book.

66	22	5
140	7	1
116	1	1
15	9	1
64	8	4
41	3	4
140	10	7

"What is a book cipher?" asked Pearl.

"It's a code used to send messages. When two people have the same book they communicate by giving the page number, then the line, and finally the order of the word. He must want us to use this book so look on page 66, line 22, fifth word in."

Dede quickly found the page, line and word, "The word is address," she said.

"So far so good," said Josephine. "He's giving us an address. Keep going."

"Four, eighteen, Fourth, Street, Box, thirty-five." Dede completed the cipher.

"That's Waterton Bank," said Pearl. "The key must unlock a safety deposit box."

"Let's go then," said Cleo. "We can walk from here."

"We'll wait in the lobby," said Dede as Cleo made her way to the teller.

The teller got a key and walked Cleo into the room where the deposit boxes were kept. They both used their keys to open box 35 and the teller left. Cleo took the only envelope out of the box and returned the box to its place. She patted her tote as she passed the waiting ladies and they left together.

"It's an envelope," Cleo said. "Let's go to Dede's and open it there."

"This is so exciting," said Pearl. "I just hope it's not another clue."

"I've lost all my excitement," said Josephine. "I just want it to stop."

"Prepare yourselves for disappointment," said Dede. "That way you'll be super excited if it's real."

As soon as Dede's front door closed behind them, Cleo opened the envelope and unfolded the letter inside. It read:

CONGRATULATIONS!
IF YOU ARE READING THIS LETTER,
YOU ARE THE WINNER OF THE GERALD
PARK CHALLENGE. YOU HAVE FOLLOWED
DIRECTIONS AND MADE AN EXTRAORDINARY
HIKE INTO THE BEAUTIFUL FORESTS OF THE
OREGON COAST RANGE, DISCOVERED THE
BENEFITS OF NATURE'S BLESSINGS AND SHOWN
PERSEVERANCE AS WELL AS INTELLIGENCE IN
BREAKING THE MANY CODES. KUDOS TO YOU!!!
PLEASE CALL THIS NUMBER TO TAKE
OWNERSHIP OF YOUR $1,000,000 PRIZE.
1 800 1000000
GERALD PARK

"That's it," cried Cleo, "I'm done with this shit. I won't give them my bank account number or my social security number. This is the cruelest scam ever perpetrated on senior citizens."

"It's not a scam," said Dede. "We just have to be patient. I'm sure Gerald Park wants to make a big deal out of this. You know, Gerald Park handing the winner a huge check standing in front of television cameras and photographers, the whole enchilada."

"Let me handle it," said Eleanor. "I'll have my attorney make the call and we will all remain anonymous. When the money is cleared, we will split it five ways so each of us will have control over what happens to it."

"Excellent, I'm going home to take a nap," said Josephine.

Eleanor went directly to her lawyer with the letter and handed everything off to him. She instructed him to deliver half of her share to the women's crisis center which he was happy to do. Eleanor planned to buy a new car with the other half. Her car had a badly dented rear end.

When she got home, she sat down in her office and studied the evidence they had collected from the crime scene. The most interesting thing was the empty snuff box. Even though it looked like a snuff tin, it wasn't a snuff box at all, but an empty tin for nicotine pouches. The brand was SYN. She wondered what brand Tip had used and if this could be the connection between the two deaths. Had Tip killed Monica, dumped her body in the woods, and left this piece of evidence behind? Then there was the oddity that Pearl had rolled up in a leaf. It did look like gum, but it wasn't. It was a small pouch. Eleanor googled nicotine pouches and studied the images that came up and sure enough, Pearl's odd little something looked much like a nicotine pouch that had been used and tossed aside. Things were beginning to click into place, but Eleanor didn't want to believe Tip was the guilty party. If he was, what was his motive and who killed him? She needed to find out who that attractive woman at Monica's memorial was and figure out why Tip was watching her. Josephine had pictures and Dede would know who she was. Eleanor pinned the evidence on her murder board and spent the rest of the afternoon working on her poetry.

Eve's Rebuke

In the garden's quiet shade,
Where whispers soft, temptations made,
You point your finger full of spite,
And say I led you from the light.

The apple gleamed but it was yours,

To take or leave, to open doors.
I spoke, I offered, yes, it's true,
But who, my love, did follow you?

With every bite you made a choice,
The serpent's hiss was not my voice.
I played but one, a fleeting role,
But you're the keeper of your soul.

You say I led you to the fall,
But you were the one who heard the call.
I didn't twist your hand, or mind,
Your own desires made you blind.

So blame not me, this fruit, this lie,
For all you've lost beneath the sky.
The sin was yours, not mine to bear-
Your failure's weight is yours to wear.

I did not make the path you trod,
Your will was free, your heart, your God.
I took the fruit, it was you who ate,
So take the blame, and face your fate.

For in the end, it's plain to see,
You sinned the same, compared with me.
So hold your guilt, and understand-
The fault, dear man, was in your hand.

Eleanor sent a message to Angus inviting him to dinner and began to create a meal worthy of him. It would not include apples.

Angus sighed with satisfaction. The beef tenderloin melted in his mouth and the rosemary roasted potatoes were the perfect complement. Even the mixed green salad with beets, feta, and walnuts tasted like love to him. He wondered what Eleanor had in store for dessert. Eleanor sipped her cabernet and watched Angus lean back in his chair. She loved cooking for someone who enjoyed her gift as much as he did, but she also knew she wouldn't love it every day, three times a day. She wouldn't love it when it became expected, routine, a chore.

"There's something I want you to see," Eleanor said.

Angus wondered if it was an apple pie, but knew better when Eleanor led him to her office. "I've studied the evidence we found near the crime scene and wondered what you thought of this." She showed him the tin and the pouch. Angus looked closely at the tin and asked, "Where did you find this exactly?"

"We didn't go down the slope where the body was. We found it on the road. Cleo and Pearl walked back from where we cut wood and found the tin and pouch along the way," Eleanor said.

"There are hundreds of treasure hunters up there and lots of trash. This could belong to anyone." Angus picked up the bag that held the gold earring. "Where was this?"

"Pearl and Cleo found that in a bird's nest near the crime scene. I suppose it could belong to anyone too, but the pouch might have DNA that could tell us who had it in their mouth. Right?" Eleanor persisted.

"That would be a long shot," said Angus. "Not everyone's DNA is on file."

"What if it matches Tip Kent's?"

"You think he killed Monica Fischer?" Angus asked. "What do you think his motive could be?"

"I don't know," Eleanor admitted. "Maybe Klara killed her and he disposed of the body to protect her. Maybe Klara thought Monica was a gold digger and did it for Jesse's sake."

"Tip was at the Red Shed until midnight the night Monica was killed. He was an old man who only had access to a small rental car and now he's dead. I don't think it was him," Angus said. "I don't think Klara did it either. It takes strength to strangle someone as fit as Monica then drive them to a remote location and dump their body."

"I thought Monica was hanged," said Eleanor.

"Do you, now? Why would you think that?" Angus asked suspiciously.

"I don't remember exactly where I heard it, but someone said there was a leak that a noose was found around her neck," said Eleanor.

"Dede?" asked Angus.

"Maybe," Eleanor said.

"Good to know," said Angus. "Sometimes gossip is just that, gossip." He obviously knew something he wasn't going to tell. "What's for dessert?"

"Apple pie," Eleanor said. She had obviously changed her mind about the apples.

In the morning Eleanor did her workout and walked the beach. She was feeling stronger every day. After a shower and change of clothes, she decided to walk to Klara's house with a piece of her apple pie. Harry Stone was just leaving as Eleanor approached.

"Eleanor, what a pleasant surprise to see you here," he said. "My, my by the sparkle on your finger, it looks like congratulations are in order."

"Thank you," Eleanor said. "I didn't know you were a friend of Klara's."

"Well, I heard about her loss and came to cheer her up," said Harry.

"Sweet," said Eleanor, "I hope you were successful. Nice seeing you." She knocked on the door hoping Harry Stone would go away, but he lingered.

"Who's the lucky man?" he asked.

"Who said it was a man?" Eleanor said and watched his eyes grow round with surprise just as Klara came to the door.

"I'll be off then," he said as he strode quickly to his car. She wondered if he was as big a gossip as Diamond Dan.

"Oh Eleanor, how lovely to see you. Please come in." Klara saw Harry turn around and waved to him in a friendly way. Wouldn't it be funny if he thought Klara was her lover?

"I brought you a piece of apple pie." Eleanor handed the plate to Klara and they settled in at her kitchen table. "Is Harry Stone a friend of yours?"

"No, I was never friends with him and don't want to be. He was just here to see how desperate I was for his company."

"I see," Eleanor measured her words carefully. "I've heard he's quite the ladies' man."

"Could have fooled me, I thought he was looking for a loan," Klara said. "He brought me these flowers, but I'm not ready to take on another man. I don't think I ever will be, not because Tip was so wonderful he can't be replaced, but because I just feel free. That must seem terrible to hear right now, but it's the truth."

"I can understand that. It's easier to love a man when you don't live with him. They're so needy," said Eleanor. "They absolutely have to eat three meals a day, wear clean clothes, and … well you know."

"If that's how you feel, what's the big rock doing on your hand?" asked Klara.

"Right now, it's decorating my finger," said Eleanor and they laughed.

"I guess we can't live with them or without them," Klara said. "Sometimes keeping Tip home at night was as easy as puttin' socks on a rooster and other times he carried me on a silk pillow. I think I'll keep Harry Stone at a distance, like I do skunks and bankers, although I'm not adverse to a friend on a lonely night."

"Good idea," said Eleanor. They chatted for an hour or more, one story leading to another before they came back around to Tip and his bad snuff habit.

"I cleaned out all his snuff paraphernalia. No more spittoon or tins," said Klara. "It was rather cathartic."

"Did you find any pouches to suggest he was trying to quit?" asked Eleanor.

"No, just a stockpile of his regular MrSnuff. Do you want to try some?" Klara offered.

"No thank you, Klara. I should be going. I didn't finish today's crossword puzzle," Eleanor said and immediately changed her mind. "I *would* like to take a look at his stash. A tin of snuff looks a lot like a tin of nicotine pouches. Maybe you missed one."

"I really don't know what to do with them and I don't know why he brought so many on this trip." Klara carried a small box with about a dozen tins of snuff to the table where Eleanor carefully examined each tin to be sure it wasn't a tin of pouches. They were all MrSnuff.

"Thanks for coming with the pie. It sweetened my day," Klara said.

"If you need anything, Klara, I'm just a call away," Eleanor said.

When Eleanor walked, her brain went into hyperdrive. If there was no sign of nicotine pouches among Tip's things, where did he get the pouch found in his mouth that was laced with strychnine? Surely Klara would have noticed if he used an entire tin of pouches, yet there wasn't a partially used tin either. It had to be from someone at Monica's memorial service, or maybe it was Klara who poisoned the pouch and threw out the rest. She didn't seem overly grief-stricken. Didn't she say she felt free? Eleanor needed to see the photos Josephine took that day. She needed to identify the woman who caught Tip's eye.

Eleanor glanced at the flashy diamond ring and wondered if she had made a mistake accepting Angus' proposal. It might have been just as effective to let people think she had a girlfriend, but that wouldn't have kept Angus' widows at bay. They would just have a long engagement. Maybe the longest engagement in the history of romance. Everything would be all right, or so she thought.

Fiona McBride and Margo descended on Waterton like a damp rag on a warm fire. They planned to stay with Angus and were hell-bent on destroying the romance they thought Eleanor had tricked Angus into by some nefarious method. Being his older sister, Fiona thought she had the right to interfere in his love life and she expected Margo and Angus to get back together after he retired from working homicide even though Margo had no intention of ever moving back to Waterton which she considered beneath her.

"I don't know why you insisted on visiting Angus in this godforsaken place," Margo said as they drove their rental car to Sand Beach. "Couldn't you have invited him to Los Angeles where we could at least be near civilization?"

"He wouldn't have come," Fiona said. "He's so involved with that woman he can't see to leave her to visit his only sister. Surely, you can help me put a wedge between them. You know what he likes and once he liked you."

"I'm not sure I want him back," said Margo. "He's handsome and all that, but he's also demanding."

"He's also very rich now," Fiona said. "I'm sure Eleanor knows that too. He's so besotted with her he probably told her all about the billionaire who left him a fortune in his will. Homicide detectives don't get much in the way of pensions, so it was a windfall for Angus when that man died and felt grateful to him for solving his wife's murder. I'm happy for him but if she gets her hands on it instead of you … It just makes me so angry I want to spit!"

"It would be nice to have money," Margo admitted. "I'd like to have another facelift and some body sculpting done."

When they drove into his driveway, Angus came out to help carry in their bags. It was then Fiona saw the ring and her heart dropped. They would have to develop a new plan. If Angus married Eleanor, it would be more difficult to get rid of her.

"I wish you'd called before coming. I'm not sure it's safe for you to stay here," Angus said after packing in all their luggage.

"Why wouldn't it be safe here?" asked Fiona who couldn't imagine anything happening in the sleepy little village.

"Well, there have been some murders and unfortunate incidents around here lately." Angus really didn't want to go into it. "A man broke into my house."

"I'm sure we'll be quite safe with you here to protect us," said Margo flirtatiously.

"But I won't be here," said Angus. "I'm staying with Ellie until we catch the guy. It might be better if you get a room at the motel."

"Nonsense," said Fiona, "we'll be fine here. If you want to desert us for her, go ahead. I'm sure we are perfectly capable of taking care of ourselves, after all we're used to living in the big bad city."

"If you're trying to make me choose, I'm telling you right now, I'm staying with Ellie. He's threatened her and she needs protection," Angus said.

"Oh, who is this very bad scary man threatening Eleanor? An old flame perhaps? If you know who he is why don't you just arrest him and lock him up?" Fiona taunted.

"Are you hungry? I could make a little snack for you. You must be tired after your flight and it's a long drive from the airport," Angus offered, silently thinking of poison.

"Thank you but I couldn't eat a thing," said Margo batting her false eyelashes.

Angus studied his ex-wife. She had aged since he'd last seen her. Her hair was bleached blond and she was extremely thin. The only plumpness he saw were her lips and they looked like red swollen bee stings below two furry caterpillars acting the part of eyelashes. The skin on her face was stretched taut over her cheekbones and caked with makeup. If he didn't know better, he would guess she was a clown ready for her next performance at the circus. What had happened to the natural, wholesome woman he had married? Evidently, she was now under the influence of his sister Fiona who cared about looking young no matter the cost.

"You're right, Fiona, you'll be fine here," Angus said thinking they would scare the pants off Andri Frost if he encountered them looking the way they did. "Why don't you two take a rest downstairs and I'll take you out for dinner tonight."

"Are you leaving?" asked Fiona.

"I need to take Bones out for a walk. I'll be back soon," Angus said as he gathered Bones' leash and took the dog outside.

"Eww, I didn't know he had a dog inside his house," said Fiona watching the black lab frolic beside Angus as they headed up the hill.

"I didn't notice an unpleasant smell, and he seems to be rather well behaved," said Margo.

"Are you talking about Angus or the dog?" Fiona cackled. "We may have to change our plans. Breaking the two of them up may be more difficult than I thought. He didn't tell me that he married her, but that's definitely a ring on his finger. What is it that would put Angus off a woman?"

"I don't know," Margo said moving toward the kitchen. "I'm hungry."

"Oh yes you do," Fiona said, "If she was a cheater or a liar, he could never tolerate either, and you were both. He'll never take you back, Margo, so we'll have to convince him that she's unfaithful, or maybe convince her that he's still interested in you."

Fiona had seen the way Angus looked at Margo and it wasn't the look of a man who was interested. It looked more like pity. She would have to do something to make Margo more appealing. "We'll start tonight at dinner. Eleanor won't let her sugar daddy go by himself if she knows you're here."

Angus walked Bones to Eleanor's house to warn her about the uninvited guests. Feathers flew to Bones's head and proceeded to chatter, "Hello, hello, give me a kiss."

"He never asks me for a kiss," Angus sighed. Eleanor pecked him on the cheek. "Why are you here? It's not lunch time."

"What? Is that apple pie all gone?" he asked.

"No, I saved some just for you." Eleanor led him into the kitchen where she served up a piece of pie and ice cream. "Is there something you want to tell me?" she asked.

"Did I interrupt your work?" Angus asked. "I know I should have called first, but I was operating on emergency mode."

"What's the emergency?" Eleanor asked. "Does it have to do with food?"

"Fiona and Margo are here." Angus said as if he were delivering a death notice. "I'm not ready to explain the ring."

"Well take it off," Eleanor said simply. "There's no reason for them to be involved in our plan. How long are they staying?"

"I'm not sure. They didn't tell me they were coming, and I think they already saw the ring," Angus said sadly. "I need to ask a favor."

"No, I'm not going to take them off your hands, cook for them, or commit any crime to rid you of them," Eleanor said firmly.

"Would you come to dinner with me tonight?" he asked sweetly.

"Are they going to be there?" asked Eleanor suspiciously.

"Yes," he said.

"I don't know, I need to work on my poetry," she hedged.

"If you come, I'll reward you," he said raising his eyebrows.

"Have you been holding back information about the murders?" Eleanor asked.

"So, you'll come?" He smiled activating his dimples.

"Ok, maybe we should take off our rings until they leave town. I don't feel like dealing with their opinions either."

"That's just cowardly," Angus said. "I'm disappointed in you, Ellie. I've told them about the break-in and that I'm staying with you tonight. What kind of husband would I be to leave you unprotected from a lunatic?"

"What if Andri Frost comes back to your house?" Eleanor said.

"I can't protect him. If he comes back to my place, he's going to have to deal with Fiona and Margo. He's on his own."

Eleanor admired the ring on her finger, mesmerized by the flashes of light that it threw off as she moved her hand. She did not look forward to spending the evening with Angus' sister and his ex-wife. They belonged in a different world from the one Eleanor inhabited. She liked her life full of the natural beauty that surrounded her, the wind, rain, ocean, friends whose hair had turned white and whose bodies soft, exposing the core of their character expressed by kindness, wisdom, humor, and recorded by the lines on their faces. These were what she loved and who she loved. She left the ring on and dressed for dinner putting on a brave face as her only façade. She only hoped the information Angus promised would be worth it.

Angus chose Chez Pacifica for their fine dining experience. The last time he ate there had been with Helen Pence and he wanted to impress Fiona and Margo as well as make a new memory with Eleanor, preferably one that would blot out the one with Helen.

Eleanor noticed the extremely high prices and wondered at Angus' extravagance as he ordered the Pacific Northwest rib eye with cauliflower puree, asparagus, and wild mushrooms, by far the most expensive choice on the menu. This set the tone for his guests who also ordered it. Eleanor thought it odd since Fiona and Margo hardly ate any food at all. Eleanor ordered jumbo scallops with grilled corn succotash, creamy tarragon orange reduction, and microshoots as well as a very dirty martini with extra olives. She hoped it might help her enjoy the evening.

"This is a lovely restaurant," Fiona said glancing around at the elegant table setting, the fancy chandeliers, colorful flower centerpieces, and the ocean view. "It's very romantic. Do you come here often?"

Angus was suddenly struck mute. He didn't want to lie, yet he had no intention of telling Eleanor he had taken Helen here. "This is the first time Eleanor, and I have been here," he finally said. "We have our own special place, but I thought you might like this, Fiona."

Eleanor noted his discomfort and gave him the side eye, picked up her martini and took a long sip. She wondered if Margo's presence was making him uneasy. She certainly hadn't noticed any residual feelings, but his marriage to Margo had never been a topic of discussion between them. Eleanor assumed they drifted apart because of his work and then divorced when she refused to live in a small rural town. Then there were hints that he had been wounded by her in some way. She began to study Margo more closely. She was an attractive woman, very thin and tall, with blond hair and beautiful brown eyes. It was obvious that she had work done to correct the sag of old age and her lips were infused with something that made them look too large and unnatural. Eleanor thought if she hugged her, Margo would feel like a mannikin instead of a real person who had no soft curves, only hard edges.

Fiona was similar and looked quite stunning in the dim light, but on closer inspection she was an old woman doing her best to look young. There's only so much plastic surgery one can do. What interested Eleanor was finding out who these women really were.

"What prompted you both to visit Sand Beach?" Eleanor asked.

"Well, we came to see, Angus, of course," said Fiona. "I miss my little brother and he evidently doesn't have time to visit me."

"You're looking very handsome, Angus." Margo said, "You must be working out."

Angus ignored her flattery but stiffened when he felt her bare foot run up his leg beneath the table. He frowned and shook his head. It was clear what she was doing and it made him angry.

"Eleanor's writing a book of poetry about women," Angus said and saw Eleanor glance his way in surprise. She hadn't told him that, only that she was working on a new book.

"Does that pay the bills?" asked Fiona. "I know several writers who say they can't live on what they make selling books anymore. Is it just a hobby?"

"Don't worry about me, Fiona," Eleanor said, "I can pay my bills just fine. What is it you two do?"

"I travel, shop, do the party circuit, and generally enjoy life," Fiona said.

"I like to read," Margo offered.

"What are you reading?" Eleanor asked.

"I just finished an article in *Cosmopolitan*, that's a magazine, about why men ghost women after three months. Did you know there's a scientific reason for that?"

"I imagine there may be several reasons," Eleanor said. "Maybe he's not into them."

"Hmmm, I guess that's pretty much the reason," Margo admitted as the waiter brought a bottle of champagne to the table.

"This is for the lovely lady with the diamond ring, with congratulations from that gentleman at the table by the Ficus tree," the waiter said. Everyone at the table craned their necks to see who had sent the champagne. Eleanor spotted Harry Stone and Klara smiling at them happily. "Excuse me," Eleanor said as she got up and walked over to thank them.

"Thank you for the champagne," Eleanor said as she touched Klara's hand. "Are you two having a date night?"

"It's not a date, just two lonely people spending an evening together," said Klara. "Who could refuse a fancy dinner at an elegant place like this?" Obviously, Klara had decided to keep Harry Stone at a distance only when it suited her, knowing full well his intentions might be questionable.

"I wanted to let you know how happy I am for you and Angus," Harry Stone said as he stood and kissed Eleanor on the cheek. "I'm just sorry I didn't get a chance to know you better before he took you off the market. Klara filled me in on the fact that neither of those ladies at your table were your lovers. I must say, Eleanor, you had me going there for a while."

"Well, thank you both," Eleanor said as she took her leave and returned to her table.

Angus raised his glass of champagne to Klara and Harry as Eleanor returned to the glare of Fiona and Margo. "I don't usually like champagne, but this is particularly delicious knowing Harry Stone must have paid a fortune for it," he said.

"Okay, just what is happening here?" asked Fiona. "Did I miss your wedding or what?"

Angus just smiled and kissed Eleanor with a passion that couldn't be denied.

"Okay, McBride, I've fulfilled my end of the deal, now spill it," ordered Eleanor tossing her jacket on the back of a chair.

"I love it when you go all dominatrix," Angus said. "How about we consummate our marriage first."

"What are you talking about? I've been waiting patiently for you to give me some information about the murder case," Eleanor said.

"That's not what I promised," Angus said, enjoying every minute of Eleanor's frustration. "If you remember, I said I would reward you."

"I see." Eleanor did not like being played for a fool.

"Do you, now?" Angus said moving in for a neck nibble which Eleanor smoothly avoided.

"Just what did you have in mind?" Eleanor asked.

"Let me show you." Angus moved in once more and Eleanor swiftly stepped away.

"I see now that you don't have any information," Eleanor said. "I should have listened to Harry Stone when he said you were losing your touch."

"He said that?" Suddenly Angus was no longer interested in rewarding Eleanor with kisses. "When did he tell you that? Just how friendly are you with Harry Stone?"

"Not as friendly as you seem to be with Margo. Are you sure you don't still have feelings for her?" Eleanor said.

"Ellie, where did that come from? We just had dinner with Fiona and Margo and now I'm here with you."

"Don't think I didn't notice the way she was looking at you, '*You're looking very handsome, Angus. Are you working out?*' and the way she played footsy with you under the table didn't go unnoticed either."

"Ellie, your observation skills are improving. That's very impressive," Angus said, "but don't be fooled by those two troublemakers. I don't know why they came here, but now I think they plan to meddle in our relationship. Don't fall into their trap, Ellie."

"Angus, I think it's time you told me about your relationship with Margo and why it ended in divorce."

"I think I'd rather tell you about the noose we found around Monica's neck," he said.

When Angus went back to his house the following morning, Fiona and Margo were still asleep. He wasn't at all surprised to find Margo in his bed along with Bones. She'd be mortified to wake up next to a dog, but Angus suspected Bones would be equally terrified to see Margo's morning face. He quietly called Bones but wasn't prepared for Fiona's startling appearance and yelped in surprise almost backing into a nearby lamp.

"What's your problem?" Fiona all but shouted waking Margo who lifted her sleep mask to reveal bloodshot eyes that squinted in the morning light. Fiona continued her rant while Angus stared at the creature whose bloated lips kept moving even though encased in what could only be a face bra that would have scared even Frankenstein. Her hair, a tangle of extensions much like Medusa's serpents.

"We had a very late night thanks to your friend. We need our beauty sleep and here you are at this ungodly hour making enough noise to wake the dead!"

"Apparently I have," Angus said after finding his voice.

"Just what do you mean by that, Angus McBride?" Fiona said angrily.

"Fiona, I was trying to be quiet," Angus said. "I'm sorry if Bones was a problem. I'll take him out. Please go back to bed."

"I wasn't talking about the dog," Fiona continued. "I was talking about the pale guy in the hoodie who came sniffing around here in the middle of the night. I heard something and went upstairs, then saw him through the window and assumed he was a friend of yours, but when I turned on the light and opened the door, he ran away like a scared little rabbit."

Angus almost laughed but thought better of it. If Andri Frost had come in the middle of the night and had seen Fiona in her nighttime regalia, he deserved to be scared, but what was he up to? Both his truck and Fiona's rental car were parked out front, so Frost must have known someone was home. Angus went outside to check for signs that Andri tried to break in but found nothing. It wasn't until he and Bones were leaving that he noticed Fiona's rental car. Someone had scratched BITCH on the driver's side door and slashed two of the tires. Andri must have figured Eleanor's car was getting some needed body work done and it was her rental. How surprised he must have been to see Fiona at the door! Angus could only imagine how she must have appeared to him with his limited vision illuminated by the bright porch light. Angus chuckled all the way to the beach as Bones ran ahead in wild doggy delight.

Eleanor showed up on the beach after she finished her morning workout to meet Angus for breakfast at Susanna's. "Did you see Fiona's rental car?" she asked.

"Oh yeah," Angus said, "I've already called Officer McGraw. We need to bring this idiot in before he hurts someone. Andy found his campsite in the forest but he's moved, probably several times. It's a big area to cover. Like most who break the law, he comes out after dark. I'm sure it's also because he's sensitive to light. I can only hope Fiona scared him away from my place for good."

"Do you think he killed Monica?" asked Eleanor.

"I don't think so," Angus said. "If he did, I don't understand why he's still here. It may be that he's only interested in perpetuating the Bigfoot myth and has nothing to do with the murder. Let's get some breakfast."

Eleanor and Angus sat at the table usually reserved for the Do Nothings and ordered Suzanna's special breakfast skillet for Angus and eggs and bacon for Eleanor. "I've been thinking," Eleanor began, "There was a woman at Monica's memorial that seemed to interest Tip. I saw him looking at her a few times as if he knew her. She was an attractive woman maybe in her forties with long brown hair. I watched her put her plate down at the table where Tip was sitting, but I didn't recognize her. Maybe she knows something."

"Everyone there has been questioned," Angus said. "If she knew anything I'm sure someone took her statement."

Eleanor sighed. "Dede was talking with her before Tip died so I'm sure she knows who she is. Angus, do you think the two murders are related?"

"Maybe, but I don't think Tip killed Monica."

"What about the noose? Was Monica hanged because someone thought she was a witch?"

"I think it was staged to look that way," Angus said. "There was no evidence of a hanging on any of the nearby trees. The rope was new and cut short. The coroner said she was strangled not hanged."

"So you think it was someone who wanted to threaten women who practice witchcraft?"

"Are you going to eat that piece of bacon?" Angus asked.

Eleanor watched as he put the bacon on his plate thinking he was acting more and more like a husband.

Eleanor met the ladies at the Boat House where they insisted on knowing more about her ring and what it meant and asking all kinds of personal questions. It was so overwhelming Eleanor swore them to secrecy and told them the truth.

"You mean you're not going to marry him?" asked Pearl, who evidently thought that was mean.

"It's an engagement of sorts, a very long engagement," Eleanor explained.

"It's a beautiful ring. Do you think Angus bought real diamonds or are they as fake as your marriage?" asked Josephine.

"It doesn't matter to me," Eleanor said, "as long as it keeps the widows away."

"Is he wearing a ring too?" asked Dede.

"Men don't usually wear engagement rings," said Cleo.

"Yes, he's also wearing a ring," Eleanor said. "The most important part is we are making a commitment to see each other exclusively. That's all that anyone really needs to know. His sister, Fiona and his ex-wife, Margo, are here visiting. Angus didn't want them to see his ring. I'm sure it's because Fiona doesn't approve of me and would rather have Margo back with him. They seem to be two of a kind and Angus wants to avoid any conflict with his sister."

"Is he moving in with you?" asked Dede.

"No," Eleanor answered so quickly the others were stunned into silence. "Now if we could please change the subject, I'd like to know who that woman at Monica's memorial was that caught Tip's eye. She was fortyish, attractive with long brown hair. I saw her talking to Dede earlier."

"I talked to a lot of people at the memorial," said Dede thoughtfully.

"I took pictures of everyone," said Josephine, pulling out her phone. Eleanor took it and scrolled through several photos until she spotted the woman.

"There she is," said Eleanor.

"That's Malady Manning," said Dede. "Her husband, Malcolm, worked with Monica at City Hall."

"Why are you interested in her?" asked Pearl.

"I thought Tip was interested in her. He kept looking her way and then sat at the same table. I just thought it was odd," Eleanor explained.

"Malcolm Manning was on our list of misogynistic men," said Dede.

"Maybe we should send him an anonymous note too," suggested Pearl. "None of the other suspects have reacted."

"He's very charming," said Dede, "And he seems to adore his wife."

"Maybe Tip was just admiring Malcolm's wife from afar," said Josephine.

"Oh, I also learned that Monica was not hanged but strangled. The noose found at the scene was staged to make it look like a hanging and that bit of information was conveniently leaked," Eleanor said.

"What do you think that means?" asked Cleo.

"The murderer wanted people to think she was hanged," said Josephine, "But why?"

"Because she was a witch," said Dede. "Someone wanted everyone to think witches were being killed."

"Maybe, but the police didn't disclose that information, so how did it get out?" asked Eleanor.

"I heard it from someone," said Dede, "but I don't remember who told me. I think it was someone at a city council meeting."

"The tarot card was also left there to throw suspicion on Madame Patruska," said Eleanor. "It doesn't make sense to me. Why send a message that says witches are being hanged and then try to implicate someone people think is a witch as the murderer?"

"Then there's the shoe that was planted at The Oracle," said Cleo. "Maybe it wasn't planted there and Madame Patruska *is* guilty."

"Guilty of what?" asked Dede. "Maybe it was a message to Patruska saying she was guilty of sticking her nose into other people's business. She was involved with the crisis center."

"I like Madame Patruska," said Pearl. "I don't want her to be guilty."

"I think Tip's murder is connected in some way," said Eleanor. "I just don't know how."

"I'm not giving up on the husbands of the abused women," said Pearl. "One of them has to be the guilty one here."

"I agree, but how would they know Monica was involved with their wives? That was confidential," said Eleanor.

"Maybe there was a leak," said Dede.

"Andri Frost is still in the area," said Eleanor. "If he killed her, it wouldn't make any difference to him if she was a witch or not. His motive was revenge for getting him fired and humiliating him. Once she was dead, he'd be smart to get out of town. Angus doesn't think it's him and that makes me think he knows something we don't."

"He's probably not the one," Cleo said. "I think one of the husbands did it. He somehow found out that Monica helped his wife leave him so he killed her and made it look like she was hanged as a witch to send a message to all the other witches that they would be next."

"And if she was a witch, public opinion would be against her since witches are evil," said Josephine.

"Is Helen Pence still in the hospital? She certainly would have played into his hands by calling for a committee to discover witchcraft in Waterton," said Dede. "I think we may have averted a public catastrophe by getting her locked away."

"Maybe they were in it together," suggested Josephine.

"I'm sure they had no connection whatsoever," Dede said. "Helen Pence is a good person who snapped, she isn't a murderer."

"I bet she was a misogynist just like those men," said Josephine.

"Maybe there's a secret misogyny group in town," snickered Cleo.

"Probably not since most misogynists don't know they hate women, especially women," said Pearl. "I'm going to visit Madame Patruska and tell her about Malcolm Manning so she can send him a letter."

"You haven't told Angus about our little scheme have you, Eleanor?" asked Dede.

"Absolutely not," Eleanor said, "We're still on the hook for obstruction of justice for hiding the shoe."

"No wonder I can't sleep at night," said Cleo. "We'd better solve this case before the police find out what we've done."

"Perhaps we're going about this whole thing the wrong way," said Eleanor. "We're depending on gossip instead of facts. Let's see what we can find out about Andri Frost. Why would he be here and stay here? There must be something we're overlooking. He came to Angus' during the night and slashed the tires and scratched *bitch* on Fiona's rental car. If he's not the killer, he's still an evil man."

"For heaven's sake, why would he do such a thing?" asked Pearl.

"He's obviously a man who holds onto a grudge," said Josephine. "He must think you live there, Eleanor. I hope Angus is still staying with you at night."

"Evidently Fiona scared him away with her nighttime facial, but she may insist on Angus' protection now that she knows what's at stake," Eleanor said.

"Are you afraid?" asked Cleo.

"I haven't been, because he doesn't know where I live," said Eleanor.

"It wouldn't be hard for him to figure it out, especially after seeing Fiona at Angus' house," said Dede.

"Why haven't they caught the guy and locked him up?" asked Pearl.

"'The woods are lovely dark and deep'," Eleanor quoted Robert Frost's poem.

"If Angus needs to protect his sister, we could always have a sleepover," suggested Cleo.

"Let's do it," said Eleanor who wanted to give Angus a welcome break and time to spend with his sister. And so, the plan was set in motion.

The coffee group ladies carpooled to Eleanor's later in the afternoon with snacks and food for dinner as well as a bountiful supply of wine. The plan was to do a deep dive into Andri Frost and design a way to lure Malcolm Manning out if he was Monica's killer.

"I made lasagna," said Cleo. "It's ready to pop in the oven when we're ready for dinner."

"Here's the garlic bread, and a bottle of Chianti," said Pearl.

"I brought ingredients for my special green salad," said Josephine as she deposited it in Eleanor's refrigerator.

"The angel lemon meringue pie is for after dinner, and the cheese and crackers are for before," said Dede.

Eleanor had laid out a charcuterie board of meats, cheeses, fruits, and vegetables and added Dede's crackers to the mix. "It might be best if we do the serious work before we have any wine," suggested Eleanor who set out a pitcher of water, ice, and glasses.

"We all brought our canes just in case you know who pays us a visit," said Cleo on her way out to bring them in from the car.

"Good idea," said Eleanor. She had her weapon of choice near the sliding door to the deck. "You should move the car into the garage," said Eleanor, "If Frost comes here, I wouldn't want him damaging your car, Cleo."

"I just brought a baseball bat," said Pearl who didn't own a cane.

"I've already done a little research on Andri Frost," said Dede. "My friend from Orick was able to get some financial information on him. Don't ask me how because I'm sure it was illegal, but I think it tells us a great deal about why he's here." The ladies gathered around Eleanor's dining room table and studied the report that Dede offered.

"He's gone into business, creating a company selling items based on Sasquatch!" exclaimed Josephine.

"What better way to market his brand and get free publicity than to plant big footprints in the forest where hundreds of treasure hunters are gathered?" said Cleo. "It explains why we saw the boots with the fake feet in his tent."

"When I talked to the Do Nothings, they complained that Bigfoot paraphernalia was for sale all over town," Eleanor said. "I have to give him credit for taking advantage of the situation."

"I've noticed several stands along the highway selling hats, mugs, keychains, almost everything you could want with a Sasquatch logo on it," Dede said. "He's here to make money."

"Maybe he didn't even know Monica was here," said Pearl.

"Or maybe he's an opportunist who killed her when he realized she was," said Josephine.

"How do we find out if he was here when she was murdered?" asked Cleo.

"If we could catch him, we could ask him," said Eleanor.

"What do Sasquatch eat?" asked Josephine, "If they like lasagna, we could set some outside to bait him."

Dede was furiously typing on her laptop. "It says here there is no credible evidence that they prefer any specific food but are opportunistic in what they eat based on what is found in their environment. The words 'there is no credible evidence' occurs over and over in this article."

"That's because there is no credible evidence that they exist at all," said Josephine.

"That's why the Bigfoot hunter, Andri Frost, has to create evidence and manufacture the footprints to keep his investment alive," said Eleanor.

"What's the name of his company?" asked Cleo.

"It's called Sasquatch Supply Co." said Dede, "**Unleash the Wild. Gear up with Sasquatch Supply Co.** They sell everything from soap to …" Dede began to laugh and read on, "Invisible Camouflage Suit—for blending into the forest without a trace. Warning: May cause confusion in your own reflection.

Sasquatch-Sized Boots—A pair of boots so big, they double as kayaks. Perfect for stepping into the wild with style (and stability).

Bigfoot-Sized Snacks—The ultimate protein bars made with forest-grown, organic ingredients guaranteed to fuel your inner cryptid.

Hairy Beast Beard Oil—for the rugged, untamed look. Gives your facial hair a wild, Sasquatch-inspired glow.

Monster Footprint Stamps—Leave Sasquatch-sized tracks everywhere you go. Great for adding a little mystery to your walk."

"And there you have it!" said Josephine. "He didn't even have to make the footprint stamps himself. His company provided them."

"He's funny," said Cleo. "I can't help it. I'm starting to like this guy."

"I'm sure the police have all this information on him if he's a serious suspect in a murder investigation. They've probably known ever since the footprints were discovered to be fake," said Eleanor.

"Do you think they still suspect he's guilty?" asked Dede.

"I bet they know if he has an alibi," Eleanor said. "Angus has kept me in the dark."

"And yet he's staying with you to protect you from this man," said Pearl. "He knows he's dangerous."

"He may be dangerous, and still not be the murderer," said Dede. "Let's look at Malcolm Manning. I took some personnel files from city hall. Let's look through them and see if there are any red flags."

"I'm going to Google him and look at his online history," said Josephine.

"I'll check out the file on Monica Fischer," said Pearl.

"I'll open a bottle of wine," said Cleo and she disappeared into the kitchen.

After several minutes of silence, a sharing of information began with Cleo's rating of the wine.

"I really like this red blend," she said. "It pairs nicely with this soft cheese and makes me see clearly that Malcolm Manning is too good to be true. No, wait. There is a very nasty complaint in here filed against him by Monica Fischer."

"I saw that too," said Dede.

"Monica Fischer's file depicts her as a troublemaker. There is a counter-complaint against her filed by her coworker, Malcolm Manning, who claims she came on to him and tried to take credit for his ideas concerning a more efficient way to use funds in the renewal project," said Pearl.

"I know for a fact that it was her idea," said Dede. "She came to me with it weeks before he proposed it. I can't believe it's still in her file."

"Who's responsible for what goes into the file?" asked Pearl.

"Human Resources, that would be Eva Blount," said Dede. "I don't know her well, but Mr. Manning is looking more guilty by the minute. He could have known about her past at Orick if he did a background check on her and used it against her when she turned out to be a threat to him at work. The fact that she won a defamation suit against Frost didn't seem to matter."

"We need to talk to Eva Blount," said Josephine.

"Don't forget that Tip was watching Manning's wife at the memorial," said Eleanor, "My gut tells me something else was going on there."

"The police have gone through these files already," said Dede. "Manning may be a person of interest, or they may have discounted the complaint against him because they believe Monica was a troublemaker."

"If there are misogynists on the force, it makes sense they would take the man's side," said Josephine.

"I know that Angus is not a misogynist," Eleanor said, "but I'm not sure if he is deeply involved in working this case. There was that whole thing with Helen Pence, the concussion, now his sister and Margo, and of course, me. I can't believe Andrew McGraw is one either. Do you remember who told you about the noose found at the crime scene, Dede?"

"Yes, it was Eva Blount," Dede said slowly. The silence that followed was profound.

"Just what can you tell us about Eva Blount?" asked Josephine.

"She's worked at city hall for ages and is older, but not as old as we are. She seems very nice and old fashioned in her thinking. I remember her saying some revealing things now that I think of it. How her husband made all the major decisions in their relationship because he had the brains and God's blessing. She often deferred to men and was eager to serve them and take care of their needs by baking for them and bringing them coffee as if she were their mother. I never gave it much thought. She was very nurturing but not to me. Pretty much asked me if Mark approved that I was mayor. I think she would have liked to stay home and not work at all, but she needed the health insurance. Her husband runs a dairy farm."

"So, it's possible she took Manning's side against Monica's complaint of sexual harassment. Was there even an investigation?" Josephine asked.

"I don't recall," Dede said, "Wouldn't surprise me if they just buried it because they didn't like the optics. Monica hadn't been here that long. Look at the date here. If he was harassing her, it's still an ongoing investigation. I'll check into it."

"My guess is it's no longer an issue," said Eleanor. "Monica Fischer is dead. I wonder how they like those optics."

"How would Eva Blount know about the noose?" asked Pearl.

"Maybe Manning told her about it, knowing she'd spread it around because she didn't approve of witches or beautiful women who file harassment complaints," said Josephine.

"That's if he is the one who killed her, but what would be the purpose of a noose other than a message to other women who might be witches?" asked Eleanor.

"Maybe he thinks all women are witches or perhaps it has some other meaning and nothing to do with witches at all," said Cleo. "I'm going to put the lasagna in the oven."

"My head hurts," said Pearl. "Let's take a break and let some of this information marinate."

They poured the wine and nibbled on cheese as the sun sank lower in the sky and provided them with a beautiful orange and crimson sunset.

Angus sat on his leather couch and faced the angry judgment of Fiona McBride. "I cannot understand you, Angus," she scolded, "I know you're a man, but I thought you were smarter than most. How could you fall prey to the oldest trick in the book. '*The way to a man's heart is through his stomach.*' You are a fool to trust her. Have you told her about your windfall? I saw that ring she wore and I'm sure she's already had it appraised. She's nothing more than a money-grabbing whore who plays at writing poetry because she's too stupid to put a proper sentence together."

"I've heard enough, Fiona." Angus sighed. "I don't owe you an explanation for what I do with my money or who I love."

"I know who you *should* love. Margo and you have history together. She put up with years of neglect from you while you worked endless hours for little money and now when you can actually provide for her, you turn to Eleanor. It's not right and it's not fair!" Fiona continued her rant while Margo sat silently in a chair. Her long legs crossed and a pout on her swollen lips. He wondered if she thought she was sexy.

"I'm getting a drink. Would you like one Margo?" Angus asked politely ignoring Fiona altogether. He went to the kitchen and poured two large whiskeys. He didn't think Margo wanted him back in her life at all, but she would definitely like the money. She would squander it on more plastic surgeries and outrageous outfits to prove she wasn't an old woman. He thought about just giving it to her to shut Fiona up, but had already considered the idea of doing something good with it. He admired Eleanor for giving half of her share of the million-dollar prize money to the women's crisis center. She hadn't told him about it, but Mark had said Dede wanted to do the same. If he was honest, he liked having the money. Just knowing it was there if he needed it. It felt like a security he'd never known. He'd always known that Eleanor had more money than he did and now he felt on equal footing with her. She was generous with her wealth and he wanted to be generous too, but not to Margo.

Margo took the drink gently caressing his finger as she did. He watched her and wondered how she drank with those lips. "So, Margo, you're very quiet. Do you want to get married again?" She sat up straighter in the chair and uncrossed her legs suggestively.

"You're still a very handsome man, Angus," she said. "I wouldn't say no if that was a proposal."

"Are you willing to sign a prenup?" he asked and watched her frown and squirm. "I have several expectations you might find unappealing. First, I expect you to live here as my wife in Sand Beach until I die, second, I expect my wife to be truthful and faithful or leave the marriage with nothing; third, my wife must bring something to the relationship besides need." When Margo didn't respond, Angus smiled. "I don't wish you ill, Margo. There was a time when I loved you, but that time has passed. Let's just be kind to each other and part as friends."

Fiona stood and paced the room. Things were not going as she expected. Margo was proving too selfish or just too stupid to get the job done. She was supposed to lure Angus into a compromising situation so Fiona could confront Eleanor with Angus' infidelity. Instead, Margo sipped her drink and stared off into the distance chewing on her fat lip. Finally, Margo excused herself. "I'm going to take a shower," she whispered into Angus' ear, "maybe you'll join me for old time's sake." Angus watched her walk away and continued to nurse his whiskey.

The coffee club ladies ate their lasagna, drank their wine, and laughed until their faces ached.

"I never noticed that chipped tooth before, Dede," said Pearl.

"It just happened yesterday," Dede said, "I was draining the very last of the soup I'd made in my Crock-Pot into my mouth when the pot slipped and hit my tooth."

"Oh, my goodness, I've done that a hundred times but never broken any teeth," confessed Cleo. "Those Crock-Pots are so heavy."

"Does it hurt?" asked Josephine who did not drink wine and retained some semblance of kindness.

"Only my pride," Dede admitted. "I'm seeing Dr. Babbity next week. Of course, I may need a shot of tequila to deaden the pain of embarrassment."

Eleanor knew she'd had too much wine when she began to laugh at everything even when it wasn't funny. "What do you want to do after dinner?" she asked. "We can watch a movie, play a game, or just sit around and talk."

"I brought Cards Against Humanity," said Cleo. "It's a very naughty game for horrible people."

"Well, let's play that after we clean up," said Pearl.

"How do we play?" asked Josephine.

"All I know is it's a little like Apples to Apples only there's a Card Czar instead of a judge and that person is chosen because they were the last person to poop, unless Hugh Jackman is playing and then he goes first," explained Cleo.

Simply reading the directions sent them all into fits of giggles. They decided Eleanor should be the Card Czar since none of them wanted to admit when they last pooped or even that they ever pooped at all and Hugh Jackman wasn't playing.

Eleanor drew a black card. "Check me out, yo! I call this dance move …" ______. Eleanor read each white card the other players contributed to finish the sentence. "Tentacle porn, tap dancing like there's no tomorrow, pooping back and forth forever, smegma. I don't know what smegma is but it sounds nasty. I'll go with tap dancing like there's no tomorrow."

"Good grief, Eleanor," said Cleo, "That one makes way too much sense and isn't even naughty. You should have picked pooping back and forth forever." Then she proceeded to illustrate the dance move by squatting first one way and then the other.

"I gather that was your contribution," said Eleanor. "My decision holds. Who gets the point for tap dancing?" Josephine raised her hand.

Josephine then became the Card Czar and drew a black card.

"Shouldn't we at least find out what smegma is?" asked Pearl. "I'll just Google it quickly on my phone."

"Beat ya to it," said Dede. "It's a secretion around the genitals of mammals that is white and smells bad."

"Ewww," said Pearl. "There's even a picture of it here." They all crowded around Pearl's phone to see, as if none of them had ever seen genitalia before.

"I can't say I'm a better person for having learned that fact," said Eleanor.

"That's why this game is for horrible people," said Cleo.

"Click here for …" _______________. Josephine read. Once she had the white cards she continued, "Full frontal nudity, permanent orgasm-face disorder, getting naked and watching Nickelodeon, the magic of live theatre."

"I wonder what orgasm-face disorder looks like," said Dede.

"You know," said Cleo who opened her mouth and wrinkled her forehead in her version of what it might look like."

Eleanor pressed her lips together in an attempt to stifle a laugh. Dede couldn't stop herself and then full hysteria began and wouldn't quit.

"I'll choose full frontal nudity. This is the most disgusting game I've ever played," said Josephine. "It is truly for horrible people."

"Absolutely not for refined ladies such as ourselves," added Dede.

Cleo began putting the game away. "What are you doing?" asked Pearl. "I haven't had my turn as Card Czar yet." There was more laughter and some snorting until Pearl drew her card and read, "What's my secret power?" And everything went off the rails from there. The coffee ladies began to adlib revealing things they had done in their youth and vowing never to repeat a word of it outside their inner circle until finally Cleo did put the game away.

"Is the wine all gone?" asked Cleo as she moved to the couch.

"Yes," lied Eleanor who was only looking out for Cleo's good health.

"That's an interesting pin you're wearing," said Josephine.

"Madame Patruska gave it to me for protection from those who would do me harm by looking at me. It's called a Nazar amulet," Eleanor said.

"It does look like an eye," said Dede taking a closer look at the cobalt blue pin with a white circle in the center. "Protection from the evil eye."

"I don't believe in that," Eleanor said. "I stuck it on this sweater when she gave it to me and forgot to take it off." She turned when she heard Cleo snoring and began to laugh. "I guess none of us have the stamina to stay up late anymore."

"It's one of the joys of old age," said Pearl. "I can fall asleep anywhere now."

"What do you think Angus is doing?" asked Dede.

"I'm sure it isn't playing Cards Against Humanity," said Eleanor "I can't imagine being in the same house with an ex and a bossy cow older sister. They aren't nearly as much fun as you are."

"I know people who still enjoy the company of their exes," said Dede. "And a few who even get along with their siblings." As if on cue, the telephone rang. "Probably Angus calling for help."

Eleanor answered and listened without speaking. What she heard was disturbing but did not surprise her. "Thanks for the update, Fiona. Goodnight."

"That was Fiona?" asked Pearl. "What did she want?"

"She called to tell me to give the ring back, because Angus had proposed to Margo and was in the shower with her now and if I didn't believe her, I should come over and see for myself," Eleanor said calmly. "Angus warned me not to be drawn into their plan to break us up. She doesn't like me and thinks I'm after Angus' money."

"What? That's an outrage!" Josephine said. "Let's march down there and punch her in the nose."

"You just want to see Angus in the shower," accused Pearl.

The idea sent them into peals of laughter that caused Cleo to snort even louder, but the laughter died suddenly when there was a loud thumping sound coming from the deck.

"What is that?" whispered Dede.

"Probably the wind blowing something against the house," said Eleanor moving to the sliding glass doors and turning on the outdoor lights.

"Don't go out there!" cried Cleo who was now awake. "In the movies there's always a monster or a murderer outside that kills the brave one when they go out to investigate."

"It's probably Fiona, come to scare us," said Eleanor stepping outside and into the arms of a large hairy beast that glared at them through the window causing them to scream bloody murder. The screaming combined with the wild chaos of four panic-stricken old women looking for weapons was enough to give them all coronary embolisms and would have made for an excellent funny home video.

Pearl grabbed her baseball bat and the others eventually found their canes as they raced to Eleanor's rescue bumping and pushing each other as they tried to exit at the same time. Fortunately, Josephine had the good sense to turn off the indoor lights so they could see what was outside. What they saw shocked them. Eleanor struggled to free herself from the creature that could only be the well-known but seldom seen Bigfoot, and she wasn't winning the fight. She stomped on its huge feet and kicked as it lifted her off the ground in an attempt to carry her away. It was at least seven-feet tall with long brown hair that hung in tangled strands from its head to its huge hairy feet. Suddenly the creature cried out in pain and let go of Eleanor long enough for Pearl to swoop in with her bat and give it a hard whack on the back. Emboldened by Pearl's bravery, the others went into action using their Cane Fu training to trip and bring down the poor beast until it curled up on the deck floor in a fetal position whining in fear and pain.

Josephine and Cleo sat on the animal while Eleanor ran back into the house and reappeared with a roll of duct tape. Together they wrapped the tape around the feet and with a great deal of effort turned it onto its belly and tapped its arms behind its back. The cryptid never had a chance.

"I think it's crying," said Cleo.

"How did you get loose, Eleanor?" asked Josephine.

"I stabbed it with the pin from my sweater," said Eleanor. "Let's get the mask off so we can see who's in there. I know it's not really Bigfoot. It only stinks a little." The beast made some ugly noises meant to scare them, but they knew they were in control. It took some time to find a zipper hidden under all the hair, but they were rewarded with a close up of Andri Frost when they pulled the headpiece off. "I knew it would be you," said Eleanor. He only squinted into the light. His white face streaked with sweat and blood.

"Madame Patruska's pin did protect you after all," said Josephine pulling the pin from Frost's costume.

"What do we do now?" asked Pearl.

"Let's find out what he knows," said Dede, shining a flashlight into his already tortured eyes.

"Why are you here?" asked Cleo. The beast only growled.

"We know who you are," said Eleanor, "but what I don't understand is why you want to hurt me?"

"Because you hurt me!" he yelled. "You laughed at me and I'm tired of being the butt of everyone's joke."

"I laughed at the thought of you making an indecent proposal to me, an old woman who could be your mother. That hardly constitutes a reason to ram my car, break into my friend's house and damage their property. You should be ashamed of yourself," Eleanor scolded. "You could have killed my friends with your scare tactics tonight. Don't you think of anyone but yourself and your imagined slights?"

"I'm bleeding," said the monster as he wiped blood from his cheek where Eleanor's pin had pierced him.

"Did you kill Monica Fischer?" asked Josephine.

Andri Frost looked up in surprise. "No, I'm not a killer. I just came here looking to make money off the Park Challenge. I knew there would be lots of people swarming the forest looking for that treasure. I've been following many of them all over the state taking advantage of their interest in Bigfoot. You have no idea how much money I've made selling them merchandise from my company. I'm a successful businessman. Why would I kill Monica Fischer? She was nothing."

"You seem like a petty, vengeful man, maybe you wanted to hurt her the way you tried to hurt me," Eleanor said, "to get revenge. We know what you did to her and how she made you pay for it."

"The police are looking for you as a person of interest," said Cleo. "Maybe we should call them now."

"No, they already know I wasn't even here when she was murdered. I have an airtight alibi for April 5. I was in jail for disturbing the peace a hundred miles from here. You women are all alike, cruel and stupid."

"I wouldn't call *us* stupid. You're the one bound in duct tape wearing a Bigfoot costume in the middle of the night, captured by five old ladies with canes," said Dede.

"I'm sure I can press charges for trespassing, assault, and criminal mischief," said Eleanor.

"Go ahead," he dared, "Even bad publicity is good for business."

Eleanor really wanted to poke him with her pin again, but someone was ringing the doorbell. "Keep an eye on him," she warned as she went to answer the door.

Angus stood outside with Feathers perched on his shoulder, his wet hair giving proof to Fiona's statement that Angus had been in the shower. "What's going on here, Ellie? Feathers flew to my house squawking about Bigfoot and intruders. Bones barked so loud all the neighbors woke up and started calling to complain."

"He must have flown out the sliding doors when we were occupied with an intruder," Eleanor explained taking Feathers to his cage. "Come and meet Bigfoot." She led him to the deck where the coffee ladies posed proudly over their collar like hunters with their kill.

By the time the police arrived, took Andri Frost into custody and Eleanor's friends had gone home, it was almost morning. Angus' hair had dried and Eleanor was too stimulated to sleep.

"Is it alright if I eat some of this lasagna?" asked Angus as he dished it and warmed it in the microwave.

"Eat it all," Eleanor said. "It gives me heartburn."

"Did you ladies drink all this wine?" Angus pointed to the bottles that sat on the counter. Without answering Eleanor, he gathered up the bottles and took them to the recycling bin in the garage. "I'd guess you had a very good time tonight, at least until Mr. Frost arrived uninvited."

"And did you have a very good time too?" Eleanor asked.

"Absolutely not. Dinner was some vegetarian casserole that involved kale and then Fiona yelled at me for loving you instead of Margo. Then Margo used all the hot water so I had a cold shower and Bones went nuts creating bedlam and confusion, the neighbors called and then I saw Feathers and rushed over here thinking the worst. But it all ended well. Andri Frost won't bother you anymore, but I suppose there will be hell to pay when I go home."

"Then don't go home," Eleanor said.

Angus looked deeply into her eyes and thought he saw sadness there. He wondered if she knew he had been tempted by Margo, remembering the young woman he fell in love with and wishing things had turned out differently. He had been curiously aroused by her whispered invitation to join her in the shower and wondered what it would feel like to touch her, hold her again.

"Don't feel that you have to stay, Angus. I understand that you have guests to take care of and we both need some sleep.

You do what you need to do," Eleanor said and gently caressed his face.

On the way back to his house, Angus wondered how Eleanor knew. She had to know. The look in her eyes, and her departing words signaled something dark and final. Maybe it was just his guilty conscience and she really didn't know, but he wasn't guilty of *doing* anything. He hadn't joined Margo in the shower, but he'd thought about it. Was that cheating? Maybe he was radiating guilt and she was picking up on it. Angus' brain was too tired to think straight. He hoped Margo wasn't sleeping in his bed. When Eleanor said he should do what he needed to do, did she mean get Margo out of his system? Was she giving him permission to cheat or just telling him to get some sleep?

Eleanor took a long hot shower. She took extra time scrubbing Bigfoot's stink off her body and even though she was beyond tired she sat up watching the sun rise thinking about what Fiona had said and how Angus seemed somehow different. If Angus shared more than a shower with Margo, could she forgive him? Would he tell her? Eleanor knew Margo from when she was still married to Angus, but she didn't know what their marriage was like. There had been hints about her being unhappy in a small town but there had to be more than that for them to divorce. Lots of people who divorced got back together.

Whatever spark drew someone to another at first could resurface later. Margo was staying in Angus' house day and night perhaps reminding him of the good times they'd shared. Fiona was there too, making sure Angus didn't forget he once loved Margo, planting the seeds of doubt and mistrust in what Eleanor had taken for granted in their own relationship. Eleanor wondered if Angus found Margo's false eyelashes and plumbed up lips attractive. She'd obviously had a boob job too. Whatever Angus decided to do about Margo, Eleanor could live with it. She was surrounded by a loving family and good friends. Angus was more than a friend and she would miss him if he left her, but she'd survived worse. Having made peace with whatever might be going on in Angus' heart, Eleanor finally fell asleep.

Eleanor slept badly, tossing and turning while dreaming the worst about Angus and Margo who ran away together leaving Eleanor to care for Fiona who continued to be mean and vindictive only from a wheelchair to which Eleanor was inexplicably chained. In her dream she tried several times to kill her but the witch would not die. First, she tried poisoning her food, but Fiona refused to eat and continued to taunt her for being old. Then she tried stabbing her in her heart, but evidently Fiona had replaced it with a plastic one that went on working despite being damaged. Then she shot her with the gun Angus kept by his bed, but the bullets merely bounced off her hard head and shattered the picture of Eleanor that Angus kept on his nightstand. It was becoming apparent to Eleanor that she was stuck with Fiona as long as she continued a relationship with Angus so Eleanor took off the ring that Angus put on her finger, broke the chain and Fiona finally disappeared.

When she woke, the sun was shining, but Eleanor felt an emptiness inside that defied explanation. As far as she knew she had lost nothing, yet the ache of longing was there just as it was when her girls had gone away to college, and Walter had left their home. So, she wasn't surprised when Angus showed up later that afternoon with the announcement that he was going back to California with Fiona (and Margo) to help her settle some financial affairs dealing with an inheritance. He only asked that she take Bones and pick up his mail while he was away. He didn't say when he would be back and she didn't ask. The only hopeful detail was he still wore the ring she gave him. It wasn't long after that Eleanor received a text from Fiona that read, "YOU LOSE."

Eleanor spent the rest of the afternoon in her office writing.

The Hater

She stands with grace, her beauty bold,
Yet in her gaze there's a hidden stain,
Silent hate, whispered disdain.

She sees the world through a different lens,
For she believes she is different, elite,
In her mirror, no flaws, no defeat.

Other women – irrational, weak,
Manipulative, petty, dishonest at best,
While she, the exception, stands above the rest.

A fierce competitor, she plays the game,
To tear down a sister, to use for a prop,
It's what she will do, to climb to the top.

She wears her beauty like armor of steel,
Fights every battle for her survival,
Sees every sister as her archrival.

She is the thing she most despises,
Denying the sisterhood, forgetting her birth,
In her quest for power, she's lost her own worth.

She doesn't value what women provide,
A space to uplift, to comfort, to grow,
In her mind, it's a threat, each woman a foe.

She's aligned herself with the power of men,
The sisterhood fractured, the bond turned to dust,
She sees not the unity, only mistrust.

For denying her sisters, she's utterly lost,
One day she'll know what betrayal has cost.

It was time to get outside. Eleanor walked to Angus' house and was greeted with love and affection. At least Bones was happy to see her as shown by his wriggling body and wagging tail. She stroked his shiny black coat and spoke to him softly, "So he's left us both, Bones. I know he'll be back for you, so don't worry. Until then, you and I are going to be buddies." Angus' house was quiet, the kind of dead quiet that existed in abandoned houses.

Eleanor wandered from room to room looking for something that might give her a little hope that he was coming back to her too. The living room was neat and tidy, and the kitchen was almost bare of any semblance of food. She was reluctant to enter his bedroom, afraid of finding something too personal there. She picked up his pillow and buried her face in it but tossed it down when she recognized the scent of a woman's perfume. His closet still held his clothes and dresser drawers were full of his socks and T-shirts. Sticking out from under the bed Eleanor found a pair of red lacy underwear. Good grief, what had she expected? Maybe Angus had given up his room to Margo. He was staying with her to protect her from Andri Snow after all. Assume nothing, assume nothing, it only makes an ASS of U and ME. Eleanor really wanted to believe the best of Angus, she loved him.

She wandered into the bathroom and found a condom wrapper in the garbage. That's when she knew. This was all Fiona. Margo was too old to worry about getting pregnant. Angus didn't keep those in his house. She looked in the medicine cabinet. There wasn't a box of them there. She went downstairs to the guest room. This is where Fiona slept. The bed had been stripped and blankets folded neatly and topped with pillows. Angus' bed had not been stripped on purpose. It wasn't even made. The wrapper had been planted there. It was the only thing in the garbage. Fiona assumed Eleanor would check out Angus' house, snoop through his things and come to the conclusion that she wanted Eleanor to believe was the truth. Hadn't Angus warned her that he was afraid they had come to meddle in their relationship and not to fall into Fiona's trap? Okay then, Eleanor would trust Angus. She certainly didn't trust Fiona.

She left the house and she and Bones spent the rest of the afternoon frolicking on the beach before they picked up Angus' mail and returned home where an interesting message awaited her.

Eleanor, it's Patricia Venga from The Oracle. I need your help. I sent a message to Malcolm Manning and this afternoon he came to the shop while I was out. I caught him in my surveillance camera. I don't know what he wants but I believe it's a sign that he's involved in something sinister. Come to The Oracle when you can. I've called the others.

Eleanor called her back but there was no answer. She tried Dede's cell phone and learned that the coffee group was meeting at Madame Patruska's house to form a new plan. Eleanor put Bones in the car and drove there just as the sun was setting.

"Look who's come late to the party," said Cleo, "And she's brought a date."

"Who's a good boy?" cooed Pearl upon seeing Bones who immediately loved her because she smelled of bacon. "We were just taking a break from planning and enjoying a few nibbles."

"Sorry, I wasn't near my phone most of the afternoon," Eleanor said. "What's happened?"

"Nothing really," said Patruska, "Pour yourself some wine, Eleanor. I have a frontal lobotomy and we'll fill you in on the most recent happenings." She handed a glass to Eleanor and offered her a seat at the table while Cleo and Dede began to laugh at Patruska's latest spoonerism. This caused Patruska to concentrate on what she had just said and made her more determined to speak slowly and clearly. "I sent a shoebox to Malcolm Manning with the note inside saying I had discovered the shoe he planted and had proof of his involvement in the murder of Fonica Mischer. He showed up this afternoon while I was out and I'm sure he is the puilty garty. I didn't know what to do. I called everyone but no one came, so I closed the shop and came home afraid he might come back.

"We don't know what he intended to do, but we do know that he knew where the shoe was planted or he wouldn't have come to your shop," Eleanor said as she poured a glass of wine from the bottle in front of Madame Patruska.

"Is it possible he may have come for another reason?" asked Josephine.

"He's never come to the shop before," Patruska said.

"What have you planned before I got here?" Eleanor asked.

"Nothing clever," said Cleo, "We thought at least two of us should be with Patruska until this is resolved, so Josephine and Pearl are staying here overnight."

"I can be at The Oracle tomorrow, but I'll have to bring Bones. Angus is out of town," Eleanor said.

"I have meetings tomorrow so I can't be there," said Dede.

"I can be there tomorrow," said Cleo.

"Where are your meetings, Dede?" asked Eleanor.

"City Hall," Dede said.

"What if you plant the shoe in his office?" asked Eleanor. "Then we can alert the police and he'll have to explain it to them."

"But what if he's kept the shoebox and shows that to the police?" asked Dede "They might trace it back to us somehow. Then we're back to being criminals."

"I was the one who sent the message. You wouldn't have to be involved," Patruska said. "It's the least I can do to repay you for helping me. Otherwise, I might have been implicated by the planted evidence."

"Do we know where Manning lives?" asked Josephine.

"Yes," said Dede, "He lives near me, just a few houses down the street."

"Our best bet is to plant that shoe in his house and get the shoebox back," Josephine said.

"Or plant the shoe in his office, where the murder probably took place anyway, and break into his house and get the shoebox." Cleo said.

"It might be difficult to get into his house, since Malady hardly ever leaves," Dede said. "At least her car is always parked on the street."

"Do we know if his house has been searched by the police?" asked Eleanor. "He should be a person of interest since they worked together."

"Maybe we could plant the shoe in an outbuilding," suggested Pearl.

"If they searched his house, I'm sure they searched his outbuildings," said Eleanor.

"I just want to get rid of the shoe!" said Dede.

"Let's plant it in Helen Pence's house," said Cleo. "I never liked her and it's close."

"Is she home now?" asked Dede, "I see a light on over there."

"Don't go to the window!" hissed Josephine. "It might be Malcolm Manning over there. He knows where Patruska lives."

"Well, that would be just perfect!" said Eleanor, "If he's broken into her house to spy on Patruska, he probably has left his DNA on something, so we could hide the shoe there. I bet the police haven't searched *her* house."

"Wait, wait, wait," said Josephine, "We don't know that he's over there for one, and we don't have the shoe."

"Okay, we have to get the shoe and then plant it ASAP," said Dede. "I think I know a place the police may not have checked in his office, but it may not point the finger at him. Lots of people go in and out of there."

"What about in his car?" asked Pearl.

"Yes, his truck!" said Eleanor. "That would make so much sense and there could be no doubt it was him then."

"Unless, it was Malady. Maybe that's why her car is always on the street. She probably drives his truck. I bet he walks to work," said Cleo.

"I think I've had too much wine to think clearly," said Pearl.

"It's a good thing you're staying here tonight," said Eleanor. "Maybe we'll be better able to sort this out in the morning. I'll try to find out if Manning is a suspect and if his truck was searched."

Eleanor took Bones, drove home, and got ready for bed. She thought about calling Angus but decided against it. It didn't feel right to her to appear needy. Just as she was about to crawl into bed, the doorbell rang. It was Officer McGraw.

"Good evening, Mrs. Penrose," he said, "I know it's late but Angus asked me to check on you to make sure you're okay. I guess this whole thing with Andri Frost has had him worried."

"That's very sweet of you," Eleanor said. "I'm relieved that Mr. Frost is no longer a threat and I'm fine, thank you. Have you heard from Angus?"

"Not since he asked me to look in on you before he left. He's doing some investigating … oops, I'm not supposed to tell you anything about it." Officer McGraw had slipped up.

"Oh, you must be talking about Malcolm Manning and the murder case," Eleanor adlibbed.

"He told you about that?" McGraw seemed surprised, "I thought he wanted to keep you out it."

"Don't worry, he didn't tell me anything important," Eleanor said. "I'm curious though, when someone is a person of interest, do you search their homes? I'm only asking because I'm doing research for a new book."

"If we have their permission, we might," said McGraw. "But we're in the early stages of this investigation and only searched Monica's home and her office. I have to admit it's been a challenging case since there are so many possible suspects and very few leads. We were able to eliminate Andri Frost who was our main suspect and now we're looking into other persons of interest, including those who worked with her or had relationships with her. Sometimes an investigation is tedious and slow work … a process of elimination. Not like in books where it's all neatly tied up in a day."

Eleanor was amazed at how much information Officer McGraw was giving to her. If she knew she could coax people to talk by using her writing as a ruse, she would have done it earlier. She wondered if it would work on Angus. "It is getting late, thank you for stopping by, Andy. Are you able to go home now?"

"Yes, my shift is over, so I'm headed home now. Good night, Mrs. Penrose."

Eleanor closed the door with a smile. Angus was working the case, not pursuing Margo, a bit of information that made her happier than learning about a possible site for the shoe. Eleanor was finally getting into bed when the phone rang.

"Hello, Sweetheart," said Angus, "Are you missing me?"

"Absolutely," said Eleanor, "But there is someone here with me right now. We were just going to bed."

"What! I've only been gone a day and already you've replaced me," Angus said.

"Well, he's not a very good replacement, although he does smell bad and often begs for food," Eleanor teased.

"Are you okay? Not scared and lonely?" Angus asked.

"I'm fine. When are you coming home?" Eleanor asked.

"Soon, I'm just tying up some loose ends and I'll be back. I miss you."

Eleanor was happy.

There was no need to rush to The Oracle in the morning. Madame Patruska didn't open the shop until after ten, so Eleanor had time to complete her daily routine. While walking Bones along the beach she thought about Malcolm Manning and puzzled over his motive for murder. Could he be so competitive and insecure as to kill someone for their office skills? Maybe there was more to the story. Did he have a history of anger issues? Did he fear Monica would destroy his career with her claim of sexual harassment? Eleanor wondered why Malady stayed with him when she knew of his attraction to other women. Maybe she didn't know about the sexual harassment complaint since it seemed to be buried by his friend at work.

If only they could talk to Malady. Maybe Angus was investigating Malcolm's past and was finding out things they couldn't even imagine. If Malcolm became a suspect, a search could be just a phone call away. They really needed to get busy. The problem, of course, was where to plant the shoe. Where was Monica killed? Even if they knew for sure that Malcolm had killed her, it seemed wrong to plant evidence. What if he didn't do it and they were wrong and he went to prison because of their meddling? Eleanor couldn't live with herself. If Angus knew what she was doing he would probably want nothing more to do with her. He'd probably testify against her in a court of law, but what could they do at this point? It seemed they were in too deep to get out now. Eleanor thought about going to Officer McGraw and confessing, then realized how late it was and hurried home.

Madame Patruska was in the shop and opened the door to Eleanor when she arrived with Bones. "Good morning, Eleanor, I'm hery vappy to see you today. I keep telling myself not to be frightened, but it isn't helping."

"Were there any problems last night?" Eleanor asked.

"No nothing. It was a quiet night except for the snoring," Patruska said. "The lights next door went out soon after we turned out ours."

"Did you see any cars that aren't usually parked in your area?"

"No, sorry I don't pay much attention to cars, and I hidn't dear anything out of the ordinary. Our neighborhood is usually very quiet."

"Well, if someone was at Helen Pence's house last night, they had to leave sometime," Eleanor said. "Unless they were waiting for you to leave so they could break into your house and look for the shoe. Oh, what if they were planning to hurt you but saw that you weren't alone? I'm texting Dede." She sent off a text asking if Manning was at work. "I'd like to see the video from your security camera."

"Certainly," Madame Patruska said and showed Eleanor to her computer in the back room. Eleanor sat at the computer, pulled up the video and watched a dark green pickup truck pull up in front of The Oracle and saw Malcolm Manning get out and come to the front door. He read the sign that showed the store hours. Eleanor didn't think he looked so much nervous as annoyed that the shop was closed. Then she saw him do something that clinched his guilt for her and linked him to Tip Kent's murder as well. He pulled out a tin of nicotine pouches and put one in his mouth. She could just make out the brand that read SYN. It was hard to keep her excitement under control, but excitement turned to fear as she heard the bell over the door ring and looked out from the back room to see Malcolm inside the shop.

Eleanor didn't know what to do. She had her phone and sent off a quick message to Dede saying Malcolm was at The Oracle and set her phone to record. She heard Madame Patruska ask if she could help him. That's when he pulled out the shoebox from a plastic bag he was carrying. Eleanor stayed out of sight and listened quietly hoping Bones, who had been laying under the computer table, wouldn't cause any problems.

"Yes, I think you can help me by explaining why you sent this box to me with this stupid message inside," he yelled. Bone's ears perked up at the menacing tone in Manning's voice and a low growl came from his throat. Eleanor stooped down and tried to soothe him even though her own heart was racing. What could Manning do to Madame Patruska? Was he here to silence her, threaten her, or kill her?

Madame Patruska took the box and looked it over carefully. "Why do you think I bent you this sox? I don't sell shoes here and I've never seen you or this box before now. Was there something inside that came from my shop that you would like to return?" Eleanor thought Patruska was handling the situation marvelously. How could he explain his appearance here without admitting his guilty knowledge?

"You witch, I know you sent the box and this note …" Eleanor grabbed a random box and stepped out of the backroom nosily interrupting Malcolm and breaking the tension between the two. Bones stood by her, attuned to her fear, every muscle tensed and ready to attack.

"Excuse me, Madame Patruska, but a delivery came in this morning and I don't know where to put these items." Malcolm's head swiveled toward her, his face red, his neck bulging over his collar. He was infuriated and now there was a witness and an angry dog.

"I'll be back later and we'll settle this then," he warned and stormed out of the store leaving the shoebox and the note behind. Madame Patruska ran to the door and locked it. She was shaking.

"Come back here and sit down," Eleanor said. "I'll make some tea and we'll figure out the best way to play this."

It didn't take long for the coffee group to gather at The Oracle.

"What do we have?" asked Josephine getting right down to business.

"Malcolm Manning was here in a rage with the shoebox and note," Eleanor said.

"So, he did murder Monica," said Cleo, "And now we have the incriminating shoebox."

"Yes, but look at this video," said Eleanor as she ran it. "What do you see?"

"A murderer," said Pearl.

"A murderer in need of a breath mint?" said Josephine.

"Look closely at the tin," hinted Eleanor.

"It's a snuff box," said Dede who had left her meeting claiming a family emergency.

"It's a tin full of nicotine pouches, and it's the same brand that we found at the crime scene in the forest and the one in Tip Kent's mouth full of strychnine," said Eleanor.

"That means both murders are connected," said Josephine, "but why would Manning kill Tip?"

"Maybe Tip saw something he wasn't supposed to see," said Pearl.

"It has to do with the wife," said Eleanor. "Tip kept eying Malady Manning at Monica's memorial. He was sitting at the same table with them."

"She must be involved in some way," said Dede.

"Maybe she killed Monica because she was jealous," said Cleo, "Love is a strong motive."

"So is revenge," said Eleanor. "If she knew about it, perhaps she was angry at Monica for the harassment complaint that could ruin them."

"Can we get rid of the shoe now?" asked Dede.

"This throws a new wrinkle in our case," said Eleanor. "If Malady did it, planting the shoe in Malcolm's truck would make him look guilty. I can't stand the thought of planting evidence unless we're sure and maybe not even then. We need to find the facts."

"What if they did it together?" asked Josephine. "It's her truck too."

"I don't have a problem planting the shoe to incriminate Malcolm," said Cleo. "He did it. He knew to come to The Oracle because he planted the shoe here to get Madame Patruska in trouble. He's guilty."

"What if we go to Officer McGraw and tell him what we've done? That we found the shoe here, sent the shoeboxes, the note, everything. We could show him the video and the nicotine tin evidence. I've even got Malcolm recorded on my phone threatening Madame Patruska," Eleanor said.

"We'd still be risking obstruction of justice," said Dede.

"And we haven't solved the case. Now that we've found a link to the double murders, it's a whole new ballgame," said Cleo.

"I could go to Officer McGraw with the evidence and tell him I just found the shoe. Do you think I would still be a suspect?" asked Patruska.

"That may be our best bet," said Josephine, "But I think we should try to solve this ourselves."

"You aren't afraid for Madame Patruska?" asked Pearl. "Maybe she should leave town again."

"I wish Angus were here to help us," said Josephine.

"He's not," said Eleanor, "and I'm afraid he'd be very angry if he thought we were planning to plant evidence in a murder case."

"What should we do?" asked Pearl.

"I don't know," said Eleanor, "but I feel like using my lock smithing tools. Let's see if the Mannings have any rat poison in their garden shed. The more proof we get the better."

A few hours later, after dark, the group gathered at the Manning's shed in their black velvet stakeout uniforms while Dede wined and dined the Mannings inside the Pacific House Restaurant.

"We'll just unlock this padlock with my magic sanded keys, get in, search for evidence and get out," said Eleanor.

Pearl and Josephine were posted at the corner behind a hedge to watch for anyone who might witness their activity. The neighboring houses were dark and appeared to be empty except for the one on the other side of the hedge. Josephine texted that the coast was clear even though she felt a raindrop on her face.

Eleanor tried two of the keys while Cleo held a flashlight. The third key opened the lock and the two snoops slipped inside the garden shed.

"This place is chock full of stuff," said Cleo as she bumped into a lawn mower and worked her way around several other obstacles to get to the shelves in the back.

"Be careful not to touch anything," warned Eleanor as she searched a cabinet full of tools.

"There's a lot of bug spray, slug killer, and … bingo! Here's the rat poison," said Cleo. "It's right out front. He didn't even try to hide it."

Eleanor was oddly quiet. She was looking through a large manila envelope full of pictures. "Cleo, take photos of these with your phone. I think we stumbled onto something we weren't expecting."

"What am I looking at?" asked Cleo as she prepared to take pictures of what seemed like more pictures.

"It looks to me like x-rays of broken bones and pictures of a bruised and battered Malady Manning!" said Eleanor.

"Where did you find them?"

"They were hidden in the very back of this cabinet," Eleanor said. "I don't think we need to search for anything more. I'm beginning to piece this together."

When Cleo finished taking pictures, they put the envelope back in the cabinet, closed and returned the padlock to the door, leaving everything as they found it, then walked nonchalantly to where Josephine and Pearl kept watch.

"Let's wait for Dede back at her house," suggested Eleanor. "We need to plan our next move."

"I've got Patruska on the phone," said Pearl. "She's retrieved the shoe from the tunnel under The Oracle, and is waiting for us to tell her what to do next.

"Tell her to bring it over to Dede's and be quick. We need to get into Malcolm's truck and plant it where he won't see it," said Cleo.

"We need to get out of here before they come back. If he sees our cars here, he may get suspicious," said Eleanor who was so convinced of his guilt now she had lost all scruples about planting the shoe. Josephine texted Dede and said they needed more time. As soon as Madame Patruska arrived with the shoe, Cleo and Eleanor walked back to Malcolm's house hoping the truck wouldn't be locked, but luck was not on their side. His truck was armed with a security alarm so they quickly went to plan B, which meant breaking in to the garden shed again. Eleanor's fingers were stiff and crampy even in her gloves, so it took longer to open the lock. Cleo was getting anxious and then began to hiccup. Finally, they were back inside the shed where Eleanor opened the cabinet and shoved the shoe to the back next to the envelope with the pictures. Just as they were leaving the shed, lights came on around the corner and they recognized Dede's car pulling up to the curb outside the Manning's house. They froze in the shadows and waited until Dede drove away and then followed the line of shrubbery to the sidewalk and sauntered innocently away.

"I hope we're doing the right thing," said Eleanor.

"My heart is beating like a drum trapped in my chest," Cleo panted.

They walked all the way around the block until they got to Dede's without passing the Manning house. The other partners in crime had fled the scene. They picked up Dede and drove to Patruska's house where Josephine and Pearl were waiting.

"It was so dark in the shed, I just took pictures without really seeing what they were," said Cleo as the group gathered around Cleo's phone.

"These are obviously x-rays of broken ribs," said Eleanor. "And this is Malady with multiple bruises on her neck and face. It looks like someone tried to choke her."

"We don't know what caused these injuries," said Pearl. "She could have been in a car accident."

"Then why hide them in an envelope in a cabinet in a garden shed?" asked Eleanor. "There was money in there too. I think she was going to leave him."

"Look closely at this one," said Josephine. "It's of two people kissing."

"That's the man that came to The Oracle," said Patruska. "That's Malcolm Manning, and there's more going on there than kissing."

"The woman's face is hidden," said Josephine. "Maybe the other photos are clearer."

The ladies studied the photos of the couple in various positions without their clothes. "Go back," said Cleo, "I want to see how they did that!"

When Dede saw the photos, she thought the woman might be Monica Fischer but couldn't be sure.

"Wow," said Eleanor, "Malcolm Manning having an affair with Monica Fischer would put a twist on things."

"Do you think she was blackmailing him?" asked Dede.

"Maybe Monica was becoming a problem so he killed her," said Cleo.

"Or Malady hired someone to take these pictures, found out about the affair and killed her," said Josephine. "It doesn't make sense for Malcolm to hide these pictures and money in the shed. It's more likely this is Malady's evidence."

"Unless it's the blackmail money he was going to pay for those pictures and then didn't have to because he killed her," said Cleo.

Pearl said, "What if it's not Monica? It doesn't make sense that she would have an affair and then claim sexual harassment or that she claimed sexual harassment and then had an affair."

"It doesn't fit her character either," said Josephine. "She didn't like men hitting on her, stealing her ideas, and disrespecting women, so why would she stoop so low as to have an affair with her boss who is also an abusive man?"

"What if Tip was involved somehow?" asked Cleo. "Monica may not have been the person we thought. Maybe Andri Frost was her victim too."

Eleanor put her head in her hands, "What are we doing? Dede, please tell me you learned something tonight that will make sense of this mess."

"If Malcolm was having an affair and Malady knew it, there was no indication of that tonight," said Dede. "He was very charming and attentive to her and she was hanging all over him."

There was something they were overlooking, something Eleanor knew but couldn't retrieve. Maybe it would come to her later. The coffee group ladies decided they needed time to process this new information.

Eleanor thought Klara might provide new details. Perhaps she knew things that no one thought were important before but with the discovery of the photos might be revealing. Hoping to ply her with food and drink and get a different perspective, she called Klara and invited her to dinner. At the last minute, Harry Stone dropped by Klara's house and with Eleanor's permission, he tagged along.

Eleanor cooked a special dinner for Klara but knew there would be enough to feed Harry Stone. It wasn't that she didn't like Harry, but Angus had insinuated that the man was a player and she didn't want Klara to be hurt by someone who might take advantage of a widow's grief. This would be the third occasion Klara had spent time with him since Tip had died. What did the man want and why did Klara keep company with him after she told Eleanor she would keep him at a distance? Did Klara want something too? Perhaps Eleanor could provide a buffer to protect Klara from an unscrupulous man.

Feathers flew to the door to welcome Eleanor's guests who arrived with a delightful white wine to pair with the crispy fried chicken that she was serving. It felt good to have company and she had high hopes for a pleasant evening. She opened the wine and offered Harry a choice of whiskey which he accepted graciously. Bones sat silently in the kitchen hoping something delicious would find its way onto the floor and into his mouth.

"Dinner is almost ready," Eleanor said. She had done most of the work earlier in the day and just needed to finish the sour cream mashed potatoes and toss a green salad.

"Can I help you?" offered Klara.

"Sure," Eleanor was glad to get Klara alone in the kitchen. "Harry, maybe you'd like to go through my collection of vinyl albums and select some easy listening music."

Harry nodded and wandered into the living room. It wasn't long before the two women in the kitchen heard the lovely sound of Chopin's "Nocturne in E Flat Major." They looked at each other and smiled.

"Is that why you keep seeing him?" asked Eleanor.

"That and other things," said Klara. "He's talented in many ways."

"Okay then, as long as you're going in with your eyes wide open," said Eleanor.

"Let's get all greasy around the mouth," said Klara as she carried the salad to the table that was elegantly set and romantically lit with candles.

"You don't have to call me twice," said Harry who approached the table and pulled Klara's chair out for her.

Eleanor noticed his empty glass and offered a refill which he eagerly accepted.

"This is delicious, Eleanor. It's no wonder Angus wanted to marry you. Where is that lucky man anyway?" asked Harry as he dug into his meal.

"He's visiting his sister, Fiona, in California," said Eleanor.

"Wasn't she just here? I could swear that was her at the restaurant the other night."

"Yes, it was. She and Margo were here for a brief time."

"Oh, I know Margo," said Harry, "I bet there isn't a man in Waterton who doesn't."

"She is a striking woman," said Eleanor sweetly.

"I mean *knew* her in the most intimate way," Harry said. "She was well known in certain circles here. I'm surprised Angus hasn't told you about why they divorced and why he dislikes me so much."

"Harry, please don't embarrass our hostess," said Klara in an attempt to stop him from revealing too much of an unpleasant story.

"No, Klara, I want to know," Eleanor said.

"It's an old story really, not very unique at all. A beautiful woman left alone by a workaholic husband finds comfort in the arms of other men. I think it started in California and Angus thought he could save his marriage by moving her to a new place where no one would know her history, but life here didn't excite her and she soon picked up where she left off. She wasn't very smart, but she had some tricks that made her desirable. It's sad really, I think Angus loved her."

"That is sad," said Eleanor.

"Don't feel too sorry for him, Eleanor," continued Harry, "the ladies loved him, still do, and he took advantage of that. I don't know if he just wanted to hurt her in return or if he stopped caring at all and found comfort wherever he could, but he's no angel. That's why I was surprised to see a classy lady like you with him. I knew Walter, fished with him a few times and he was a stand-up guy. He loved you, there was no doubt about that."

"Have you ever been married, Harry?" asked Eleanor who inside was shaking to her core to learn such intimate details of Angus' history.

"Oh yes, a few times, but I'll never go there again," he said. "Good women are hard to find and if you fall for one like Margo, it can ruin your life."

"I imagine the same is true for finding good men," Klara said. "You need to clean up your own backyard before talkin' trash."

"Klara, what do you know about my backyard?" Harry said as if he were offended.

"Just what you told me now," Klara said. "You're about as low as a snake in a wagon track. You slept with Angus' wife and then blamed her and him. What about you? Were you married to one of those bad women then?"

"I may have been between marriages at the time," he said.

"But they weren't. That makes you an adulterer, not a good man." Klara continued, "I still like you. Don't get me wrong. You're more fun than a barrel of monkeys, but I don't respect you anymore."

"Could you respect me, Eleanor?" Harry laughed, "I think Klara and I are through."

"Well, there's a lid to fit every skillet, but you don't fit mine," Eleanor said.

That cracked Klara up and her laughter spread to Harry and Eleanor who were all wise enough to know that there is something good about everyone. You just have to find it and love them for it.

When they left, Eleanor realized she had learned absolutely nothing new about the murder case, but something interesting about Angus.

The next morning Angus called to let Eleanor know he was thinking of her and would be home that evening. She could have been angry with him, but she wasn't. There was always something, a deep wound, that caused Angus pain and distrust. Now that she had an inkling of what it was, she felt certain that she could help him heal. There were many things to love about him and his past may have taught him how to be a better man . After completing her exercise routine, she walked to the shore to enjoy what looked like a spectacular day. The sun was shining, birds were singing, Angus was coming home and everything was right with the world except there was confusion with the case of Monica Fischer's killing. As she neared Suzanna's on her way home, she spotted Klara on her way inside. Remembering her failure to question her more about Monica at dinner, Eleanor decided to try again and followed her inside. The Do Nothings sat at their usual table and waved to her as she sat down near Klara.

"Do you mind if I sit with you?" Eleanor asked.

"Goodness no, I love your company and I'm so sorry I brought that boring old gossip last night. I hope you won't hold it against me," Klara said.

"No, of course not, I learned something about Angus that I've suspected for a long time. I already knew there were lots of women in his past. It's not surprising since I've seen how they throw themselves at him. He's been unlucky in love and that's wounded him. He's not the same man that he was when he was married to Margo." Eleanor said. "It would be foolish of me to hold any gossip against you. I just regret we didn't get a chance to chat more about Tip and how you are coping with it all. Have there been any more developments? Are you still a suspect?"

"I don't know anything," Klara sighed. "I'm just living day to day and as far as I know, I'm still a suspect. Do you know anything?"

"I was wondering what you knew about Monica. What kind of a person was she? Has Jesse told you anything more about her?" Eleanor probed.

"Like I told you before, I only met her that one time and she seemed very smart. It takes time to really know someone. Jesse did say she had trouble with men. It was like she emitted a signal she didn't mean to send that said, *Here I am and you're welcome to me*," Klara said.

"Did Jesse get the signal?" Eleanor asked.

"Maybe he did, but he's pretty good at listening and talking things through. He'd get the opposite signal right away if it was given, if you know what I mean," Klara said. "Jesse may have been interested in the beginning, but when she didn't want to go there, they became friends. He told me she had some bad experiences with men that left her with a lot of baggage."

"I imagine that's why she involved herself with the women's crisis center," Eleanor mused.

"Oh, I didn't know that," Klara said.

"I guess it was confidential," Eleanor said. It was then she remembered something she heard at Monica's memorial. "I'm sure there will be a break in the case soon, Klara. I better get going. See you later." Eleanor hurried home with Bones racing ahead. She needed to call the coffee group for an emergency meeting somewhere they could talk and not be overheard.

Eleanor was the first to arrive at Dede's house but didn't have long to wait; everyone was curious to know what Eleanor had to share.

"What's so important?" Cleo asked, excited that there might be a break in the case.

"I remembered something," Eleanor said. "It might be an important connection or mean nothing at all, but I know how the crisis center's confidentiality may have been hacked. I think it was Molly Fiori who said no one was supposed to tell who they saw there or who helped those women leave their husbands. Most of the women found safe places to go where their abusers wouldn't find them, but one of the women went back to her husband after she left the crisis center. What if that woman was Malady Manning and what if she told her husband Monica was the one who helped her?"

"You think that was his motive for killing her?" asked Dede.

"But why would Monica have an affair with Malcolm?" asked Josephine.

"Maybe that wasn't her," said Pearl. "Dede wasn't positive."

"Diamond Dan told me Malcolm had many affairs. That woman could be one of them and not Monica. Let's look at those pictures again," said Eleanor. "By the way, would you send me the pictures from the memorial, Josephine? Maybe there's something we overlooked."

"I don't know," sighed Dede, "It might not be Monica, but it's definitely Malcolm, and the fact that these pictures were hidden in the garden shed means Malady knew about his infidelity. They acted so much in love the other night I almost believed they were happy."

"Of course, Malady knew. Diamond Dan said he slept with her whenever she wanted revenge for Malcolm's cheating. He is a big gossip, but somehow this all rings true," said Eleanor.

"If Malcolm knew about the pictures, he would have destroyed them instead of hiding them in the garden shed," said Josephine. "She must have been collecting evidence to divorce him and pretending to be in love with him to keep him ignorant of her plan."

"Malady definitely did the yard work," said Dede. "Malcolm was just bragging about her talent for landscaping and choosing the most beautiful flowers to plant in their yard when we were at the Pacific House. I have other news to report," Dede continued. "The police picked up Aaron Cambell and brought him in for questioning regarding the murder of Moncia Fischer. Evidently, he got drunk at the Red Shed and was bragging about killing a witch and leaving her in the woods to rot. He claimed she deserved it for meddling in his business."

"Oh my," exclaimed Eleanor, "Mary Cambell is his wife. I met her at the memorial along with two other women Monica helped get safely to the crisis center. Didn't we send a shoebox to him?"

"Yes, but he never responded," said Pearl. "I wonder if he knows Malcolm."

"Maybe he didn't know about the shoe, because he didn't do it," said Josephine. "He may have heard about her murder and was just mouthing off in a drunken rant."

"Or maybe he didn't know that Malcolm planted the shoe, because he wasn't involved with dumping her," said Cleo.

"If Malady told Malcolm he may have told the other men. Who knows, maybe they were all involved," said Eleanor. "Maybe Malady told them Patruska was involved with the women's crisis center and that's why they decided to set her up. It's all about revenge!"

"Malcolm is a smart man, a charming man. I wouldn't be surprised if he kept details to himself. The less the other men knew the less they might leak, and I think Malcolm may have been the source of many leaks," Dede said. "The thing about the noose was supposed to be kept quiet. Yet it came out, giving credence to a rumor about witches and linking Patruska to it because lots of people already believe she's a witch."

"I think the killing of Monica was an act of opportunity committed out of anger. Strangulation isn't planned. If Malcolm planned to kill her, he would have done it differently," said Josephine. "Imagine he was angry about her success at work and then he finds out she's helping his wife leave him. Maybe it was Monica's idea to collect evidence to get a divorce. Malcolm confronts her in a fit of rage and strangles her. Then he takes her body to the forest to dump it and gets the idea to make it look like she was hanged by some witch hunters. So, he takes a piece of rope, puts a noose around her neck and throws her down an embankment."

"Later he finds her shoe in his truck, and plants it at The Oracle to implicate Madame Patruska, but this part doesn't make sense to me," Eleanor said. "Even if Patruska was a witch, why would she kill another witch by hanging? That's what witch hunters do."

"Why didn't Patruska say something about Malady?" Asked Pearl.

"Patruska didn't know Malady," said Cleo. "We don't know when or for how long Malady was at the crisis center. I bet Malady used a fake name, so Patruska might not have made the connection to Malcolm, but he may have known about her."

"That's possible," said Dede. "I remember Patruska saying she used her tarot cards as a kind of therapy. What if Malady went to The Oracle to have tarot readings and used an assumed name? Maybe there's a file on her that Malcolm was looking for and that's why The Oracle was ransacked."

"We should go to The Oracle and ask Patruska about it. She might recognize Malady from the memorial photos," said Eleanor.

"Patruska has gone to stay with her sister," said Pearl. "She thought she would be safe there and not a problem for us."

"It's in the hands of the police now, so I say we keep our heads down and wait to see what happens," said Josephine. "If the husbands are all involved, I'm betting they turn on each other."

"There's still the mystery of Tip, the nicotine pouches and his murder," said Eleanor.

"Let's take one murder at a time," said Pearl. "Maybe they aren't related."

Eleanor left Dede's feeling uncertain and hopeful at the same time. She stopped at the grocery store for steak, potatoes, and fresh greens and at the liquor store to replenish the Crown Royal that Harry Stone had consumed. She wanted Angus to feel certain of her affection.

When Angus knocked on Eleanor's door later that afternoon, she was surprised that he was so withdrawn and cold. There was no peck on the check, no hug, no friendly greeting at all. He said he wasn't feeling well and just wanted to take Bones home even with the aroma of apple pie wafting from her kitchen. There would be no reunion dinner. Eleanor was disappointed, of course, and worried about him but thought he might just be tired from traveling and would be himself in the morning after a good night's sleep.

After taking the pie out of the oven, Eleanor decided to look at the pictures Josephine had sent of Monica's memorial. First, she glanced quickly through them, then went back and focused on those of Tip and Malady. There was one of Tip seated at the table next to Malcolm Manning; Klara must have gotten up to fill her plate because her chair was empty. Eleanor noticed something of interest on the table that looked familiar but she couldn't see it clearly even after zooming in on it. Suddenly her heart was pounding with excitement. If it was what she thought it was, she had Malcolm Manning dead to rights for Tip's murder. Maybe it would be clearer on her computer. She rushed to her office brought up the photos and zoomed in on the one particular item on the table she wanted to see and there it was. Between Malcolm and Tip was the tin of nicotine pouches with **SYN** on the label. That and the video of Manning at the door of The Oracle putting a pouch in his cheek was certainly enough evidence to make him a suspect in Tip's murder. Eleanor was beside herself with this discovery and hurried to Angus' house to tell him.

When Angus opened the door Eleanor rushed in without even noticing the grim look on Angus' face. "Angus, I've discovered something you must see," she said pulling out her phone and showing him the picture. "It's a tin of nicotine pouches like the ones we found at the crime scene and the one in Tip's mouth. It proves the two are related and Malcolm Manning killed them both."

"I see that. We already know Manning was at the scene. DNA from the pouch you found there came from him. It doesn't prove he killed her."

"Angus, I'm sorry. I know you must be tired," Eleanor said looking into his scowling face. "I'll leave and let you rest."

"No, don't go," Angus said. "We need to talk."

Suddenly Eleanor was afraid. She'd never seen Angus so serious and knew those words could only mean something bad was to follow. Maybe she was right when she thought he and Margo had rekindled their love for each other. She'd let optimism cloud the truth and now the truth was painfully clear.

"Should I sit down?" she asked.

"No, this won't take long. Being with Margo has dredged up some old feelings and I can't be with you anymore. It's important to me that I'm honest with you and you have to be honest with me. I have baggage, I know that, and I thought I found something with you that was real, but it isn't." Angus spoke slowly and Eleanor heard him clearly, at least she heard the part about dredging up old feelings with Margo and then she quit listening. It was everything she feared. She had nothing to say. She took off the ring, put it on the table by the door and walked away. Angus watched her until she disappeared from view, then he picked up the ring and sighed.

Eleanor's mind reeled on the way back to her empty house on the hill. "I should have known. I should have prepared myself for this. I opened my heart and now it hurts, but I'm not sorry I did it. There isn't anything I would do differently. Angus deserves to be happy and if he is happy with Margo, I have to be happy for him. We were happy for a while. I'm not going to cry, I'm not going to cry," she said as big tears rolled down her cheeks and fell on her sweater. "Okay, I'll only cry until I get home, then I'm moving on.

Angus will probably sell his house and move to California. Until then, I refuse to take a different route to avoid him. I won't be forced from my habits because of him. Why was he so mean about it? I've never seen him so grumpy. I think I'll go home and eat the entire apple pie." But when she got home, she had no appetite.

She went to her office and tried to write. She wrote Angus a long angry letter full of hurt and then tore it up. Then she wrote another one wishing him and Margo all the best and tore that one up too. If what Harry Stone told her about Margo was true, how could Angus go back to her? He must be a fool. Her respect for him waned with every minute that passed. Finally, she went to the kitchen and put the steak and the pie in the freezer. Looking at them just made her think of Angus. She poured herself a drink from Angus' bottle of Crown Royal and turned on the television. She needed something to take her mind off her pain. When a romantic movie came on, she turned it off. Eleanor was done with romance.

Angus went to the refrigerator and found it empty. He'd have to go down to the Anchor to get dinner and only imagine dining with Eleanor again. She'd never invite him for pie again either. It made him angry to think of Harry Stone sitting at her table or sharing her bed. It was Margo all over again. Cheating and lying. He'd opened his heart to her, trusted her, thought he knew she was different and now he knew she wasn't. As soon as he left, Harry Stone was at her house. Andrew McGraw had seen Harry's car parked at Eleanor's when he was looking out for her, making sure she was safe. She didn't even try to deny it, just took off the ring and left. It was a simple admission of guilt. Angus thought about getting his gun and killing the bastard, but that wouldn't bring back what he thought he had with Eleanor. How could he have been so wrong about her? All her virtues ran through his mind, never had she given him a reason to doubt her. Why would she fall for Harry Stone? The guy was a snake.

Now every time he opened his empty refrigerator, he'd think of her, and he didn't want to think of her now. He went into his bedroom to unpack his suitcase. He'd get some dinner later. He saw the unmade bed and cursed Margo for not stripping it and putting on fresh sheets. The pillow even smelled of her perfume. He tore the sheets angrily off the bed and saw the red lace panties on the floor. What was she thinking? Margo was lazy and a horrible house guest. She and Fiona told him to pack out the luggage and they would tidy up. He hadn't gone back inside because he was so eager to get them to the airport and out of his life. They probably left their towels in the bathroom too. He collected the sheets and when he went into the bathroom he discovered the condom wrapper in the garbage. Now his detective senses came to life. This had Fiona's signature all over it. Had Eleanor found these things when she came for Bones? Did she think he and Margo were back together? Is this what pushed her into the arms of Harry Stone? Angus stuffed the laundry into the washer and considered the evidence. Then he drove to Eleanor's house to get the facts.

Before he even got to her door, he could hear the music. It was the Everly Brothers singing "Bye, Bye Love" at full volume. He caught a glimpse of Eleanor dancing around the living room singing along with a glass of whiskey in one hand and a hairbrush in the other. He couldn't help but smile until he heard the lyrics she was singing and remembered why he was there and rang the doorbell. Eleanor continued to dance and sing until Feathers did a fly-by and caught her attention. She came to the door while the music continued to blare.

"Angus McBride," she said, "What do you want?"

"May I come in?" he asked politely, thinking she looked more beautiful than ever.

"I don't think so," said Eleanor, "Feathers and I are having a party." It was obvious to Angus that Eleanor was more than a little tipsy.

"We have unfinished business and need to talk." Angus walked past Eleanor, went to the record player and turned the music off.

"Well, you're a party pooper," Eleanor sulked, "I'd offer you a drink, but I don't want to."

"Ellie, I think you may have gotten the wrong idea," Angus began but was interrupted.

"Don't call me that," Eleanor was angry. "You can call me Mrs. Penrose."

Angus thought this might be the wrong time to have a serious talk with Eleanor, but figured she would be more likely to tell the truth under the influence, plus he found her quite amusing, so continued. "Mrs. Penrose, did you leave a pair of red lacy underwear in my bedroom and a condom wrapper in my bathroom?"

"I refuse to answer any of your ridiculous questions unless my lawyer is present," she stated emphatically as she plopped down on the couch.

"I see," Angus said sitting across from her and continuing his questioning despite her request. "Did you or didn't you invite Harry Stone to your house while I was away?"

"Yes, and no," Eleanor said vaguely. "He was here but Klara invited him."

"Are you having an affair with Harry Stone?" he said suddenly serious.

"There's a lid for every kettle, but his doesn't fit mine, and unlike you, I take my promises seriously. Now I think you should leave before I call the police and have you thrown out for being a two-time fool." Eleanor stood and walked unsteadily toward the door. Angus walked with her but didn't want to leave. He really just wanted to hold her and tell her how sorry he was that he'd misjudged her. He'd put the pieces together and got it wrong. He was a fool. Eleanor wasn't Margo. He had jumped to conclusions, made assumptions and hurt her, all because he had a wound that he couldn't heal. "We're not finished, Ellie," he said.

She opened the door. "Give Margo my regards," she said, "And Angus, don't come back."

When Angus got to his truck, he could hear the music and lyrics lamenting lost love.

Eleanor woke early and didn't feel good. She blamed it on the three fingers of whiskey she'd had for dinner. She got in the shower and let the water wash all her pains away, made a pot of coffee, and settled down with the morning paper to do her puzzles. Feathers watched over her shoulder helping whenever he could. After a piece of toast and several cups of coffee, Eleanor took stock of her situation. She felt pretty good about almost everything. Having a broken heart wasn't really all that painful, she decided. Like Klara, she felt free. She completed her workout and began her walk to the beach, passed Angus' house without even turning her head and finished two miles in record time. A woman didn't need a man to be happy, but she might need a lawyer if anyone found out what she and her cohorts in crime had done. They needed to solve this case and do it fast. She called Dede and then went to her house to discuss her latest observations.

"I see the tin of nicotine pouches," said Dede. "What did Angus say about this when you showed him?"

"He said they already knew Malcolm was at the scene of the crime because his DNA was on the pouch that we found there, but it didn't prove he killed her," Eleanor said. "But I meant to show him that Malcolm killed Tip and the pouches connect the two crimes. Somehow my brain got muddled." Eleanor knew exactly what had muddled her thinking but didn't want to discuss it. "I've been thinking about where Monica was murdered. Officer McGraw told me they had searched her office and her home, but nowhere else. I think that means it must be one of those places."

"If it was her office, I would know," said Dede.

"Then Malcolm killed her at her house," Eleanor said. "Do you know where she lived?"

"Yes, but what would we gain by going there?" asked Dede. "The police probably scoured it for evidence already."

"I don't know," said Eleanor. "Do you want to find out?"

"I think we should wait until we learn more about what Aaron Cambell gave the police. It may be that they have enough to indict him," Dede said. Eleanor had to agree.

"Let's send these pictures from Monica's memorial to Patruska and see if she recognizes Malady Manning. It's possible Malady was going to The Oracle under an assumed name. If we knew it, we could look through Patruska's files and learn more about her," Eleanor suggested.

"Eleanor, are you alright?" asked Dede, "You seem distracted and I see you're not wearing your ring."

"Oh, I gave it back," she said nonchalantly. "It turns out Angus is still in love with Margo. I don't need that kind of drama in my life."

"So, you're finished with Angus?" Dede tried not to sound shocked. "I can tell you unequivocally that he would never take Margo back and I know this because I saw what she did to him. She cheated on him with half the men in this town and lied about it. It broke him and for a long time he was a jerk, but he finally divorced her, found his footing, made some good friends like Walter and Mark, and then you. There are only a few people here who really knew what was going on and we tried to keep it quiet. He didn't need a scandal on top of his pain, so I'm sure he isn't still in love with Margo. You better do a little detective work and find out the facts."

"Why didn't you tell me this before?" Eleanor asked.

"It isn't my story to tell, Eleanor," Dede said. "Angus should be the one to share his story when he's ready."

"Does this mean you don't want to break in to The Oracle when we discover Malady's alias?" Eleanor asked.

"Of course I want to," said Dede. "Let me know what you find out."

Eleanor texted the picture to Madame Patruska and received a reply immediately. "I recognize that woman. She came to me for a tarot reading and said her name was Lacy Bobbit. She was referred by the crisis center. I remember the name and thought it funny since she claimed her husband was cheating on her and she wanted to cut off his instrument. Get it? Bobbit? It was maybe the least believable alias ever. She was angry and we worked through her emotions using the cards as starting points. She came several times and then stopped abruptly. Feel free to check out her file since I don't remember everything I put in the notes."

Eleanor called Dede and they planned to go to The Oracle that evening. Eleanor brought her lock-picking tools because Dede didn't want a repeat of their earlier attempt to get into the shop from the underground tunnel. Even though Eleanor was a little rusty she easily breached the lock and they were inside within minutes with little trouble. They went directly to the secret space behind the wall and looked in the file for Lacy Bobbit. "It's all so easy when you have the right tools for the job," said Dede as she sat at the table covered with a black tablecloth.

"It also helps to know what to look for," Eleanor said sitting next to Dede.

Lacy Bobbit: fortyish, attractive, married to a man who abuses her physically and emotionally and cheats on her with her friends. Has no close family. Father died when she was 10 leaving a daddy vacuum (possible victim of sexual abuse) Somewhat promiscuous also cheats on her husband as payback. Often verbalized she wished she'd killed her father, maybe also her husband. Telephone call from heaven, possible ruse. Something is off with her. Estranged from mother for years, (blamed her mother for not stopping abuse?) mother died recently. Seems to vacillate between loving and hating men.

"I wonder what Josephine would make of this," Dede said.

"Nothing good," said Eleanor. "I wonder who her friend is who cheated with Malcolm. Maybe the woman in the photo. I wouldn't want to be her friend, and Madame Patruska doesn't look so good to me either. She gets close to people, finds out their story and uses it to make a living as a medium. I can see why someone might want to get revenge on her."

"Yes, but a great deal of her information is based on gossip and rumors," said Dede. "Let's get out of here before we're tempted to look into other files."

Eleanor thought she might want to see what was in Angus' file, but reminded herself that she was done with romance and didn't want to know. She could understand Malady's desire to kill her husband and maybe even her friend, but couldn't condone the actual act.

"What if Malady put the strychnine in the pouch to kill her husband?" asked Eleanor.

"Then he would be dead," said Dede.

"Not if she only poisoned one pouch and then waited for him to use it. Sort of like Russian roulette, only Tip got the poisoned one," Eleanor said.

"It could happen any time and she wouldn't even have to be with him. It feels right," said Dede, "Are you going to tell Angus your theory?"

"No, I think I'll tell Malady."

Before Eleanor went home, she stopped at the Farm Store and bought some nicotine pouches and some rat poison.

In the morning, Eleanor received a large bouquet of flowers from the local florist. It was made up of all the white blooms that symbolized forgiveness; roses, tulips, hyacinth, and lilies. There was even a small stem of a bleeding heart in the mix. She assumed these were from Angus and wondered if they were meant to say he was sorry about Margo, or he forgave her for having an affair with Harry Stone. Eleanor didn't even read the card but threw the bouquet in the trash.

Later, there was another delivery of red roses. Eleanor knew red roses meant passion and threw them in the trash as well. It wasn't long before Angus appeared at her door.

Eleanor opened the door but said nothing. "Good morning, Mrs. Penrose," Angus said, "Do you have time to set some things straight?"

Eleanor bit her lip and then stepped aside to let him enter. Feathers did not leave his perch by the window but glared at Angus from a distance. Eleanor didn't offer a word of welcome or any word at all but gestured toward a seat in the living room.

"I think I owe you an explanation," Angus said sitting on the couch with his elbows on his knees and leaning toward Eleanor who settled on a seat across the coffee table. "I asked Officer McGraw to check on you while I was away, not to spy, but to make sure you were safe. When he told me there was a car that belonged to Harry Stone parked at your house, I admit, I went to a place from my past when I was married to Margo. The situation dredged up some deep and ugly feelings. Then I saw what Fiona and Margo left in my house for you to find; the unmade bed with Margo's perfume, the lace panties, the condom wrapper, and assumed you thought the worst of me and found some comfort with Harry Stone. It was all a misunderstanding based on assumptions and I'm sorry that I misjudged you. I'm sorry I didn't trust our love for each other and jumped to a conclusion without talking to you. I know better and I know I don't deserve you, Ellie, but I want you and only you."

Eleanor listened. "Would you like a glass of water?" she asked as she went to the kitchen to get a drink for herself. Angus followed her there where he noticed the red roses in the trash. He scowled because he knew he hadn't sent them and wondered where the bouquet he ordered was.

"What's this?" he asked innocently. "Do you have another admirer?"

"I thought they were from you," Eleanor said without apology or explanation.

"You didn't read the card?" Angus asked picking it up out of the trash. Eleanor snatched it away before he could read it. He realized she was still angry with him even after his sincere act of contrition. "Ellie, tell me what to do to make this right."

"Angus, I don't want this drama in my life. You were right when you said you had baggage and you will bring it into every relationship you have until you unpack it and get the healing you need. I love you, but I can't fix your brokenness, only you can. Get some real help, see someone who has the skills to help you work through your distrust and suspicions. You are smothering me. I didn't know how much until you told me you couldn't be with me anymore. I suddenly felt free. This cycle of hurt and uncertainty followed by romantic gestures of flowers and forgiveness is not for me. I thought I wanted romance but what I really want is something real," Eleanor said, "something you said we don't have."

"Do you mean you love me but don't want me in your life?" asked Angus. The look on his face almost broke Eleanor's heart.

"Of course, I love you and want you in my life," Eleanor said, "but until you can trust again, you will keep hurting both of us. I saw the clues Fiona and Margo left, but I remembered what you told me about falling into their trap and trusted that you loved me. I trusted you. It wasn't until you told me you had dredged up feelings for Margo that I lost faith in us. If it helps you, we could get counseling together, but until things change, I'm afraid this love affair is over."

"It was never an affair for me, Ellie, but I hear you and I'll respect your wishes," Angus said sadly. "Can I still see you, as a friend?"

"Sure," Eleanor said but pushed him away when he moved close to kiss her. "As a friend."

When Angus left, Eleanor dug the flowers out of the trash, put them in vases and read the cards.

The red roses were from Harry Stone who said: "Come away with me!" It made her laugh. At least there was no pretense there.

The white bouquet was from Angus who said: "I love you, forgive me!" Eleanor would enjoy the flowers, but had no intention of going away with Harry or forgiving Angus. She would never go away with Harry Stone and releasing Angus depended on him. She searched her office for photo albums from the past, sat on her couch and relived a simpler time when Walter shared a life and a love with her that was true and real.

It was time for a family dinner. Eleanor needed to be close to those she loved unconditionally so she invited her two daughters, Amy and Erin, their husbands, Taylor and Ben, and all the grandchildren, Elise, Addie, Wesley, Ruby, and Mitch for an Easter celebration. It was the first time Elise brought a boy to the festivities. His name was Sean and he was tall, with dark brown hair and eyes. Eleanor thought he was handsome and very polite as Elise introduced him, and he gave Eleanor a sweet bouquet of lilies. A romance was just the beginning for Elise, and just ending for herself and Angus. Hopefully there would be many loves for her first granddaughter and little heartache.

It was a rainy day on the Oregon coast making an outdoor hunt for eggs unpleasant. Plastic eggs filled with money were scattered around her house in the most ridiculous of places. There was even one in the toilet tank in the guest bathroom. Eleanor had done a count and a double count of all the eggs and after an intensive search by the junior snoops all but one was found.

"All I do is win, win, win!" bragged Erin as she counted her money which added up to more than anyone else.

"You are too competitive," Taylor sulked. He never liked losing to Erin who somehow always caused him one kind of injury or another each year. Last year, she pushed him into sticker bushes and the year before caused him to fall on his Easter basket smashing it. That's why it was held together with duct tape. "I think this hunt should only be for the kids."

"Sounds like a loser talking to me," Erin said. Eleanor never knew how much of their banter was based on friendly teasing or genuine dislike. Fortunately, they never took it too far.

"Why not put your money on the line with a friendly game of poker?" Amy challenged.

"Excellent idea," said Ben who went to set up the card table.

"What about us?" Wesley said.

"Let's play *Birds and Binoculars*," said Addie.

"I'll play," said Mitch, "But not for money. I'm keeping mine in my pocket."

"What is *Birds and Binoculars*?" asked Sean.

"It's a card game, much like *Go Fish*," said Elise. "You gather like birds into flocks of three and the player with the most flocks at the end wins."

"If you get a binocular card, you get to look at everyone's cards," said Ruby.

"And there are dirty bird cards that allow you to steal flocks from other players," said Elise. "It will be easy once you start playing."

They sat on the floor holding their cards close to their chests while Feathers flew around from one shoulder to another telling secrets and spreading lies much to the joy of the children.

"All I do is win, win, win," Erin sang again after taking all of Taylor's money in a dramatic bluff that left him rolling his eyes.

Even though rain fell nonstop, the festivities continued with more board games and a competitive piano playing contest. Then there was a knock-knock marathon with everyone joining in and asking "Who's there?" until their bellies ached from laughing or groaning in disgust.

"Knock, knock," said Elise.

Who's there?

Somebody.

Somebody who?

Somebody who can't reach the doorbell!

"Knock, knock," said Addie.
Who's there?
Butter.
Butter who?
Butter be quick. I have to go to the bathroom!

"Knock, knock," said Sean.
Who's there?
Cheese.
Cheese who?
Cheese a nice girl.

"Knock, knock," said Erin.
Who's there?
Honey bee.
Honey bee who?
Honey bee a dear and get me some water.

"Knock, knock," said Wesley.
Who's there?
Howl.
Howl who?
Howl you know it's me unless you open the door?

"Knock, knock," said Ben.
Who's there?
Ben.
Ben who?
Ben knocking for 20 minutes already.

"Knock, knock," said Wesley.
Who's there?
Dwayne.
Dwayne who?
Dwayne the bathtub — I'm dwowning!

"Knock, knock," said Mitch.
Who's there?
Nobel.
Nobel who?
No bell, that's why I knocked!

"Knock, knock," said Eleanor.
Who's there?
Mustache.
Mustache who?
I mustache you a question, but I'll shave it for later.

"Knock, knock," said Addie.
Who's there?
Wooden shoe.
Wooden shoe who?
Wooden shoe like to hear another knock-knock joke?
"Noooooooooo!," they all cried and the game was over.

They gathered around the table and ate an Easter feast of tenderloin roast, twice-baked potatoes, fruit salad, green beans, and chocolate cake while they caught up on the exciting things life had brought them over the weeks they had been apart. There were sports events to remember, feats of daring, friend drama, musical recitals, and concerts. School was coming to a close and there was a calendar that Eleanor knew would keep her busy for the next month … too busy to miss her friend. No one asked about Angus or why he wasn't there. They must have assumed he was with family of his own. Eleanor hoped he wasn't alone.

"The community center along with the Rainy Art Gallery has hidden several glass balls on the beach, if you find one, you get to keep it," said Eleanor. "Since it's so miserable outside, I don't think there will be much competition. Let's put on our rain clothes and go for a hunt."

"Yeah!" They shouted and scurried away to find coats and boots.

The adults looked out the windows to see if others were on the beach. "It looks like a small window of opportunity," said Erin. "I see a blue patch."

"Well, I see a glass ball from here," said Taylor as he raced to the door to beat Erin."

"This never ends well with them," warned Amy as she and Ben followed close behind.

Eleanor took up the rear making sure all the children were ready to go. They knew better than to run down the hill, but walked as fast as they could leaving Eleanor to her own pace. As she passed Angus' house, she noticed how dark and empty it appeared and a pang of guilt shot through her for not inviting him to the gathering, but she felt it was necessary and walked by quickly. She heard from Josephine that he was seeing a therapist and knew she had done the right thing.

By the time Eleanor reached the beach everyone else had scattered in search of the glass balls. She watched Elise and Sean holding hands as they searched the shore for a treasure that might become a keepsake, a memory of a youthful romance, but Eleanor could see their real focus was on each other. Erin raced ahead of Taylor to grab a glistening gem before he could get to it, a continuation of their competitive nature. Amy walked by herself toward the tunnel, probably solving the world's problems in her active mind and generous heart. Ben followed Erin with a prize in his hands, always ready to give his wife her heart's desire. Addie and Ruby ran like wild horses over the sandy expanse happy and free, hair flying in the wind. All her beloved children in different stages of their lives. They had so much life to live, so many opportunities ahead and countless milestones to experience. Eleanor hoped they were happy.

She searched the edges of the shoreline where the driftwood collected and was rewarded by the gleam of a small green globe and put it in her pocket. The beach was almost deserted except for a man and his dog who walked in her direction stopping to speak with her two grandsons and pointing in the direction of the tunnel. She knew immediately it was Angus and Bones. Eleanor watched Max wrap his arms around him as Mitch squatted to love on Bones. Then the boys ran off toward the tunnel, ready for an adventure. Angus watched them for a while and continued toward her.

"Hello, Ellie. Not a lovely day for a walk, but I did find an unexpected treasure," he said looking at her in a meaningful way. "And this glass ball too." He pulled a beautiful cobalt blue orb from his pocket. It gleamed as a bit of sunlight broke through the clouds and lit the cerulean swirl giving it life. "Here you take it, give it to the grandkids. It makes me think of your eyes."

"Thank you, Angus," she said. "Where did you find it? Maybe I can find another blue one to match it. This green one matches your eyes." She handed it to Angus who smiled and his dimpled cheeks touched her just like they always did.

"How have you been?" he asked even though he already knew she was fine. It hadn't been that long since she told him they could only be friends.

"I'm good, and you?" she asked.

"I miss you," he said. "I miss the Knock-knock jokes."

"Who's there?"

"Olive," he said sadly.

"Olive who?"

"Olive you, do you love me too?"

"Always," she answered.

She noticed he still wore her ring.

Eleanor waited in a booth in a small diner outside of town. When she saw Malady Manning, enter she waved and watched the younger woman walk toward her with a smile on her face.

"I'm Eleanor Penrose, you must be Malady Manning. I'm so glad you could meet me here. Please sit down."

"It's lovely to meet you," Malady said. "I was intrigued by your invitation and have no idea how I could be of use to you, but here I am."

"Well, I'm writing a book of poetry about women," Eleanor explained. "I need inspiration. After all I'm just one woman with my one story and I'd like to include some experiences that are different than mine. I'm older and you are younger. I'm a widow and you have a husband and no doubt a history before him that might bring out new ideas. I'd love to hear your story."

"I'm flattered," said Malady. Eleanor could tell she was honored to be a muse for someone's writing.

"I brought some of the poems I plan to include in the book, just to give you a sample of my work." Eleanor pulled out two pages from her tote bag and watched as Malady read them.

"I love this part about being born a woman and it sealing my fate, possessed, repressed, undressed. I can certainly relate to this. Maybe our stories are not so different," she said as she looked up. "My father died when I was young. It was the greatest gift I can imagine. He was a horrible man. We were wealthy and still he beat me and my mother, made us feel that we were nothing, but she never left him because what would the neighbors think? 'One must always keep up appearances she said. I always said I would never allow a man to abuse me like that, but now I understand how difficult it is … was for women to make it on their own in a world ruled by men, especially men of power and wealth."

"How long have you been married?" Eleanor asked.

"Too long, nineteen years," she sighed. "Sometimes I wonder how people do it. I don't know why I'm telling you this. I pretend to be happily married, but it's all for show. My husband cheats on me every chance he gets, sometimes with women I thought were my friends. This poem you wrote about the hater. I know them. They've betrayed me for a ride to the top. I don't trust women or men anymore. I'm alone somewhere in the middle with no one to trust. Poor me."

"What skills do you have?" Eleanor asked.

"What do you mean?" Malady was at a loss.

"You seem like an intelligent woman. Do you have a college degree, computer skills, communication, arts? What can you do to support yourself and give back to the world?" Eleanor asked. "If you aren't happy, change. Why don't you leave him? You don't have children that need your support," Eleanor probed. "Why stay?"

"I'm afraid," said Malady. "I don't know how to support myself. I can play piano and dance. Perhaps I could give lessons, but I don't think I could live on that income."

"You won't know until you try," Eleanor said. "I think you are a very resourceful person. Then she brought out a bag from her purse and gave it to Malady. Inside were the nicotine pouches and rat poison.

Malady looked in the bag, her eyes grew large and her face went white and that was all Eleanor needed to know.

"What is this?" Malady feigned innocence but it was too little too late. If Eleanor had any doubt about Malady's guilt it was displaced by her reaction. It was clear that Malcolm didn't kill Tip. It was Malady.

"We both know what it is," Eleanor responded. "It was supposed to be freedom for you, but Malcolm offered a pouch to Tip and, unfortunately, it was the one loaded to take Malcolm out of your way. It worked for your father too, and no one suspected you then. You were just a little girl, but you knew even then about rat poison."

"You are a crazy lady!" Malady laughed and began to fidget in her chair. "You can't possibly prove any of that. It's libel."

"I bought these items at the Farm Store. Maybe you didn't know when you purchased yours that they keep a record of poisons like strychnine. They know when it was purchased and who bought it. If you paid with your card, they know you bought the pouches at the same time," Eleanor spoke slowly, calmly and without judgment. "When did you know Malcolm killed Monica? Did he kill her because she wouldn't sleep with him? Was that the last straw?"

"You don't understand" Malady said knowing now that she had been found out. "Monica filed a harassment complaint against him. It would have ruined his reputation," As Malady pleaded, her face changed into that of an innocent child and tears filled her eyes. "You have to believe me. I had nothing to do with him choking her. I didn't even know what he'd done until I found her shoe in his truck. I recognized her black suede pump right away and thought they had made love in his truck, but she wasn't like that. I knew she wouldn't have anything to do with him in that way. She was good." She squeezed her eyes tight forcing the tears to trail down her cheeks. Eleanor listened without interruption.

"He has a violent temper. It was my fault he found out Monica was helping me gather evidence against him so I could divorce him." Her shoulders slumped and she bowed her head. "I always make a mess of things. I wasn't supposed to tell who helped at the crisis center, but he has a way of tricking me into revealing things and then he went to confront her. He didn't mean to kill her. I know how cruel he can be when he's angry, but I don't think he meant to kill her."

Eleanor found a tissue in her pocket and handed it to Malady who wiped her tears away careful not to smudge her makeup and twisted the tissue in her perfectly manicured little hands as she continued her story, now as an angry woman instead of a little girl. Eleanor marveled at the transformation.

"When I showed him the shoe, he threatened me. He told me I would go to prison as an accomplice to murder. It wasn't supposed to be Tip. Malcolm killed Tip. He remembered him from the casino when he helped me after Malcolm yelled at me and pulled my hair. He offered the pouch to Tip at the memorial for Monica." Malady paused to take a sip of water. Her eyes cutting up to the ceiling as if looking for her next words. "My mother poisoned my father. It wasn't me who put rat poison in his snuff. If you say one word about me poisoning anyone, I'll sue you for everything you have, your house and all your money. You can't prove that I poisoned that pouch."

"Malady, if you are smart, you will go to the police and tell them everything before your husband lets you take the blame for any of this. For all we know, he may be there right now testifying that you killed Monica in a jealous rage, and poisoned Tip accidentally while trying to kill him."

Malady's eyes widened as she stood and hurried out of the diner. She left in such a hurry she didn't see Dede, Josephine, Cleo, and Pearl sitting in the booth behind them recording every word.

"Wow, this is the best kind of stakeout," said Pearl. "No heart palpitations or disguises, and now there will be lunch."

"Thanks for researching Malady's family, Dede. I think that was what really threw her into a panic, saying more than she should," said Eleanor.

"Don't thank me. I didn't do it all by myself. Once I remembered her maiden name was Striker, I told Angus. It was Angus who went to California to investigate Malady's past, her wealthy family and her father's mysterious death. There was speculation that he was poisoned at the time but nothing was ever proven. He died while the mother was away visiting family, so she had an alibi. Malady was only ten years old and never a suspect. That was more than thirty years ago but interest in the case was renewed when the mother died recently and confessed that she saw Malady putting rat poison in his snuff."

"That's crazy, if she saw her putting poison in his snuff, why didn't she stop her?" asked Pearl.

"She was dying, and very conscious of how things looked in society but evidently didn't care so much about leaving a positive legacy for her daughter after her death," Dede said. "It's still not clear if her deathbed confession was believed. Blaming her ten-year-old daughter was an awful thing to do, but people continued to think she was the one who did it because of her self-centered obsession with how things look. For all we know they did it together. I'm not sure there's any possibility of indicting Malady for her father's death at this point."

"Maybe her mother wanted to confess to get into heaven, but in the end just couldn't do it because of the optics," said Cleo.

"Everyone wants a clean conscience before they die," said Josephine, "It must have been a heavy burden for her to still try to make herself look innocent at the end."

"I'm hungry," said Cleo, "What looks good?" The ladies studied their menus.

"I don't believe it," said Eleanor, "There's a Bigfoot Burger on the menu."

"I simply refuse to eat anything with "foot" in it," said Cleo.

"Really, they should have called it a Sasquatch Sandwich," said Josephine.

"What's in it?" asked Dede.

"Bigfoot Burger: Made with a double patty of venison burger for the wild adventurous taste, sauteed wild mushrooms to add an earthy forest flavor, slice of bold cheddar, extra crispy onions, smokey bacon and wild berry jam served on a thick and chewy pretzel bun," Eleanor read.

"There is a Sasquatch Sandwich: a giant open-faced pulled pork sandwich topped with candied bacon, pineapple, and creamy coleslaw served on a massive hoagie bun. All served with extra-large fries or onion rings," read Josephine.

"I think I'll have the Cobb salad," said Dede.

"Sounds good to me," said Pearl.

"I feel like living adventurously," said Eleanor, "Want to split a Sasquatch Sandwich, Cleo?"

"I'm in," said Cleo.

Josephine chose a peanut butter sandwich with blueberries on the side.

As they waited for their meals to arrive, the conversation continued about the case.

"Do you think she'll go to the police?" asked Cleo.

"We'll just have to wait and see," said Josephine. "She doesn't seem to trust anyone."

"Do you think she'll really sue you, Eleanor?" asked Pearl.

"Of course not, I haven't published anything about her yet and once it's in the newspaper it will be public. Besides, she doesn't have anything I want to write about."

"She's all bluster and bluff," said Dede, "just like most people are who slap a lawsuit to intimidate, get something for nothing or to shut people up."

"There seems to be a lot of that lately," said Josephine. "I heard of a woman who sued a weatherman because his forecast was incorrect."

"I know," said Cleo. "Remember that woman who sued McDonalds because she burned herself when she spilled her coffee and claimed it was too hot?"

"There was a class action suit against Subway because their advertised foot-long subs were only eleven inches long," said Dede.

"Then there was the man who sued his workplace because his job was too boring," said Pearl.

"Don't let Andri Frost see the menu here. He'd probably sue for brand infringement, "said Eleanor.

"He probably owns this place," said Dede.

"Now you've ruined it for me," said Eleanor.

"What do you think will happen when Malady finds the shoe in her cabinet?" asked Dede.

"She'll think Malcolm put it there to make her look like the murderer," said Eleanor. "Whatever happens, we're clear. She stated that she found it in his truck."

Everyone breathed a sigh of relief.

"I hope it doesn't come back to bite Madame Patruska in some way," said Pearl, "I've grown very fond of her."

"What happened with the evidence against Malcolm anyway? Angus said they didn't have proof that he killed Monica," asked Eleanor.

"Well, they did. I'm sure he's in custody as we speak. He was careless and left his DNA at the crime scene and at Monica's house. Police found a deck of tarot cards at Monica's with his fingerprints all over it. The Lovers card was missing. Did you know you can get fingerprints off a victim's skin? Malcolm Manning strangled her in a fit of rage, stuffed her in his truck and tried to make it look like a group of witch-hunters did it. He told some of the guys he worked out at the gym with that there was a coven of witches that were indoctrinating their wives. It was all based on a letter Helen Pence wrote to the editor of the local newspaper denouncing witchcraft."

"What happened to Helen?" asked Eleanor.

"I heard she was evaluated and put in a facility where they could assess her condition," said Josephine. "It's possible she could come back if it was just a matter of drug interactions."

"Oddly enough, Helen Pence and Eva Blount were friends, so Malcolm was able to use Helen's house to spy on Patruska because Eva had a key to Helen's house which she gave him. She has a lot to answer for and will most likely be looking for a new job. Malcolm used her like he used most women, charmed her and got her to take his side and do his bidding. Anyway, he learned who was at the crisis center because Malady went there during a crisis of her own and then came back to him and revealed that Monica had helped them all to leave their abusers. That and the advice she gave Malady to divorce him was what made him so angry. He hated that Malady revealed personal information to Patruska, so she was on his list as well and that's why he broke into The Oracle to find any information she might have had and plant the shoe." Dede said.

"Were those men we sent the shoeboxes to involved in the killing? Did Aaron Cambell turn on him?" asked Josephine.

"Those three were the ones who worked out at the gym with him. They were all abusing their wives. Aaron admitted that they often got together and laughed about how they could keep their women under control. When Malcolm told them he had killed a witch to teach the others a lesson, Aaron wanted to take credit for it and blabbed in a drunken rant, but he really knew nothing. That's why none of them responded to the notes. They knew nothing about the shoe. It was all Malcolm." Dede said.

"How do you know all this Dede?" asked Josephine.

"I'm the mayor. I know everything."

Eleanor woke with an entire day ahead of her with nothing on her to-do list. The murders of Monica and Tip had been solved, family celebrated, poems written. She rolled out of bed and the quiet of her home settled down on her like a heavy blanket. Even Feathers seemed subdued. When she opened the door to his cage, he refused to come out. Even the gray foggy morning conspired to muffle her joy. She forced herself to dress and complete her workout, make coffee, and work her daily puzzles. When she saw the fog begin to lift, she decided to walk down to the beach and treat herself to breakfast at Suzanna's.

Determined not to change her routine, she strode past Angus' house without looking to even see if he was home. That's what she told herself, anyway. It was hard not to notice his truck parked outside, but there was no other car there. Her mind wandered to Helen Pence and her Mini Cooper that caused Eleanor so much hurt when she saw it parked there. What would happen if she came back to Waterton, and when would they know her final diagnosis? Maybe Dede would tell her, since she knew everything. Eleanor hadn't really thought much about the secrets her so-called friends kept from her. They knew about Angus' harem of food donors, and Eleanor had to admit she must have known too, but it was before she loved him, before she saw Helen Pence sitting on his couch. It was something she'd put out of her mind.

Dede knew about Margo and all the gossip surrounding that part of Angus' life. Even Walter must have known about Angus' painful divorce and yet he never told her any details, at least none that she remembered. If Walter were still with her, he might remind her that he had told her, but she just wasn't interested then. Angus was reluctant to talk about Margo and why they divorced, perhaps he didn't reveal the details to Walter, but Walter must have known. Men weren't immune to gossip. Dede and Mark were his friends and they knew. Eleanor tried to remember a time when she knew Angus and Margo as a couple, but had only a few flashes of them together. She remembered how beautiful Margo looked and how aloof and unhappy she seemed on Angus' arm at a dance at the Elks Club.

They came to dinner once with a group of other friends and Margo sulked while Angus drank too much and laughed too loud. Angus was a fishing buddy for Walter and Eleanor didn't give him a second thought until Walter began inviting him to dinner. It was a slow and easy transition from Walter's fishing buddy to Eleanor's frequent dinner guest who helped her when Walter sunk deeper and deeper into his dementia. All the baggage that he carried had always been there, just as he had always been there whenever she needed something heavy moved, something broken fixed, something sad shared. Eleanor realized she missed him. She was so into her head she was surprised to find herself on the beach with the ocean's surf nearly at her feet and Klara standing beside her. "Oh, good morning, Klara!" Eleanor said.

"It's a good thing you weren't driving," she said, "Surely, we would have had a collision. Where were you just now?"

"Just thinking," Eleanor said.

"About anyone I know?" she winked knowingly.

"Maybe," Eleanor said. "Now that the murders have been solved, will you be going back to Atlanta?"

"Leaving this afternoon. Harry's driving me to the airport. That way I don't have to inconvenience Jesse. We've already said our goodbyes." Klara said.

"Harry huh?" Eleanor smiled, "I thought you were keeping him at a distance."

"You don't think Atlanta is far enough?" Klara laughed. "Don't worry, I'm just using him to do the heavy lifting. I wish I could chew the fat with you a little longer, but I've got a flight to catch. I've enjoyed your company more than you know. If you ever find your way to Georgia, give me a jingle." Eleanor gave her a hug and Klara left adding weight to her already heavy heart. Good byes were becoming more frequent but no easier to bear. As she turned away from Klara's receding image, she spotted a familiar one in the distance walking toward her. A man, whose black dog was running loose toward her, surprisingly made her heart skip a beat.

She picked up her pace and met the dog whose wiggly body and joyful greeting lifted her spirits. "Hello Bones, are you such a good boy?" She squatted, looked into his sparkly brown eyes and gave him a good rub. In her pocket she found a cookie treat and rewarded Bones for his friendliness. By the time she stood Angus was there. 'Hey, who said you could feed my dog?" he said. "I know you have ulterior motives, one being to steal his affection away. Maybe you should get your own dog."

Eleanor smiled at his attempt at grumpy possessiveness. "I already have a cantankerous pet bird who seems down in the dumps lately. I think he misses his friend, Bones. Want to bring him over for dinner?"

"Tonight?" Angus' face lit up briefly before he collected himself.

"Sure, why not?" Eleanor asked, "Unless you have other plans."

"No, no other plans," he said. "Sex?"

"Right, I'll see you at six." Eleanor continued on her walk already planning a menu for the evening meal.

Angus watched her walk away to see if she would look back but turned to go seconds before Eleanor turned to watch him as he threw a stick for Bones.

Eleanor drove to the butcher where she purchased two dry-aged prime Angus New York strip steaks, put together a chipotle marinade, dipped the steak in the marinade, and placed them in the refrigerator. She took a nap, plucked a couple of chin hairs, and had a long soak in the tub.

By six, Eleanor had taken her apple pie out of the freezer, prepared a red wine butter sauce, set the table for a romantic dinner, and took some extra time to make herself feel pretty.

When Angus rang the bell, Feathers flew to the door with his favorite refrain warning Eleanor of intruders. Eleanor opened the door and Bones raced inside eager to chase his bird friend around the living room. Angus stood in his white shirt and blue jeans staring at Eleanor as if for the first time. She could smell the scent of Old Spice before he stepped inside and wondered if the evening would be awkward given their recent misunderstandings but there was no time for wondering. Angus moved to her, took her in his arms and kissed her long and hard. She didn't think, getting lost in the moment. Angus picked her up, kicked the door shut and carried her into the bedroom. It was the only time she left the sauce too long on the stove.

Needless to say, dinner was delayed. Angus started up the grill while Eleanor started over on the sauce.

As they finally sat down to eat, Angus looked at Eleanor with interest, "I didn't know you could do that," he said.

"Well, I *have* been working out," she said.

"I see," Angus took a bite of his steak. "This is delicious, Ellie. I have to admit you are a marvelous cook, among other things."

"Thank you, Angus." she paused slightly, "I think we should have an honest and open discussion about your 'baggage', as you called it."

"Really, you want to talk about my baggage after what just happened?" Angus wiped his mouth with a napkin. He thought about Helen Pence's return to Waterton. He had decided not to ruin this moment with Eleanor by sharing that news with her and now she wanted to know about his sordid history with Margo. He was tempted to change the subject.

"There will never be a good time to tell me why you and Margo divorced," Eleanor said. "Once you tell me, it won't be just your baggage anymore. I can help you carry it the way you've been helping me carry mine all along."

"Ellie, your baggage is nothing compared to mine. I'm afraid you won't understand and you'll judge me. I wasn't a good man then," Angus said.

"Try me," Eleanor dared.

Angus sighed and then began his story.

"I met Margo at one of Fiona's parties. Her sister was a friend of Fiona's and they thought we'd get along. Margo was young and beautiful. I admit I was attracted to her immediately. I'd just been promoted to detective and thought it might be time to get married so I asked her and six months later we were living in a small apartment in Los Angeles." Angus paused to look at Eleanor who simply nodded. "It was hasty. I didn't know her well and didn't give much thought to what her needs were. She thought being married to a homicide detective would be exciting, but I worked long hours and sometimes got called out at night. The work was interesting to me and after a while Margo wasn't."

Angus scowled as he remembered this unhappy period. "She complained about everything: I didn't make enough money, I was gone all the time, I didn't love her. Anyway, Margo decided she would find other outlets for her boredom." He bit his lip and lowered his eyes as if what he was about to say embarrassed him.

"I knew what was going on, but she always had a good lie and I went along because it was easy. I didn't have to listen to her complaining about how much I worked, or how late I stayed out. Neither of us was happy, but not unhappy enough to change anything. This went on for longer than I care to admit. I confess I took advantage of the situation too and had affairs and one-night stands but nothing that was real." Angus looked at Eleanor for signs of disgust. Seeing only her concerned face, he continued. "I'm not going to lie, Ellie. I've been with lots of women. I'm not proud of it. Mostly they left me empty and sad. I saw some really ugly stuff working homicide and began drinking more than I should." He sighed and stared off into the distance afraid to meet Eleanor's eyes in case he saw judgement there.

"To make a long story short, Margo began sleeping around with some of the guys I worked with, and I couldn't take it. They all thought she was hot and she was, but when we were together it wasn't special, it was just a moment's pleasure and then nothing. I thought if I could get her away from there, we could make a fresh start. Waterton looked good to me, but it wasn't the place that was the problem, it was us. We didn't make each other happy.

She just started sleeping around here too. I wasn't any better until I met Walter."

Angus finally looked at Eleanor. She saw his face transform as if a dark cloud lifted. "He set the bar high on what it was to be a good husband. You were lucky, Ellie. When we fished together, he talked about you and his family, how much he loved and respected you and I wanted that. I wanted a wife that loved only me and wanted to care for me, feed me, make love to only me. Walter showed me that I had to be the person I wanted as a mate. I had to love my wife, care for her, feed her, and make love to only her. I gave it a try, believe me, but by then Margo only wanted out of this town and nothing else seemed to matter to her. I don't know, maybe she ran out of lovers. It was clear to me then that I was in love with a dream and there was no substance to our relationship. What I wanted wasn't ever going to happen to us." Angus closed his eyes as if remembering something and began again.

"Then I met you. Everything he told me about you was true. I loved the way you made me feel. I couldn't wait to be invited to your home and eat with you, listen to you, get to know you, be near you. I fell in love for the first time in my life, but I knew I'd never have you because of Walter and the love you shared for each other. It was after that I realized I'd rather be alone than married to Margo and we divorced. I don't deserve you, Ellie, but I love you and I think you love me too."

"I'm sorry you experienced that, Angus." Eleanor showed him no sign of disgust or judgment, no anger. "Everything that happens to us makes us who we are and you are a patient, caring man and a remarkable lover. Angus, you bring me joy. I'm not sure if it's just love I feel right now. I think it may be a little lust, but to quote Mary Oliver, 'Joy wasn't meant to be a crumb'."

Angus cocked his head, "Can you do that thing again?"

Eleanor winked, "Let me freshen up first."

Angus moved to the kitchen to refresh his glass of Crown Royal when his cell phone rang. It was Officer McGraw.

"Angus, I thought I'd better let you know that Helen Pence has been murdered. Her neighbor found her body in her garden this afternoon. It looks like she was stabbed in the neck with something like a knitting needle or ice pick. Considering what she did to you, I figured you'd want to be in the loop," Officer McGraw didn't give any other details.

"Thanks, Andy," Angus ended the call, shocked and a little saddened by the news. Who would kill Helen Pence? His gaze fell on the utensil in Eleanor's sink. It was an ice pick.

Love vs. Lust
In the quiet of a starry night,
Where hearts speak soft, and souls take flight,
Love blooms like roses, gentle, sweet,
A bond that's built on trust complete.

It's in the whispers, tender and true,
The depth of eyes, a view so new,
In every touch, a warmth that stays,
A steady flame that never fades.

But lust is like a fire that burns,
With fleeting heat, it twists and turns,
A hunger fierce, a sudden chase,
A passion's rush, an empty race.

It pulls you close, then lets you fall,
A moment's pleasure, no more at all,
A lightning spark, a spark that dies,
Leaving only hollow sighs.

Love is patient, love is kind,
It seeks the soul, the heart, the mind,
It weaves a tale that's long and deep,
A promise made, a vow to keep.

Lust, on the other hand, ignites the skin,
A surface thrill, where truth is thin,
It lives in flashes, bold and bright,
But fades with dawn, lost to the night.

So love, like rivers, flows and grows,
Though seasons change, through highs and lows,
But lust, a tempest in the air,
Dissolves like mist, with nothing there.
    In love, we find our hearts a home,
In lust, we search, yet stay alone,
For love is boundless, free, and deep,
While lust a shadow, you cannot keep.

Acknowledgments

A person never really knows when they inspire someone. It can happen while sitting next to them at a basketball game and they tell you they used a nicotine pouch to quit smoking. Thanks Janelle Werner. You've read all the books I've written and always want to know when the next one will be published. That makes me feel good and gives me the push I need to keep going. I hope the nicotine pouches worked.

Then there are the people you see on a regular basis whose stories and words of wisdom come out of the mouths of characters and sometimes are the characters themselves. Thank you Suzanne Weber, April Petersen, Kathryn Christensen, and especially Lyndall Bongiorno, whose Southern expressions found their way into this book.

I'm always grateful for the time and effort of the editors and publishers at GladEye Press. Sharleen and Jeff have kept me out of messy situations (maybe even out of jail) by offering the best suggestions and critiques, urging me to rewrite and revise.

Then there is Max Mulder, my talented grandson. When I told him I was struggling with the ending to this novel, he came up with an idea that surprised me. I used it and he promised to keep it a secret, which I'm sure he did. He then proceeded to read the first book in this series. Twelve-year-old boys aren't my target audience, so I hope it hasn't damaged him in any way. Thank you, Max. I'm looking forward to reading the tales you keep inside that magnificent brain of yours.

About the Author

Patricia Brown was born in Oregon City, Oregon, and attended Oregon State University, graduating with a degree in elementary education, a career she pursued for 28 years.

She currently resides in a small town on the Oregon coast with her husband, where she dabbles in the arts and enjoys the company of family and friends. *Dying for Love* is her sixth novel.

Get all the books in the Coastal Coffee Club Mystery series!

A Recipe for Dying: *The old people are dying, but no one seems to notice—after all, that's what old people do, isn't it? Eleanor and her friends set out to discover what the heck is going on!*

Dying for Diamonds: *When a mean-spirited mystery writer visiting the sleepy coastal town gets murdered, family secrets and the bonds we share are tested.*

Under A Dying Moon: *When a girl washes up on the beach and two women are found murdered, it's up to Eleanor and the gang to solve the mystery.*

Dying to Win: *Eleanor and her band of quirky friends investigate the disappearance of a Hispanic man betrothed to the young heiress of the richest, meanest, man in town.*

Hope, Faith, Dying: *Rumors swirl when sisters Hope & Faith return to their hometown to settle their preacher father's estate, prompting Eleanor and her sleuthing friends to dig up the truth about a decades-old mystery.*

Dying for Love: *When a women's shelter worker's body is found dumped in a remote area, Eleanor and her band of quirky amateur sleuths are on the case. Was it Bigfoot? Witches? The local psychic? Or one of the coastal town's misogynistic residents? And will Eleanor's relationship with Angus survive the investigation?*

Dying for Recipes: *Eleanor's binder filled with all of her super-secret recipes is missing! And everyone is a suspect! Follow the clues while enjoying twenty-two of Eleanor's scrumptious, mouth-watering recipes drawn from the pages of Patricia Brown's charming Coastal Coffee Club Mysteries series.*

Visit www.gladeyepress.com for details.

More books from GladEye Press

Follow the adventures and missteps of time-traveling PI Imogen Oliver as she recovers lost items and unearths long-buried stories and secrets from the past in this exciting series! (*The Time Tourists is available on Kindle Unlimited.)

The Time Tourists Trilogy
Sharleen Nelson

The Extraordinary Journey of a Tall Ship in a Tiny Pool Far from the Sea
Donevon Reves

With gentle absurdity and copious humor, author Donovan Reves weaves a whimsical yarn entwined with a tender love story all set in a ridiculous landlocked tall ship built in a tiny pool. As hard to describe as it is to put down, this tender fable evokes the magic of *The Princess Bride*.

I am the Wind
Cullen Cantwell

In GladEye's first YA novel, adults as well as teens will be inspired by the journey of a young long-distance runner who receives advice and encouragement from an unlikely source.

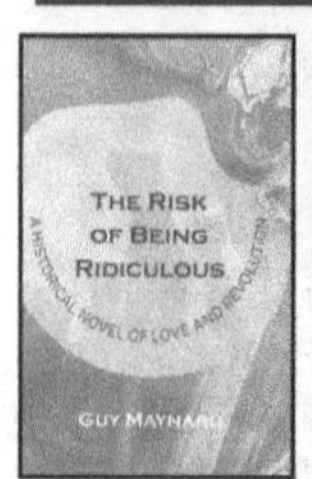

Join 19-year-old Ben Tucker for a passionate and revolutionary tale of protests, parties, trials, and a band of idealists who set out to build a countercultural utopia in the southern mountains of Oregon.

The Risk of Being Ridiculous Trilogy
Guy Maynard

*Available as an ebook on Kindle Unlimited.

All GladEye titles are available for purchase from
your local bookstore and www.gladeyepress.com.

*Federation of the Dragon
*Footman of the Ether
Jason A. Kilgore
Enter the ancient world of Irikara for
high-stakes epic fantasy adventure
in a mythical land filled with dragons
and demons, dwarves and elves,
magic and mages and gods.

Far Side of Revenge
Anne Dean
A *tale of two brothers, bound to each other but following divergent paths, this Booklife Editor's Pick,*
traces the life of Brian Boraime from his childhood
as a son of a clan king until *he was named King of all
Ireland.*

Off Route
Rick Levin
"Fearless, sensitive, hilarious and grim" aptly
describes Levin's debut novel. From the front seat
view of a public bus driver, the author navigates a
world teetering on the edge, where personal crisis
intertwines with broader systemic failures.

Black & Tan Fantasy
Randall Luce
A *Booklife Editor's Pick*, this gritty historically accurate
tale of racial identity and life in the deep South during
the turbulent early days of the Civil Rights Movement is
engaging and hauntingly relevant today.

COMING SOON *from*  GladEye Press

The Parable of Sam
Jason A. Kilgore
What if the biblical stories in Judges 13–16 were set in modern times? The Old Testament wasn't all gardens, apples, and manna from heaven. When Sam draws upon his supernatural strengh to save his friend from being mauled by a lion, his behavior begins to change, not for the better.

The Kingdom Brothers
Mike van Mantgem
Out on parole, white-collar grifter Cornelius Tayler finds himself enmeshed in a multi-level maelstrom of brutal neo-nazis, pseudo-religious gangsters, and unreliable allies who may be out to con the conman.

So Much for a Safe Landing
Susan Solomon
With a dash of humor, action, empathy, and truth, a recently retired woman finds herself enmeshed in the polarizing and perilous world of women facing tough decisions in a post-Roe v. Wade world.

Friday Night at Atonement Cafe
Jim Currie
When Native American rock musicians awaken from a coma at a hospital in the Columbia Gorge, downwind of the Hanford Nuclear Reservation, the group's charismatic leader and his followers set out on a mission to protect sacred lands and get to the bottom of the accident at Hanford.

Rereleases from Jason A. Kilgore
Around the Corner from Sanity: Tales of the Paranormal
Fourteen short stories of spine-tingling horror that will scare you AND tickle your funny bone!

Guide Me, O River and other poems